SAM CRESCENT

EVERNIGHT PUBLISHING ®

www.evernightpublishing.com

Copyright© 2021

Sam Crescent

Editor: Karyn White

Cover Artist: Jay Aheer

ISBN: 978-0-3695-0405-0

SAM CRESCENT

HIS SECRET SIN

Sam Crescent

Copyright © 2019

~◦◦•◆•◦◦~

Chapter One

Diego Leoni pounded into the woman's pussy. She was a whore to the core, and if he were to pull out now and fuck her ass, she'd let him. So long as he gave her a life she wanted, she'd allow him to do whatever he wanted to her. Even have his men use her. For now, he was just happy to pound her fucking cunt and to take everything he wanted. She was at his mercy, and she would do whatever he demanded of her.

Gripping her hips, he watched his condom-covered dick as it slid in and out of her hungry hole, taking all that he gave her. This was why he had women all over the city. No matter where he went or what he did, he had women at his beck and call, which was exactly what he wanted.

Thrusting in one final time, he closed his eyes as he spilled his release deep inside her. Jane was such a good sport, and after he was done, he pulled out of her. She flopped to her back with a sigh, and he left her alone, dealing with the condom.

"Oh, baby, that was so good. You need to come and give me some more," she said, moaning his name.

He rolled his eyes, not in the least bit interested in giving her whatever she wanted.

Washing his dick from the excess cum, he dried his hands, put himself together, and exited the bathroom.

Still complete naked with her legs spread, Jane pouted at him.

"Come on, Diego, you know you love spending time with me."

He smirked. He never spent time with any woman.

Women to him were a waste of time. Unless they were close relatives and part of his world, he didn't have the time for them. Most often they were too weak and boring. The women who were not part of his world, where he was capo, they were merely there to amuse him.

Pulling out his wallet, he counted out a thousand and put it down at the base of the bed.

"Ugh, you don't have to keep paying me money, you know. I'd gladly fuck you without the money."

"This keeps you in your place. Don't for a second think I enjoy coming here for your company."

"Diego?"

"Don't. I've heard some of the rumors you're spreading. You haven't caught me. I know exactly how many men you fuck with that pussy. My dick doesn't belong to you. It never will. Now, are you going to take the money, or do I need to silence you for the rest of your life?" He waited, allowing her to see his weapons that he kept on his person at all times. He didn't just rely on guards to do his dirty work; he was more than happy to do it himself.

"Yes, it's fine."

"Now tell me, what are you?" he asked.

He saw her jaw clench. He wondered if she'd snap and finally attack him. He wasn't being nice to her on purpose. Women always needed a reminder to keep them in place.

"I'm a whore."

"Exactly, and like good whores, you're going to learn to keep your mouth shut. We wouldn't want anything happening to you now, would we?"

With that, he turned on his heel and left the apartment. His two guards were waiting. He didn't speak to them. There was only one place to go, and that was to his club, Spice. His men knew he liked silence, as it helped him to think. If he wanted any interference, he had men, fellow capos who he went to for advice.

He didn't become capo of his city by asking for help, and he never intended to.

Climbing into the back, he pulled out his cell phone to see if there was anything urgent.

With no new attacks on the family, business was booming, and he was starting to get a little bored with his life. Also, he knew all of this was false.

Their enemies were luring them into believing truces and alliances were being met when he knew the truth. Death happened to those who failed to see the threat.

Arranged marriages, business deals never kept happiness and treaties together for long. All they did was postpone the inevitable.

He thought about his own marriage to a beautiful American woman. She'd been stunning, innocent, and had been supposed to bring together two great families and bring about peace—but it had failed.

Diego had caught his wife fucking one of his men and also discovered her treachery in selling his business secrets. He'd slit her throat and sent her body back to her father. He'd become a widower, and war had raged in the streets for two years, until he finally killed her father as well. He'd buried the entire family on his land, and made sure to keep their territory for himself. It was the biggest "fuck you" he'd ever dished out, and now at forty years old, he knew it would only be a matter of time before another bride was found for him. Leoni was a name feared and one that came with wealth and power. There was no way The Boss would ever allow him to die without heirs to take over his place. This was what he'd been born into, bred to become, and now he had to do the same for a new generation. Otherwise, his place as capo would be taken from him by his cousin.

He wouldn't allow that to happen.

Angelo was a fucking spoiled little prick who didn't know how to run anything. What he was able to do was gather rumors, hear gossip, and use it against his enemies. Each time Angelo thought he was getting dirt on him, Diego made sure to hit back. There was nothing he had to hide from The Boss.

He was powerful.

He never kept secrets, and he sure as fuck never made any mistakes. That's because he never allowed himself to get close to anyone. The men he associated with were not close friends. They were all in the same boat, and that boat could come crashing down at any moment.

Once he was caught up on all of his emails, he pocketed his cell phone and stared out the window.

When night fell over the city, the true darkness of life came out to play. He saw prostitutes on street corners, trying to get their punters for the night. Men walking the streets, looking to either score, or in the process of making deals.

Back alleys were not where the innocent should come, as it would ruin them. He'd done a lot of damage himself over the years. It's what made him a little different from other capos who ran their city. Where some were more than happy to have other men go and grab who they wanted, bring them back, and then torture them, he liked to do all of his torturing himself.

This not only dealt with the monster inside him, but it also made sure all of his men knew he was the one in charge. If they stepped out of line, they dealt with him and only him.

He didn't have time for traitors, and all of them were tortured and killed, their bodies disappearing just as they were supposed to.

After the fuck, he still wasn't happy. Usually when he was with Jane, she helped him to at least tame the beast within him. Now, he felt more wired than ever before. He should have known she'd fucking spoil things by thinking there was more between them than there ever would be.

With The Boss breathing down his neck, he knew marriage was inevitable. The wars that were raging needed to be dealt with. Every passing year they were all getting older, and as much as he didn't want to get married, he needed an heir.

The car came toward the club, and he didn't wait for his driver to climb out and open his door. He slid out, poised and always ready in case one of his enemies were lurking in the darkness. They never came out during the day. Most of them were fucking cowards.

Stepping inside the club, he ignored the women who smiled his way. Some of them were employees who were hoping to climb up the social ladder in their world, and of course to warm his bed.

He didn't need any more bed warmers, and no

woman slept in his bed. His place was always off limits. The women he used were always put in either an apartment of his choice, or a hotel, again of his choice. They followed his rules and did exactly as he said. If they couldn't follow that, then they had one nice, good fuck and were gone.

There was a city, no, a world full of women, and he intended to enjoy every single one of them. If some didn't comply, there were always replacements.

The heavy beat of the music grated on his nerves.

Leaving the main floor, he took the staff exit and made his way up toward his office, to see his security guy, the man who tried to call himself friend but Diego never made that distinction. Richard Cartwright was a security specialist. He worked with the best up-to-date technology, but he also knew there were some dangers out there that required human interference, so he offered bodyguards as well.

The only security Diego wanted was the specialist kind.

"Why are you in my office?" Diego asked.

"You do realize friends hang out with each other?" Richard turned from the screens showcasing the main club and stood beside the desk.

"And we're not friends," Diego said.

"Okay, if you want to keep on saying that."

He was starting to think Richard was dropped on his head as a baby. No matter how many times he tried to dissuade the man, he kept on coming back for more. He still hadn't cracked, and his suspicions were raised the second time Richard attempted to be *friends*. After a thorough background check, being followed, checking his routine personally, Diego had come to one conclusion: Richard was lonely.

"Business is booming, but you might want to

check on the barman. I've been here for twenty minutes, and I've seen him serve a teenager, and also sell drugs to four women, and even a few men. The cops will be all over this place, especially as there have been a string of date rape cases in the clubs."

Diego cursed, walking over to the videos. With Richard's help, he was able to see the barman in action.

The law was in their pocket, but there were times when no matter how much money and bribery you threw at them, you couldn't make certain things go away.

Grabbing his phone, he called down to the security on the main floor and explained the situation. He wanted the women who'd been given the drugs secured and the men who'd been sold something else, to also be watched and to intervene.

What these people did on their own time wasn't his problem, but he wasn't going to bring unnecessary heat into his club.

"You know, the usual nicety is to say thank you."

"What for?"

Richard laughed. "You don't make being nice to you easy."

"What I want to know is why you're still here? Why you hang around when you clearly see I don't like you." Diego stared at the man, and he simply placed a hand over his heart.

"You have a magical way with words."

"I think it best if you leave?"

"No can do, I'm afraid."

"And why is that?" Diego asked.

"Since I was here all alone, I have a personal investment in a lady. I want to make sure she's safe."

"You got a crush?" Diego asked.

"Nope, not a crush. She entered the club with your friend, and I've got a feeling she's blind."

"Why?"

"The way they've behaved, and I want to make sure nothing happens to her because the friend has done no more than abandon her." Richard grabbed the tablet that controlled the security footage.

Diego hated that his curiosity was piqued, and getting to his feet, he walked over to the screen. Sure enough, Richard had been able to zoom into one of the private booths. A quick look at the tag and Diego saw it had been reserved.

"What's the reserved name?" Diego asked.

Richard typed on his keyboard. "Belle Johnson. Ha, with special recommendations because she is blind. Damn, I'm good."

Diego looked at the screen. The girl was sitting alone, her eyes staring across the booth, but he also noticed the way she tilted her head to the side, listening to everything. Her long, raven hair was perfectly coiled and fell around her in ringlets, and her pale face made him think of an angel.

Shaking his head, he turned away, going back to his desk.

"And why does this woman have your attention?" Diego asked.

"The friend was supposed to stay with her at all times. The friend has decided to abandon her, and now she's on her own."

"You want to go and play knight?"

"For no other reason than I helped to install the security cameras. Women should be able to walk into any nightclub and have fun. That's why I care."

Diego had discovered Richard's only sister had been raped in a nightclub. She'd been fed a drug that she had reacted to. During her rape, she had a seizure, but the guy had finished what he was doing and left her to die.

Since then, Richard had made it his mission to help women.

It was a touching story and one Diego never intended to bring up during all of their meets.

The meets were not even initiated by him, but like today, he often just arrived, and it truly irritated Diego.

"If anything happens in my club, I'll deal with it."

"With all due respect, you didn't know your barman was giving out drugs to men and women. You don't even know if those men are using them to rape women. I'll keep on doing a check. You may not think we're friends, but a guy that does a thorough background check, finds out what you do, and then still questions me, I find fascinating."

"You knew about that?" Diego asked.

"I'm a security specialist. I didn't get where I am today by pretending to be good at my job."

Diego ignored him, but his gaze was once again drawn to the security screen. The woman didn't look frightened, more wistful. Her full lips called to his cock, along with other things, but he kept that little detail to himself.

Every now and then, he found himself looking toward the camera. She had a scar down her cheek, and he wondered what caused that.

Clearly, he needed some sleep. Women never appealed to him on any other level other than the basic, and he wasn't about to ever change.

****

Belle listened to the heavy music. This was one of the reasons she hated coming to nightclubs. The loud, banging music always made it impossible for her to hear who was coming. Since her accident many years ago that had left her blind, she relied on gut instinct and excellent hearing, but this didn't work, not in the club.

Where she worked, she played music and sang; that was her job. She also tutored talented kids, but tonight Melanie had asked her to come out, with the promise she'd stay by her side.

This wasn't staying by her side. This was anything *but* staying by her side. They had entered the club, and for the first hour, it had felt like a lot of fun. She'd enjoyed a drink, a couple of dances, and then she'd been escorted to the booth she'd reserved, and left.

Why did Melanie even bring her here if all she was going to do was abandon her? This wasn't fun. If she wanted fun, she could stay at home and listen to her latest audio book, or even better, make music.

Clasping her hands together, she waited for the time to pass, hearing people talk, laugh, and just be part of it all.

She had lost her eyesight really young, at about five years old. She'd been in a car accident that had damaged the nerves in her eyes. At first, she was still able to see, but soon after that ability had been taken from her, until she had been medically declared blind. For some, they thought it was horrible, the worst thing she could have experienced. For Belle, at least she got to see something before it was taken from her.

Her father was still upset by the whole ordeal. He'd taken his eyes off the road for a single minute, and in the process, it had cost his daughter her sight. She didn't hold a grudge. Life was way too short to ever hate someone for a long period of time, or to even seek out revenge for what had been done.

She knew just how short life was after burying her mother when she was thirteen. Her mother had been taken from her by cancer. It had been such a short life at thirty-three years old, and it had taught Belle to always appreciate the smaller things in life. To take risks and above all else, to live with no regrets. Her mother had told her there were many things she wished she'd done with her life and none of them she'd ever be able to do as she always put it off for the tomorrows. Knowing her mother had had regrets, she'd made sure to always live each day to the fullest, doing exactly what she wanted, no matter how scary.

Which was why she was now sitting in a booth, alone, annoyed, and a little pissed off. Actually, a lot pissed off. This was the reason she always avoided clubs. They all sounded like a lot of fun, but unless she hired a personal bodyguard to help escort her to and from the dance floor, it was useless. She had considered calling the owners and asking if she could stop by before opening to count the distance between the dance floor and booth, as that way she could do it all herself, carefully, not to bump into anyone.

She hadn't done that, and now as she sat in the booth, alone, she wished she had. She didn't even have her cell phone because Melanie had made her these stupid promises. Not she felt so fucking stupid for even believing them.

She was alone and miserable, and it annoyed her to think she'd fallen for the usual best friend line.

Her father had warned her that people were out there to take advantage. It wasn't in her nature to see the bad in people though. She liked to think they were mostly good because if they weren't, didn't that just fucking suck?

She wanted to believe there was more to people than pain, manipulation, and lies. Her father, though, had a different perspective on life. After her mother died, it had taken him a few years to start dating, but it had left him cynical. Fortunately, he was still an amazing father, and one she loved dearly, who believed in helping her live her own life, and to always venture out into the big, wide world.

Belle jumped as someone bumped into her table.

"Well, well, well, hello, sexy lady," he said.

He was a little too close, and she smelled the alcohol on his breath.

Allowing her hair to fall around her, she tried to hide how terrified she was.

The man sat down right next to her. The way he did pulled on her dress, and she gritted her teeth, trying to move away from him, hoping to create some distance, but it wasn't working.

He was stuck on her dress.

She gasped as he stroked a finger down her bare arm.

"How about you and I get out of here? I know I can totally give you the time of your life. You can ride my dick all night long. I'll give you the best cum you've ever tasted."

"No, thank you." She had never had sex before in her life.

It wasn't because she didn't want to. Most of the men she knew were friends. They helped her on a daily basis, and she adored them like brothers. When she met "the one," she always believed she'd feel it. The fluttering in her stomach, the need in her gut. All of it would count and would matter to something more.

Her mother had told her she'd find the right one, and when she did, there would be no doubt.

Mr. Smelly Breath and Touchy Hands was nowhere near the right one. He was so far not the right one it wasn't even funny.

"Could you please leave?" she asked.

Now her heart was pounding, and it wasn't for

any feeling other than a need for him to be gone.

"Is that any way to talk to a guy? I'm offering your fat ass a chance to ride some grade-A cock and you're treating me like this?"

She let out a cry as he grabbed her arm. Pain shot through her flesh and she tried to get away, but he was the one in charge here. He hurt her as he pulled her.

Just as suddenly as his touch was there, it was gone, but she sensed another presence.

"The lady would like you to leave," he said.

His voice was strong, dominating, powerful.

It sent a thrill down her spine as she listened to the guttural tones. When he stopped speaking, she wanted to listen to him again.

"Dude, fuck off. This is none of your concern. She wants me, and she likes to play hard to get."

"No, I don't," she said. "No hard to get. No nothing. I just want to be left alone."

"You fucking bi—" Mr. Smelly Breath and Touchy Hands didn't get to finish what he was saying before her savior did something.

She wished she could see what was happening.

"When a lady says no, she means no."

The man was gone, and she heard him being taken from her booth.

She wasn't alone though. She sensed her savior's presence.

"Thank you," she said.

He sat in the booth opposite her, and she looked in that direction, wondering what to do or to say.

"You're here to have a good time. I don't see why you should be forced to endure the company of someone you don't want."

She smiled. "Thank you so much for stopping him." She rubbed at her arm, the one he'd grabbed. Belle jumped as this man touched her arm.

"Sorry, I was just going to see," he said.

"It's fine. Erm, I … it's fine."

"I know this booth is reserved for you, Belle," he said.

"You do?"

"I'm the owner of the club. I have all your details, including the fact you're blind."

"Oh," she said. "I didn't mean to jump or anything."

"I should have told you."

She smiled. Some people were offended by the way she reacted. It wasn't intentional. She was so used to being in her own space that the few occasional touches often made her react in ways that she wasn't used to. Only when she was with her father did she relax. She was used to him holding her, touching her, but even still, she often tensed. He never took it personally though.

Growing up, her father had taken a day to walk in her shoes. He'd stayed at home, wearing a blindfold. This was when her mother was alive, and it had taught him a lot about what she faced on a daily basis. It had strengthened their relationship, and she loved her father.

"My friend should be here soon. I think she's dancing with someone." Again, she wasn't sure. Melanie had been vague.

"Your friend has left," he said.

"What?"

"I saw who you were escorted in with, and I watched her leave as well."

"No, that can't be. She's supposed to make sure I get home safely." Now Belle was feeling really fucking pissed off. Her friend had just left her to fend for herself. Most often she could do this. In a nightclub where she had no idea where it was, and alone, now this was unfair, and not what a friend would do. Nibbling her lip, she wondered what she could do now. Her father would be angry and demand to speak to Melanie. She didn't want to call him. He'd be upset that she allowed herself to be put in this vulnerable position. "I don't suppose you could help me?"

"You don't even know my name."

"Oh, sorry, what's your name?"

He chuckled, and she liked the sound. "Diego Leoni."

"Nice to meet you." She held her hand out, and after a pause he still hadn't shaken her hand. Just as she was about to withdraw her hand, he finally took hers, shaking it. His hands were nice, smooth, firm.

She pulled away before he did, and she liked that. It had taken her years of practice to shake hands. She spent a great deal of time with her father, and he'd talked her through the quick shake, the awkward lingering one. It had been a lot of fun.

"Have you ever heard my name before?" he asked.

"No. Sorry. Are you a celebrity of some kind?"

He laughed, and she loved the sound. "No, I'm no celebrity. Just a guy trying to make an honest living."

"I know what you mean."

"You do."

"Yeah, I work at a restaurant, Angelo's Place. I play the piano and sing. It's how I make an honest living."

"It is?" he asked.

"Yes. Everyone is always so nice there."

"I bet they are."

There was something in his tone, but she didn't understand it.

"Would you like to get out of here?" he asked. "I

can call whomever you want or book you a cab?"

"Please, a cab if it's not too much trouble."

She slid to the end of the booth and stood up, waiting for him.

"How do I help you?" he asked.

"If I can just hold onto your arm, that would be easy."

He took her hand again, making her tense, but as soon as she touched his arm, which was an impressive arm, she was able to relax.

"Is this why your friend stays with you at all times?" he asked.

"No, she doesn't need to stay with me. This is a new place, so I've not learned the general layout. When I know a place, I'm quite capable of getting around myself. It's easy, but this is all new." She was rambling, and she really needed to stop.

Diego walked her out of the club, and she was amazed no one bumped into her or stopped them.

The moment they were outside, the immediate silence was a relief. She closed her eyes and looked up to the sky.

Paused, on the street, she finally acclimated herself to the new sounds. The sounds of the street, passing cars, and the sounds of conversation of people walking by.

"Is there a car?" she asked.

He chuckled. "No car."

"Oh."

"In fact, there are no cabs. Would it be okay for me to drive you? I've got security footage that shows you leaving with me. You're perfectly safe."

She smiled. "If you don't mind. I'd hate to cause you too much trouble."

"It's no trouble at all."

"Okay."

He started to move, and she followed him. Her heels clicked along the pavement and he made a point to stop at a crossing and allow her to step off before proceeding to the next path.

"Have you done this before?" she asked.

"No, I haven't."

"You're very good. My dad when I first became blind completely forgot about the steps, and I tripped so many times. He always felt bad, especially if I fell."

"He doesn't sound like a good man," Diego said.

"Oh, he is, believe me, he is. It was all a little adjustment for us."

"You haven't been blind your entire life?" he asked.

"No." She then told him about her accident and how her eyesight was gradually lost. They came to a stop at the car, and she heard him talking to someone in a low voice. She stayed silent while he conducted his business, not wanting to get in the way.

A car door opened, and Diego helped her inside. She reached for the seatbelt, but he moved her hand out of the way and strapped her inside.

"You don't need to do that."

"I insist."

She liked that he insisted.

Sitting back, she was aware of the back of his knuckles as they brushed across her breasts. The door closed, and she waited, counting the seconds before he climbed in beside her.

Giving him her address, she felt the car move.

She gripped the door handle, hating cars. She'd always hated cars since the accident. There was a time her parents couldn't get her in one. Her fear had lessened over the years but never disappeared.

Diego didn't say anything until they got to her apartment building. Without another word, he climbed out of the car, went to her side, and helped her into her place. When she was at the door about to thank him, his words stopped her.

"I wouldn't go around telling complete strangers where you live. You have no idea who you'll meet along the way."

She didn't see him, but listened to his retreating footsteps.

Chapter Two

Diego wiped the blood from his hands, being careful not to leave any behind. His pristine white shirt was still impeccably clean, so he didn't even need to worry about burning his clothes. The body of the barman was currently being dealt with, and the warehouse where he liked to do all of his killings was being cleaned.

There would be no evidence linking him to the body or to anything else. Not that he'd ever go to prison for killing a man. He had way too many connections and knew how to dispose of a body himself.

With his job done, he grabbed his jacket and left the warehouse. The barman was a bad seed that needed to be dealt with. If he'd brought too much attention to the club, it would have caused problems. He didn't like to have the law sniffing around him, unless he was the one in complete control.

Taking a deep breath, Diego turned toward the building, knowing it had seen a lot of death. He'd burn it to the ground soon so no one could see it.

"It never even occurred to you to let him live?"

Diego had his gun out and pointed toward Richard within the next second. "What the fuck are you doing here?"

"Just out to see what took you so long."

"You do know we're not friends."

"As you can see, I don't give a fuck."

He was pissed off. Advancing on his so-called *friend,* he began to pat him down, checking him for wires. Richard put his fingers behind his head, allowing him to check.

"You don't trust easy, do you?"

"In my experience, a man with your persistence has a reason. I haven't given you one."

"Let's say I'm bored and you seem like fun."

Diego didn't find any wire, but he wasn't ready to back down. Keeping his weapon drawn, he stared at Richard. "What the fuck is your deal?"

"Simple, I've got nothing left to lose, and you seem like a fun kind of guy."

"I don't do anything in this world that's fun."

"You ever wonder why you've always been lucky, Diego?" Richard asked.

This made him frown as he looked at the other man.

"Are you more than a security specialist?" He didn't for a second believe this was all a coincidence. In his life believing the good of people got you killed.

"I didn't say I was *just* a security specialist. Let's say you and I have a common enemy, and that person is closing in." Richard pulled out a card. "I want us to talk business but not here." Diego didn't take the card, and Richard laughed. "That's okay. It's always good to be on guard." He placed the card on the floor. "I'm here as a friend."

"Why are you telling me this shit now?"

"Because when an enemy starts to gain power, it's a dangerous thing. I'm not willing to take any more risks. I won't tell you more now. Call me, and we'll talk." Richard left without a second glance.

Diego didn't drop his gun. He kept his gaze trained all around him before finally picking up the card. It was the same card Richard gave out for security details. He didn't have a fucking clue what was going on, and he didn't like it.

Seeing Richard though reminded him of his interaction a few hours ago. Where Richard knew who he was and who he was dealing with, Belle did not. The blind woman didn't react to his name. She didn't flinch or look terrified.

To Belle, he was a no one, just a guy with a club.

She couldn't see him. She'd never heard of his name.

Being with her had an addictive quality. He meant nothing to her, and he liked that.

Driving her home had been an interesting experience. It had been a long time since he drove himself. Even though he could take care of himself, his guards were there at all times to take care of him.

Pocketing the card, he couldn't think which enemy Richard could have.

Being a capo, Diego had many enemies all around the city who would like to see him fall. Turning back to the warehouse, he saw the last of his cleanup crew leave, and he made his way toward his car. His driver was already waiting to take him to where he needed to go.

"Home," he said.

Staring out the window, he watched the passing scenery, and his thoughts once again escaped to Belle. She was something else.

There was no way he could pursue her. She'd be dead within a matter of weeks. His life didn't allow him to chase after a woman. He had plenty lined up to take his cock.

With each excuse he thought of to not be with her, he couldn't help but want to break his own rules. Just for a taste. It was crazy, insane, and the stupidest thing he'd ever considered in his life. There's no way it could end well. Besides, she worked at Angelo's. He didn't know how it was possible to work in his restaurant, but she did.

He needed to take a trip there, but first, he'd demanded the employment records, and sure enough,

Belle had been working for him since she was nineteen, for a year.

She was way too young.

Rubbing at his temples, he felt the beginnings of a headache. Reaching into his pocket, he pulled out Richard's card. This man had been bugging him for some time, and it irritated him to know he seemed to always know where he was.

How long had Richard been following him?

There were way too many questions tonight and not enough answers. Climbing out of the car as it pulled up to his home, he didn't say anything as he entered his home. It was late, and there was only enough time for a couple of hours' sleep.

Just has he got to the bottom of the stairs about to make his way up to his room, he heard the sound of a throat being cleared.

Even as he wanted to take his gun out and shoot his father, he didn't. For all of his faults, his father had stepped down at the right time for him to take his place. Not many capos do that, at least not in his experience.

"What is it, Father?" he asked.

"We need to talk, son. Follow me."

He could ignore his father and just go to bed. Instead, he followed his father. After years of obedience, Diego thought he'd be over this shit by now, but it seemed no matter where he turned, he was always following his father in some way. He couldn't really question the old man's decisions. It was because of him that he'd lived a particularly long and healthy life.

"So, what is it you want?" Diego asked, going straight for the hard liquor in the office.

Diego was the only son to Antonio and Francesca, and after he was born what followed was years of miscarriages and stillborn babies until, eventually, they stopped trying for more. His father had found comfort in other women, and Diego knew for a fact some of those women had given birth. He had bastard brothers and sisters running around the world, but he hadn't gone to seek them out. They had a whole other life away from here, away from him and the chaos it meant to be in this world.

On another day, he wouldn't give a fuck, but tonight he was tempted by the outside world. Where their lives were not controlled by a Boss and he could make his own decisions, which he knew were limited right now.

His father still hadn't spoken, so Diego looked at him just before downing his hard drink in one gulp.

"Come on, what has you not only in my house, but also commanding me to do your bidding?"

"It's nearly time," Antonio said.

"What is?"

"For another wife to be found for you. You know this day would come. This city needs a wife, and you need an heir."

Diego laughed. "Remember what happened the last time you meddled and got me a *wife?* She was nothing more than a treacherous bitch."

"That was a mistake."

"It was a mistake that could have cost me my life, and this fucking city." He slammed the glass down. Rarely did he raise his voice to his father, but this was one thing he wouldn't be pushed around over. Not at forty years old.

"Diego, you know it is the only way. As capo you have a responsibility, and everyone is counting on you to get it right."

"Fuck getting it right. I don't want to get it right." He paced toward the window, overlooking the large expanse of garden. The main office was always placed in the back. There was a hidden wall filled with weapons, so it also allowed them to escape or to fight depending on how surrounded and covered they were. Diego had never once backed down from a fight, but he'd also never turned his back on his duty either.

"Diego, I know this is hard."

"You've already found her, haven't you?" Diego asked, turning to look at his father. There was only one reason his father would be here in the flesh and not send some kind of summons, and that was because as far as they were concerned, they'd found the perfect woman for him, or at least the right woman.

"You know what is expected of you. Our duty dictates what we can and cannot have. It has already been decided. You're going to be marrying Charlotte Durante."

Diego stared at his father, more pissed off now than he'd ever been in his life. His father normally didn't get pissed off or angry. He simply allowed life to take its course. After killing the barman tonight though, Diego wanted more blood, and it had yet to be sated.

"She's eighteen years old." Charlotte Durante was an ... outcast in most regards. Her mother was the first outsider to ever marry into their mafia world, and in doing so, she'd made sure all of her children would be considered outcasts. Of course, for her sons, they didn't care. They would inherit, and they'd proven their worth time and time again. The Durantes were fierce, loyal, and fucking crazy.

Charlotte, the oldest daughter, had always been pushed out at the parties and social gatherings that were required.

On a personal level, he didn't give a fuck where she came from or who. All the old-fashioned shit of marrying who they were ordered to never sat well with him, even now.

"And why is this?" Diego asked. "She's a kid."

"You know we marry young, Diego. She has a lot of years in her, and the boss is hoping you'll understand that you need an heir soon. We won't be taking no for an answer on this."

Gritting his teeth, he watched his father move toward the door.

"That's it?" Diego asked. "That's all the information you have for me?"

"There is a Sunday lunch this week. Don't miss it. It's where your engagement will be announced."

"And if I don't attend?" Diego asked.

"You know as well as I do, Diego, you will attend. It's in your blood to do the right thing."

With that, his father left the office, and Diego threw his now-empty glass toward the door. It was such a pathetic and childish move, but one he couldn't take back.

The last thing he wanted was to get married. Running a hand down his face, he was really pissed off now. If his father had pushed this, and he had no doubt in his mind that he had, then it meant Angelo, his fucked-up cousin, was making waves.

His cousin was a strong candidate to take over this city. He wouldn't make a good capo, and for years now, they had been enemies.

No matter where he was, Angelo wasn't far.

One of the reasons Diego owned a restaurant was to be a constant taunt to his cousin. Diego owned the very restaurant where Belle worked.

Could it be a coincidence? Was his cousin getting an innocent woman to lure him out of his safety net? Angelo had been wanting to take his place ever since they were kids. Their fathers were brothers, and in the process, they always made them fight for everything.

Being capo, Diego wasn't used to losing, and he would always beat Angelo at everything. It had set about so many motions as they got older that Diego knew without a doubt if he ever fell, Angelo would be the one to laugh over his corpse, if not be the one to strike him with the killing blow.

He had to check out Belle in Angelo's. If she posed a threat, he would dispose of her.

Leaving the office, he made his way up to his room. He had an army of servants, and the glass would be cleaned up come morning.

He made his way to his room, going straight for the shower. He never went anywhere without a weapon, and there were many knives laid in the bathroom. Once he stripped out of his clothes, he stared at his reflection in the wide mirror. His chest showed the years of pain and suffering that he'd not only dealt out, but had also been given, each scar a new memory and remembered victory.

Belle had her own scar, right down her cheek. It had faded, which told him the scar had happened years ago.

Stepping beneath the cold water, he embraced the burning pain of the ice. It didn't take long for the water to heat up and suddenly scald his body. Closing his eyes, he ignored the pain and just enjoyed the spray.

It felt good, or at least it did to him.

Getting married again wasn't in his plans, but he knew he was going to have to do it eventually.

He needed to have a son to start his training. Most of the capos already had sons, who, even as made men before their fathers stepped down, were ready to take on the role.

His own father had stepped down to make sure the city was constantly strong. By the time Diego took his place as capo, he'd earned the respect of his father's men, and many of his own.

Turning off the water after he finished washing, he stepped out, wrapping a towel around his waist.

He'd marry Charlotte. He was a man who did his duty, and she would give him sons and daughters. For the most part, they would always live separate lives. He would have his women, and she would have their children for consolation.

It wasn't perfect, but to him it was ideal.

He'd never been a one-woman man anyway.

****

The restaurant was busy tonight. Even as Belle played the music, she heard the hustle and bustle of activity. Conversations blended into one another. She stared down at her piano for a place to stare. When she first started working at Angelo's, she would often just look straight ahead, but several of the guests had complained it made her look weird.

She was used to the constant judgment, and rather than argue with her boss, she started to stare down. It didn't really matter to her. She couldn't see anyway, so where she looked was no different.

Drawing the song to a close, she allowed a few seconds' pause, waiting for the barman to either tell her a request that had been made or to continue. Most of the time she liked playing at Angelo's, but tonight, she wasn't happy.

She couldn't even explain why she was so unhappy or why it unnerved her to be here. Work was something she enjoyed doing, mainly because she didn't have to work. Her father came from a line of wealthy businessmen, and he invested in stocks and shares. It's why she was always able to afford the best growing up and how she had been able to still continue her love of music. He made sure all of her needs were catered to. It's why she believed her friends stuck around. They were paid to help escort her to events or to hang out with her. She did try to have as close to a normal life as possible, which was why she wanted this job. She didn't need it, but it helped her get out of her home, and not go completely stir crazy.

Teaching kids was also another passion of hers, but again, she liked to do other crazy things, like singing. Every now and then, she'd go to the karaoke bar where they knew her and the barman, Ben, was more than happy to help her onto the stage to sing.

With no requests, she put her fingers to the keys and began to play another tune. Some of the songs she played were classics and others she'd created herself, or even putting modern spins on old classics.

She just loved music, and without seeing the keys, she'd been able to get lost in the sounds, the vibrations the noise made.

After playing three more songs, it was time for her break.

Tanya, the waitress who helped her, walked her off stage and slid her into her private booth. Tanya placed her hand around the bottle of water, and she smiled to the other woman.

When she first started working at Angelo's, Tanya had been very mean to her. The other woman thought she was here to take her place but had soon realized she was only here to play music. Belle rarely talked to any of the staff.

Belle actually believed she made the other staff nervous with her eyes, the fact she couldn't see.

Opening the cap of the bottle, she heard the snap

of the lid, letting her know it was a fresh one.

Taking a drink, she became very aware of the fact she wasn't alone.

This was her booth. The steps she'd counted to make it here told her it was, and yet someone was there.

She didn't show she knew they were there. It was only a feeling she wasn't alone. Her heart began to race, and she wondered if the other person could hear it.

"Who are you?" she asked.

The chuckle she recognized but couldn't place it. Where had she heard that sound before?

"After you told me you worked here, I just had to come and see you."

"Diego?" she asked.

"You remembered my name."

"I happen to like the name. It's one of my favorites."

"You have favorite names?"

"Of course. I love the names Sasha and Leonardo. I like names. I even love the name Tanya. The waitress who brought me here is Tanya. Were you here from the beginning?" she asked.

Why would Tanya leave her alone without telling her there was a man sitting here?

"I was."

"How did you get to sit in my private booth?"

"You don't like the company?"

"I don't mind the company. It's actually rather nice." Most often on break, she was alone. She didn't mind being alone, but there were times it was incredibly lonely. It was those times that scared her because she was more tempted than ever before to leave and go back and live with her dad. She knew he wouldn't mind, but this wasn't about depending on her parent. This was about her trying to find her place in this new world. A world that didn't have them as security blankets.

"I have a lot of friends. I knew you played here and I wanted the chance to speak to you, and now I have it."

"Do you always get what you want?" she asked with a smile.

"Always."

There was something in his tone that sent a thrill down her spine. She couldn't help but smile at the sheer confidence of him.

"Well, is there a reason you wanted to come and sit with me?"

"Let's call it a hunch. I'm curious, what made you decide to work at this restaurant?"

"Have I done something wrong?" she asked.

"Of course not."

"Oh, well, I was sitting in a coffee shop one morning. Melanie had gone to the bathroom. The woman that was with me the other night."

"Does she have a habit of leaving you?" he asked.

"Oh, no, not usually." She had been pretty pissed with Melanie for leaving her at the club, but her friend had assured her she would have returned once she finished with her date. Belle knew it was all bullshit, but she refused to be drawn into any kind of conflict. It didn't sit well with her, arguments, and she had no interest in starting a fight over something so trivial like being left alone.

She didn't want to keep fighting with her friend, and she certainly didn't want to rely completely on anyone. She needed to consider getting a guide dog. It was something she had put off. She had a guide dog when she was really young, and when he'd passed, she'd mourned him for months. Her love and connection to him had been so strong, it had hurt her too much to even consider replacing him.

It was probably silly of her to think like that, but she did.

"So, you? Coffee shop?" Diego said.

"Yes, of course. I heard these two women talking about advertisements, and this place was mentioned. One of them said why not go for the piano player wanted, and the other complained she didn't have a clue how to play. When they left, I got Melanie to tell me what the job was for. I phoned up, explained my situation, they asked me to come in for a test show, and the rest is history. I have to get the waitress to help me to my seat and back to the piano, but for the most part, it has been amazing."

"You like working here?"

"Yes. I know my music is not appreciated, but I enjoy it."

"Why is it not appreciated?"

"You're in a restaurant, Diego. No one cares about the music. Just the right note for their date. They're completely enthralled by each other, and I'm okay with that." She didn't mind. She got to play music, earn a living, and feel another stroke of independence. "How come you're here and not at your own bar?"

"Like I said, I own it, so I can decide if I stay or if I go."

"That must be nice," she said. "To have complete control."

"It works out for me. What about you? What is it you like out of life?"

"Wow, that is a big thing, isn't it? Trying to figure out what I want out of life." She took a sip of her water. Belle wondered if she should lie. He was asking rather invasive questions, and it was alarming how much she wanted to hear him talk. He had a nice voice. It was deep, commanding, and sexy. Listening to him speak sent a thrill down her spine, and she could easily have him read a book to her. Now she was just having crazy thoughts, ones that didn't make any sense to her. "I think one day I want to have love and a family."

"A family?"

"Yes. I want to find a man who loves me, no matter my faults or flaws, and to settle down, have a family. I think love is the most important thing in life."

"Not power?"

"Why power?"

"If people fear you, you won't ever get hurt."

She frowned. This was a weird conversation or at least, it had fast turned so. "I don't think power stops you from getting hurt. I think power makes it so more people want to hurt you."

"How do you figure that?"

"Because, when you have power, you have something other people crave, and when others want it, there are some that won't sit idly by while you have it. They take it for themselves. Isn't that what history has taught us? Where there is a thirst for power there is war?" she asked.

"You're an interesting woman, Belle."

Tanya was back before she could respond.

"Excuse me."

She walked with Tanya back to the piano.

"Thank you," she said.

Tanya didn't say anything, just left her alone on stage. She felt a little unnerved this time. Placing her fingers on the keys, she drowned out the noise and began to play. It didn't take her long to get lost in the notes and the music. She poured her heart and soul into the piece, and as she came to the end with the final bar, she heard the clapping.

The restaurant went silent as a single person

clapped, and she knew it was Diego. He was bringing the rest of the diners to her attention, and in doing so, he made them clap.

It was the first round of applause she got, and even as it was embarrassing, she didn't stop playing the next song.

Soon after she started to play, everything returned to normal, and she played for the rest of the night until it was time to go home.

Tanya helped her off stage, but Diego was there.

"I'll take it from here," he said. He placed her hand over his and led her back toward the staffroom.

"My locker is the last one on the left."

"I can see which one it is."

She heard him open her locker and pull out her jacket. He helped her put it on, and she thanked him.

"You're taking me home again?" she asked.

"Yes."

"Can we make a quick stop first? I'm really hungry, and I could do with some food."

"You're in a restaurant," he said.

"I never eat here."

"Why not?" he asked.

"I honestly don't know. I guess it has never been on my mind to eat here. Besides, I fancy a juicy burger with lots of cheesy fries."

"That's what you want to eat?" he asked.

"You ever eaten it?"

"No."

"I can tell. Believe me, you'll be addicted before the end of the night. If we walk out of here, walk to the end of the road, turn down an alley, go left, then right, we'll come to Mary's place. It has the best food at this time of night."

"You go there regularly?" he asked.

"Enough to know my way to it from this spot. Please, I'll pay. My treat."

"You don't have to pay."

"Now I insist I pay. If you don't like it, no harm done."

"Okay, fine. We will go to this place."

"Do you walk home from here?" he asked.

"Most of the time. I've walked it so often I can get home from here."

"It's late."

"I know."

"And dangerous."

"Yeah, well, I'm trying to be more self-sufficient. I've been working here a year, and I've been pretty safe so far." She offered him a smile. She was probably staring at his chest. He seemed so tall compared to her. "Do I seem strange to you?" she asked.

"You're not strange. A little different maybe but not strange."

"Aw, I wanted to be strange."

He chuckled, and they suddenly came to a stop.

"What is it? What's wrong?"

"Nothing, just nothing."

He started walking again, and she didn't question him. She knew they were getting close by the scents. Her mouth started to salivate, and as they entered Mary's place, the other woman let out a gasp.

"Belle, I just knew you'd be here today. And look at you, bringing a fine gentleman with you as well."

"He's fine? How about sexy? You know me, Mary, I can only have the sexiest guy on my arm," she said, laughing.

Mary did the same, and she was pulled into an embrace. She flinched at first but immediately relaxed. "Then, my dear, you do not have a problem with that.

Maybe he could stop frowning and he'd be a keeper." Mary led her to a free booth. What she loved about Mary's was how busy it always was.

Diego sat down opposite her, and without even asking what was on the menu, she let Mary know she would have her usual, and also ordered for Diego, who had yet to speak.

Once they were alone, she reached across the table, feeling his arm. She felt how incredibly thick and muscular it was.

"I'm sorry. I hope I didn't embarrass you. I didn't mean anything by it. It's just a joke. Mary thinks I need to start dating, and well, you're the first guy I've brought here."

"You don't date?"

"I've not had much reason in my life to. I've been focusing on a lot of other things, like my music and my life, and just making sure I can actually do the things I want, you know. Dating is a complicated business and one I don't want to jump into." She let go of his arm as she realized she'd been holding it a little too long to be appropriate. "How about you? Do you date?"

"No, I don't date."

"Are you married?"

"No, not married. I'm a widower."

"Oh, no, I'm so sorry." Now she just wanted to hug him.

"Don't be. She was … cheating on me."

"Oh, I don't think that makes her passing any easier to bear. I'm so sorry." She tried to offer him comfort as best she could. She really needed to learn to stick to safe topics of conversations and not ones that could hurt others.

She was never usually like this. She would be careful in the future.

Chapter Three

The engagement party had gone through, and now Diego had to deal with a fiancée. At least Charlotte wasn't a demanding brat. Years of being the outcast had turned her into a quiet little mouse.

She never made waves and never demanded his attention. What it did mean was they had to be present for as many functions within the family as possible.

Like tonight, after two weeks of being engaged, he was at The Boss's house. All the capos were. It was a friendly gathering, one where the men talked business and the women, well, waited and gossiped for their men. Charlotte sat next to him, eating her food. She was a perfect wife. Delicate, gentle, and quiet.

He thought about Belle.

After dropping her off at her apartment two weeks ago, he hadn't seen her since.

He hadn't visited Angelo's Place, and hadn't seen her at the bar.

She hadn't been a quiet eater at Mary's place. He had watched her devour that burger with hunger and relish, and he'd done the same.

Walking into Mary's had been eye-opening to him. No one knew who he was, or at least had never given it away. Mary flirted with him, and Belle laughed and joked with the older woman.

Belle was loved. He got that much.

She was openly affectionate, kind, naïve, and he shouldn't be thinking about her while he had his fiancée beside him, and the rest of the men watching them. With Charlotte being an outcast, their union had caused even more gossip.

To some, they believed he'd fallen out of favor with The Boss. He hadn't, but they didn't need to know that.

Charlotte was a good daughter, and she would make the perfect wife, he had no doubt.

Unlike a certain raven-haired woman he'd met, Charlotte didn't fire his blood. Sitting next to her didn't affect him. He didn't find himself wanting to watch her.

"So, when is the wedding, cousin?" Angelo asked, sporting a fresh black eye.

Diego had been the one to give him said black eye because of him running his mouth to the servants about Charlotte. He had no love or affection for his wife-to-be, but he wouldn't allow anyone to say bad shit about her.

No man in his right mind would let another talk in the negative about his wife.

It's why Angelo had been forced to take his punishment without trying to hit back.

Diego knew there would be a consequence at some point. Angelo liked to hit back, but he always did it when others' backs were turned.

What Angelo didn't know, was he always had eyes on his cousin, always. He wouldn't allow anything to happen to his city and to those closest to him because of it.

"In four months," The Boss said. "I think this city has been in mourning too long. This will be a huge event. One that will really capture the essence of the city and bring back peace, security, and happiness."

Diego clenched his hand around the fork, and all he wanted to do was leave this dinner. Gatherings like this were a tense affair.

"I wouldn't get so comfortable either, Angelo," The Boss said. "You will be next to be married."

"I don't need to be married, sir. I'm just a mere made man."

This made all of the guests go silent. No one questioned The Boss. Even Diego never did.

"A word, now!" The Boss got to his feet, and Angelo had no choice but to follow.

Diego watched them leave, and he noticed Charlotte had tensed up.

"Will you be planning the wedding?" he asked, trying to distract her.

"My mother is preparing everything. I go for my fitting next week. She wanted me to ask you if you'd like to be part of the cake testing."

"Cake testing?"

"We need to decide what cake we'd like to have."

"Whichever you like is fine with me." This wasn't his first wedding. It didn't matter if the cake was delicious or if the flowers were from the right imports. A marriage could still end up fucked up.

Look at him, he was a widower, just like he told Belle. He simply left out the part where he was the one to make himself so.

The Boss returned, but Angelo did not.

Angelo had to go and get stitched for his insolence as The Boss had stabbed him. It was a pity they didn't just kill him Angelo was a pain and a pest, one that needed to be dealt with, but Diego seemed to be the only one who saw through his act.

After dinner, he escorted Charlotte back home, declining a drink, and made his way back across the city. He had every intention of going back to his apartment, but he instead, ended up at Angelo's where Belle was on stage, playing the piano.

He moved toward her private booth where he had a perfect view of her. Tanya, the waitress who'd been paid to help Belle, brought him over a drink.

Alone again, he watched Belle.

He didn't know why the fuck he had come back.

If he was getting married in a matter of months, he had to make plans for his wife, not for Belle. Since meeting her, she'd been on his mind, and it had only been on a computer screen he'd seen her. Once he saw her in person, heard her speak, he was so fucking drawn to her, it was eating away at him.

She didn't have a clue who he was, and rather than irritate him, it had given him a heady feeling.

When the song came to an end, she sat waiting for any requests, but none came. She always did this, and he found it such a sweet action. Waiting, always calm, always happy. She started to play, and he saw the smile on her lips.

It suddenly dawned on him he'd never seen women in his life happy. His first wife had been miserable, as had his mother when she was alive. He couldn't recall, other than a few mistresses, ever seeing women happy.

Belle looked genuinely happy playing the piano. Even to a roomful of people who didn't give a shit about what she was playing or who for. Still, she kept on doing it, for her own enjoyment? He wasn't sure.

Nothing made a whole lot of sense to him anymore, especially not why he was sitting here again, watching her.

She finished her last piece before being led by Tanya back to the booth. He stayed perfectly still, not even touching his drink in case the ice clinked in the glass. Tanya handed Belle a bottle of water and left without saying a word.

"You're back," Belle said.

"You know I'm here?"

"Yes."

"How is that possible when you can't see me?"

"I can smell you."

"Smell me. Do I smell bad?"

"No. You don't smell bad. Your cologne lingers in the air. It's how I can tell. Normally the booth is plain, no scent other than my own."

"Ah, I will have to be careful sneaking up on you."

"You want to sneak up on me?"

"Are you flirting with me, Belle?"

She gave him a light laugh this time. "I have no idea. Does it look like flirting?"

"I guess only if you want to be caught at the end of it?"

"Where's the fun in being caught? I thought the fun was all in the chase," she asked.

"Then you clearly haven't been caught by the right guy."

"Clearly not."

He noticed her cheeks were flushed, and from the press of her tits, she was aroused. *Interesting.*

"So, what really does bring you back here? Am I getting a stalker, Mr. Leoni?" she asked.

"I like to hear you play."

"You do?"

"You play it so well. I guess I'm getting addicted."

"There are worse things in life to be addicted to, I guess. Do you have a drink?"

"Yes."

"Ah, okay." She twisted the cap off her bottle, and he watched her take a sip. "How have you been?"

"You're asking about me?"

"It's what friends do."

"We're friends?" he asked.

"I don't know if we're friends, but we're certainly

acquaintances. I don't take just anyone to Mary's, I'll have you know. I save that for people I really like."

"Then I'll consider it a treat for a job well done."

Her smile was breathtaking, and he didn't want this moment to end. Yet, like all things, it had to end. The way he was paying her attention, someone would notice. He thought about Richard, and his enemy and knew he had to deal with that special request very soon.

Between his father, the wedding, and keeping an eye on the city, he'd pushed Richard to the bottom of the list of things to do.

"You're quiet," she said.

"I need to think."

"I get that. Take all the time in the world." She touched his hand. "You're always more than welcome here."

She was working in his restaurant and offering him her booth. She didn't have a fucking clue who was sitting opposite her. He'd killed men and women in the name of his family, for loyalty. By the time he was fifteen he had over five kills, most of them of men twice his age, and who were supposed to have more skill than he did.

Running a hand down his face, he watched as Tanya returned to take Belle back to the stage.

He didn't move.

He had to stop coming here for not only his safety but for Belle's. She was a weak link to him, and not just because she was a woman. Her blindness made her weak. Anyone could sneak up on her, hurt her.

It was one thing to have his enemy's death on his conscience, but it was another thing entirely to have an innocent woman.

Belle was innocent and a civilian. He couldn't keep coming here and seeing her. No matter how it seemed to calm the beast inside him. She played the piano without a single flaw.

Finishing off his drink, he'd walk her home, and then, he'd never see her again. He wouldn't have anything else to do to her.

He'd be getting married in a matter of months, not to mention the women he could call at a moment's notice.

Diego didn't get her allure. She wasn't the sexiest woman he'd ever seen, or the prettiest, and yet, he kept on coming, like a moth to a fucking flame. She had him under her spell, and there was no way out of it, not for him.

The restaurant slowly emptied, and he held her jacket. The locker that he'd known was hers had the label, "Blind Girl's Locker." He'd made sure his men had it removed and her locker cleaned up. She worked in his establishment, and she'd be treated with respect.

Tanya escorted her over to him, and Belle offered him that sweet smile.

"You always seem to surprise me," she said. "You're the perfect gentleman."

If she really knew what he was capable of and what he'd done to many women, she wouldn't ever mistake him as a gentleman.

Taking hold of her hand, he placed it over his arm and left the restaurant. This would be his last time seeing her, talking to her. Allowing himself to have the illusion of being a free man.

That's who Belle deserved. Someone who would love and care for her.

"You're still quiet."

"I've got a lot on my mind."

"I get that. Running a club must be incredibly exhausting." She rested her head against his shoulder.

"Whatever it is, it'll be all right."

"How could you even know that?" he asked.

"My mother, she always told me that no matter how scary anything was, there was always a way around it. There's a solution for everything, you've just got to be brave enough to look."

"Your mother sounds amazing."

"She was."

"Was?"

"She passed away a long time ago."

"I'm so sorry."

"It's fine, really. I've had my chance to grieve."

"I thought it never went away."

"It doesn't, but as each day passes and life makes you have to remember you're still part of it. It doesn't exactly allow you unlimited time to wait for the pain to die down. It just gets easier somehow. You take it one day at a time."

"Some things in life you need to take one day at a time."

"True. True."

"What about your dad?" he asked. He knew all about her, after running a thorough background check the moment he realized she was one of his employees. Her father was around, and he constantly checked up on her. She wasn't poor. Compared to his wealth she was, but she wasn't hurting for a good life.

"Yes, my dad. He's very protective of me and likes to look out for me as much as he can. I think he expected me to stay home all the time, but I just couldn't do that."

"Why not?"

"I don't want to live at home for the rest of my life. I want to get out there, have some fun, live a lot." She giggled. "What about you?"

"My mom passed away too, some time ago. It's just me and my dad now." There wasn't much else he could say. There's no way he could tell her he was capo of the city and she worked in a restaurant run by the mafia, not to mention he had a cousin out for his very job.

"Is he proud of you? The club was amazing. The atmosphere was intense and the music, and I enjoyed it there."

"Apart from where your friend abandoned you?"

"Yeah, that part still sucks." He came to a stop, and he placed a hand on her shoulder so she wouldn't keep walking.

"We're about to walk up the steps."

"Okay. Wow, that didn't take long at all to get home." They walked up the steps, and he walked her to the elevator. "I usually hate the elevator, but since I've got my hero by my side, I'll make an exception."

"Why do you hate elevators?" he asked.

"I don't know. Always have. It's the weightlessness of it. That feeling of floating right before a crash. I know, it's crazy."

"It makes a whole lot of sense."

He walked her out of the elevator, to her door. She already had a key ready, and he took it from her, placing the key in the lock.

No matter how much time he had to take, he had the patience with her.

He opened the door and waited.

"Thank you for walking me home and keeping me company."

"You're more than welcome." He stared down at her full, inviting lips. He wanted to kiss her, but if he did, it would only make it harder to walk away.

"Would you like to come in for coffee?" she

asked. Her cheeks were a deep shade of red.

"I've got to be heading back. Goodnight, Belle."

"Goodnight, Diego."

He waited for her to close the door before turning on his heel and leaving the apartment building.

He was more than aware of someone following him. He played it cool, passing across a street. He sank into an alcove, waiting for whoever it was to follow.

One.

Two.

Three.

He grabbed the man from behind, banding an around his neck, pulling him tight to his body, and dragging him into the nearest alley. With a blade in his hand, he slammed the guy up against the wall. A camera fell from his hand.

"Who do you work for?"

"Please, I didn't mean—"

He slammed the blade into the man's stomach and covered his mouth to stop the scream from filling the air.

"I asked you a fucking question. Who do you work for? If you do not answer me, the next one will be in your throat."

He let the man's mouth go, and he started talking.

"Angelo. He wants me to follow you. To get as much evidence on you as possible."

"What kind of evidence?"

"I don't know. Everyone you talk to. Who you hang out with. All of it. Anything he can use."

Drawing the blade from the man's stomach, he plunged it into his neck, holding him still, and staring into his eyes as he did so.

When he finally died, he withdrew the blade, wiping the excess blood on the man's clothing before putting it away. He'd clean it later. Leaving the man propped against the wall, he pulled out his cell phone to make a call to his cleaner to come and collect him.

It would only be a matter of minutes before all of this mess was cleaned up.

Picking up the camera, he had a quick look at the pictures the bastard had taken. All of them were of him and Belle, each one looking more incriminating than the last. The look on his face showed how besotted he was.

He was a fucking fool.

The camera would need to be disposed of, and he needed to get his head out of his ass and stop visiting Belle. There was nothing between them. No chance of anything, and he was only putting her in danger because of it. Pocketing the cell phone, he helped his men pack the body into the back of the car.

It was time he put a call through to Richard.

Angelo needed to be dealt with sooner rather than later.

****

"Come on, Belle. Please, you really need to do this with me," Melanie said.

Belle snorted. "I'm not doing anything with you." She walked around her apartment, grabbing the two cups she needed. In her head, she counted the steps around her coffee table, which wasn't glass. She had learned her mistake the hard way. Nothing around her apartment was breakable. She didn't own any lamps for this reason, and there were no pictures.

Her father hated her apartment, but for her, it helped to make her self-sufficient. She already had to call him to let him know she intended to purchase a guide dog. She was on the waiting list, but each time one came up, she always passed it along to the next person in line. She was still mourning her first one, but that was silly and she really needed to get over her pain.

Like she had told Diego a couple of weeks ago.

Had it been a couple of weeks since she last spoke to him? He'd not been by the restaurant in some time. There was no lingering scent of his cologne, which she was saddened by as she found his scent rather nice.

"I told you I was a horrible human being. Why can't you forgive me?"

"I have forgiven you, otherwise I wouldn't have given you five hundred dollars for the pair of shoes you just had to have, nor would I be sitting with you right now." She shrugged.

"Then please, come to the bar with me."

"Not going to happen, sweetheart. You abandoned me, in a club that I don't know." She hadn't told Melanie she'd forgiven her so quickly because of a certain Diego Leoni. She'd not even told her father either. Diego was like her little secret. The moment she told anyone, they would all judge her, and she didn't want that.

Her father would want to meet anyone who showed an interest in her. He was always so protective, and most times, she loved it, she really did. Not with Diego though.

He was a mystery, and so far, none of their interactions had resulted in large donations of money to his current venture. Not that she'd ever given huge amounts of money away. Her father would be pissed if he knew how much Melanie asked for on a regular basis. She had probably funded all of Melanie's branded shoe collection, or at least that's what she was told. She rarely wore heels as it was a danger to her.

She only granted herself that pleasure when she was sure of her escort, and that they were happy to keep hold of her.

Her thoughts drifted to Diego.

She hoped he was okay. Their last meeting he'd seemed distracted.

"I told you every single detail though."

"Even when I begged you not to," Belle said. "I don't need to know about your sex life. It's your sex life."

"Yeah, and if you actually trusted me, you'd have a sex life."

"I'm not going to have sex with a random guy. I'm not comfortable with that."

"You do realize you live in the twenty-first century, right? Guys want girls who put out fast and easy. You won't even make the cut if he can't get it in your pants."

"Make the cut?"

"There are so many women out there to compete with."

"Well, for the right guy, you don't have to compete."

"You're still spilling the same old crap about your mom and dad."

"It's not crap. They met, fell in love, and lived happily ever after."

"Your mother died, Belle."

Belle paused on the way into the kitchen. "You're being meaner than normal. Next time, find someone else to beg for money."

She walked into the kitchen, counting the steps to the sink. She reached out, feeling for the tap, jumping as Melanie wrapped her arms around her waist.

"I'm sorry. Okay, I love going out with you, and it's not me trying to be a bitch. I want you to meet new people as well. Have a life. Isn't that why we came out here? For us both to have a lot of fun."

"Oh, I know all about fun."

"Singing karaoke is not fun."

"Is not fun to you, maybe. I like it. I know this is hard for you to understand, but I happen to really like my life."

"And what if coming back to the bar, you'll meet the right guy?"

"You're going to the same bar as last time?" Belle asked. Her thoughts instantly returned to Diego.

She wasn't a stalker. She didn't go around begging men for attention.

Diego wasn't just any man though.

No, she wouldn't go to him.

The temptation was so strong.

"Come on, I even brought you a nice dress to complement those fantastic curves. Come on, what do you have to lose? This could be so much fun."

She nibbled on her lip.

"Afterward, you can even take me to Mary's," Melanie said.

"You know I only take special people to Mary's. You can't go there. There's no way you can order a cheeseburger with no fat and salt."

Melanie laughed. "That means you're coming with me."

"I'll go to the bar, but you have to promise me you won't leave me. You have to promise me, you'll dance with me, and that I'll have a good time, like you."

"You got it." Melanie hugged her tight. "We're going tonight."

"Wait, tonight?"

"It's Friday. It's one of the best times to go out. All of the edible bachelors are there."

"I think you mean eligible."

"Nope, I mean edible. They're never any good for

you if you don't want to nibble on them a little bit." Melanie took her arm, giving it a little bite.

"Not awkward or weird at all."

Melanie took her back to her room, and even as she protested, her friend always got what she wanted. Within thirty minutes, not only was she sporting a dress, but also some modestly high heels, and they were climbing into the back of the taxi.

She let Melanie take control, organizing where the taxi needed to go.

"This is going to be so much fun."

"I thought we'd be going out next week, but yay for right now." She did have plans to sit with a hot cocoa and listen to her book.

It would seem she was going to be dancing after all. The heels Melanie had put on her feet were pinching a little.

She wanted nothing more than to kick them off. Instead, she leaned back in the cab and waited, listening to the blur of the world as it went by.

All too soon the driver came to a stop. Belle paid, like she always did, and Melanie helped her out of the cab.

Melanie knew the guy on the door, and rather than wait outside at the back of the queue, they walked right inside.

The music was already really loud, and it stopped Belle from hearing where people were. Melanie was so distracted, Belle walked into a couple of people, immediately apologizing.

"Melanie, seriously, come on."

"Yes, let's go and dance."

Tripping over her own feet, she was dragged onto the dance floor. Melanie held her arms, and they were both dancing.

Belle didn't like it as she was moved from left to right, pushed and shoved. The heavy beat was making her incredibly nervous.

Melanie wrapped her arms around her neck, laughing. "I see a hot guy already. Man, he looks so hot."

"I want to go and sit down."

"I'm afraid there's no private booth this time. Do you want a drink?" Melanie asked.

"Yes, I want a drink."

Again, she was pulled in the other direction and placed on the seat at the bar. She placed her hands flat on the surface and knew Melanie had left her.

The heavy perfume that lingered in the air didn't last.

She was alone, at the same bar, and this time, not even in her privately reserved booth. She gritted her teeth at the unfairness of it. She should have known Melanie wouldn't stick around with her. For all she knew, they weren't even at the same bar.

All so she could have a chance encounter with Diego.

This was crazy.

She had never been the kind of woman to put herself in danger in the hope of seeing someone else.

"What can I get you?" a guy asked.

"Erm, are you the barman?"

"Yes, sweetheart."

"Excellent. Can I just get a bottled water? The cap still on? Thank you."

"Sweetheart, you're in a bar."

"I know. I just. Look, my friend is on the dance floor, and I can't see. Please, can I just have some water?"

She always tried to make sure she never showed how nervous or vulnerable she was, but this was so fucking hard. She wanted to cry, but she kept those tears locked inside.

The barman didn't put her drink in front of her.

He didn't come back and speak to her.

Melanie didn't return, and the bar was only getting busier, more frantic.

Closing her eyes, Belle tried to focus. She could make it out of here.

She had just gotten to her feet when someone pushed her hard. She landed on the floor as someone stood on her hand.

She cried out, but in the next second, she was lifted up. The cologne, she recognized instantly.

"Diego?"

"I take it your friend has left you again?" he asked.

The noise of the club faded, and they weren't on the street.

"Where are you taking me?" she asked.

"To my office where you'll be safe and not trampled to death. You didn't even arrange a private booth."

"Surprise. Tonight wasn't exactly planned."

"I expected more from you."

She tripped over her own heels again, and she heard him curse. In the next second, she let out a gasp as he lifted her up.

"Man, you're so strong." He carried her somewhere. She heard a door open and close, and then she was placed on a hard surface. His desk? "Look, I can take care of myself."

"You can?"

"Yes."

"Oh, please. One shove and you were on your ass."

"Technically, I was on my hands and knees."

"And you think that's any better?"

"Well, no, but, oh, please, stop doing this. Stop making this harder than it's meant to be."

"I should call your father."

"Oh, my, you're not my brother or my keeper."

"I'm doing a better fucking job of it than your best friend."

This made Belle pause. "Job? Are you, like, working for my father? Do you even own this nightclub? Has my father hired you to keep an eye on me?"

She wouldn't put it past him. He always did things like this behind her back. She knew for a fact he was paying Melanie to keep an eye on her, not that her *friend* was doing a good job of it. Other than when Melanie needed money, she rarely saw her friend. Most of the time, she was gone, doing her own thing.

"I'm not working for your father. This is my club, and I wouldn't lie to you."

"How did you know I was here?" she asked.

"I saw you enter on my security cameras. I watched your friend leave you by the bar. Just so you know, she already found someone and they left together. You need to stop hanging around with her."

Tears filled her eyes, and she heard him curse again.

"I'm sorry. I'm not usually this emotional. I'm not usually this stupid. She promised she wouldn't leave me again."

Diego cupped her face. "Fuck, baby, please, do not cry."

"I can't seem to stop."

"I can't handle it when you cry."

She sniffled. "I'm trying to stop."

He didn't let her go, and she felt his breath across

her face. It was so close.

"Diego?"

Just as she finished saying his name, he slammed his lips down on hers, silencing any more sound from her. This was her first real kiss.

Chapter Four

Diego had been pissed seeing her enter his club again. He'd been avoiding her, making sure he didn't go near her, to keep her safe. That fucking spy Angelo sent to him had gotten way too close.

So he kept his distance from her, giving her the space she needed. He'd also put the call to Richard, and sure enough, Angelo was their number one enemy. He should have known. Richard had been gathering intelligence for a while now on all the dirty backyard dealings Angelo was making.

Angelo wanted his place, but Diego was never going to give it up.

Now, as he held Belle, kissing her lips, he didn't know if he could give her up either. She was so soft, and as he took possession of her lips, never had he kissed a woman so thoroughly.

The women he used, he didn't kiss. He didn't put his lips anywhere near them.

Belle was too young for him. She should be finding a man more her own age, and even as he thought it, he couldn't stop kissing her.

She tasted amazing. Drawing her closer to the edge of the desk, he slid his hand to the back of her neck, holding her captive beneath him, wanting nothing more than to sink his dick deep inside her tight heat.

Breaking from the kiss, he trailed his lips down her neck, sucking on the rapidly beating pulse.

"You need to get rid of Melanie from your life."

"I know."

"You need to learn to take care of yourself."

She gasped as he pushed the strap of her dress down her shoulder. Just one taste. That was all he wanted. One taste and he'd leave her alone.

She moaned his name, crying out for more, and it was so fucking addictive. The sweet sounds coming from her mouth made his dick ache. Never had he been so enthralled by a woman.

He'd been with many experienced women, but hearing Belle, feeling her as she held his arms, it was fucking everything.

You can't have her.
You'll only hurt her.
Get her killed.

"Diego," she said, moaning his name.

Pulling her dress down, he saw she wasn't wearing a bra, the padding of the dress providing all that she needed. Her tits were huge with small nipples. They thrust up against his mouth with each indrawn breath.

He should put her away, not look, not even be tempted, and yet, he licked one hardened peak, and heard her moan his name. It was such a sweet sound.

One he wanted to hear again.

As he did, he sucked down hard, cupping her other tit and rubbing his thumb back and forth over her nipple.

Dropping his hands down to her thighs, he lifted up her dress, moving it to her waist. Pressing a hand to her pussy, he felt how wet and ready she was for him. Wrapping his fingers in the fabric, he tore the panties from her body with a yank, relishing her gasp.

Not at any point did she stop him.

She was so fucking stupid. Here she was in his office, kissing him back. She had no idea who he was or what he did. He killed people to protect his family and his reputation. He wasn't a good man, and yet here she still was, kissing him, not pushing away when she should.

Touching her pussy, he slid a finger between her

slit, feeling how wet she was. She moaned against his lips as he took her mouth once again.

His cock was so hard, pressed against the front of his pants. Leaning behind her, he pushed all of the papers and laptop to the floor, spreading her out.

"What are you doing?"

"I'm going to taste you." He made sure she was comfortable before kneeling before her. She had a light smattering of curls across the lips of her pussy. They were slick with her arousal. Spreading her open, he saw her swollen clit, and he licked at it, tasting her juices for the first time.

He'd never been the kind of man to go down on a woman.

Belle arched up, moaning his name.

She couldn't stop saying "Diego," and he loved it. The sound echoed off the walls, thrilling him to the core. He wanted her to be completely lost on him, drunk on what he could do to her.

He'd tried to be the gentleman, to walk away, but that was a mistake. For the past couple of weeks, he'd been miserable. It wasn't helping him stay focused, and now Belle had literally walked right into his lair.

She didn't have to come, but now she was here, he was going to keep her. It was dangerous and probably the biggest mistake he was ever going to make, but there was no turning back now.

Not when she tasted this good and felt this incredible. He teased her pussy, sucking on her clit. At the same time, he began to loosen his slacks, pulling out his cock. He was so hard it was almost on the verge of pain.

As he worked up and down his length, the tip was already leaking copious amounts of pre-cum, and he smeared it across the head.

He couldn't take it anymore. He had to be balls deep inside her.

After waiting this long, he needed to know if she'd be as tight as he imagined, as ready as he was.

Moving up between her thighs, he placed her at just the right angle, putting the tip of his dick against her entrance. He wanted to see her take him, to watch her pussy suck him in.

Sliding his cock in, he slammed in deep, and he heard her scream as well as felt her tense. Not only that, he felt the tear of her skin.

Staring at Belle, he saw the tears in her eyes, her beautiful, unseeing eyes, and he just knew.

"I'm your first?" he asked.

"Yes." She whispered the words, and she sniffled after.

His first wife had been a virgin. This wasn't his first time taking an innocent, and yet, he'd done this over his desk. He was to the hilt inside her and felt her pussy pulse around his length.

Gritting his teeth, he wanted to hit something. He gripped the edge of the desk, staying perfectly still.

Belle deserved romance. Champagne. Wining and dining.

Not this. Not losing it on top of his office desk.

Every time he was here, he'd remember this moment, and see her open before him, vulnerable, ready to take his cock.

He couldn't pull out.

Well, he *could*, but for her first time, he didn't want her to hate it. The pain would go, and as he eased back, he touched her clit.

"What are you doing?" she asked.

"Trust me, Belle. I want you to come all over my cock."

"It hurt."

"I know. It won't hurt for much longer." He'd tortured men. Heard them scream. Watched them piss and shit themselves, beg for their very lives. He'd never been touched by their antics. All it took from Belle was a whimper and he felt like the world's biggest asshole. He didn't want to hurt her, and the fact he did pissed him off. He cared about her and only wanted her to feel pleasure.

Counting sheep inside his head, he tried not to think about how perfect she felt wrapped around his length, or the feel of her wetness. When he pulled out of her, there would be blood, but he'd clean her up.

After taking her virginity, he would take care of her. There was no reason his world had to touch her.

Angelo was already being taken care of. He had men watching his cousin, not to mention Richard was on his side. He'd employ Richard to take care of her, to add extra security for her.

He could do this.

Stroking her clit, he felt her body change beneath him. At first, she was tense, non-responsive. Slowly, she started to thrust against him. He kept himself perfectly still, not wanting to hurt her or scare her.

Her cunt tightened around him, and as he worked two fingers against her clit, he stroked the other up her body to tease her nipples, touching each one in turn until she finally erupted. When she did, it was a beautiful sight. Her mouth opened as she gasped, her body trying to take more of him inside her.

When her orgasm ended, he took hold of her hips and slowly began to rock inside her. Pulling out, he saw her virgin blood on his cock. He wasn't wearing a condom. He would have to pull out. Not the best form of contraceptive, but it would do for tonight. All he wanted to do was to feel her come on him, and it had been an amazing feeling.

She began to thrust up against him, taking more of his cock. He sped up his thrusts until he was pounding away inside her. The desk was secured to the floor, and it didn't move, giving him the chance to hold her and fuck her hard.

It was a dream, and as he came, he nearly filled her pussy with his spunk. Pulling out at the last minute, he finished off over her mound and stomach, the dress taking several drops of his cum as well.

Panting for breath, he stared down at her. Placing his hand on her thigh, he saw blood and cum smeared together. He hadn't meant to touch her.

"Wait here."

"Where am I going to go?"

He grabbed a washcloth from his bathroom, wetting it with some warm water. Returning to her, he wiped the drops of cum and blood from her body. Once she was clean, he went back to the bathroom, washed his hands, and rinsed the cloth out.

When he entered his office, she was sitting up and trying to put her dress back on.

He rushed to her side, helping her, sliding the straps of the dress back into place, giving her the modesty she was seeking.

"I didn't come here for that," she said.

"I know. I know you didn't."

"I'm so sorry."

He frowned. "Why are you sorry?"

"You must think I'm easy or something. I can't believe I just did this with you. I'm insane." She tried to jump down off his desk, but he wouldn't let her go.

Holding her thighs, he kept her locked into place. "You're not going anywhere."

"I shouldn't be here," she said. "I didn't want to come in the first place."

"You didn't?"

"I didn't trust Melanie. When she said she was coming here, I wanted to see you again. Not see, obviously. Ugh, you know what I mean. You haven't been by to see me play, and I thought I had upset you."

He liked her rambling. It was cute. "You could never upset me."

"Then why haven't you come back?"

"Because I'm an asshole," he said. "I've been busy, but I've been wanting to see you."

"You're not married, are you? Holy crap, I've just had sex with a married man?"

"I told you I'm a widower."

"Oh, right. I can't think right now. I've just had sex."

"Did you like it?" he asked.

"What?"

He saw her blush, and again, it was the cutest thing.

"Did you like having sex with me?" He had never talked this way with anyone, not even his first wife.

The women he was used to knew who he was. They knew what he was capable of. Since meeting Belle, he hadn't gone to visit them.

He was losing his mind.

"Yes, I did," she said. "Erm, was I ... okay?"

Cupping her face, he tilted her head back, staring into her eyes. In this moment, he was so pleased she couldn't see. If she knew who he was, she'd run screaming. For now, he was just a man who owned a bar; he wasn't of any real importance to her or anyone else. "You were perfect in every single way."

This meant so much to him, he couldn't even

think straight. He was the wrong kind of guy for her. She should be running in the opposite direction, but no matter what, he kept coming back for more.

Taking possession of her mouth, he kissed her hard, needing her, hungry for more. Even though he'd just come, he wanted her again.

"Are you just going to walk away again?" she asked, breaking from the kiss.

"I'm not walking away this time." He was more determined than ever to make this work.

He saw her smile, and it calmed everything inside him.

"Let me take you home," he said.

"I'd like that."

First, he took her hand. He was so busy getting his dick inside her, he didn't take the time to look at her hand. "How is it?"

"It's fine. A little sore. It's not cut, is it?"

"No, it's not cut." He kissed her head.

He couldn't seem to let her go. Each time he touched her, he was hungry for more. He'd never experienced anything like this.

Grabbing his jacket, he placed it gently across her shoulders, covering her from anyone else. He didn't want any other man to look at her. She belonged to him now, and he took care of her.

Leaving his office, he nodded for his men to stay exactly where they were. His security team would follow him, but he didn't want or need them asking him any questions. He walked her out the back of the club to the waiting car. Easing her inside, he strapped her in, being careful as he did so.

Climbing behind the wheel, he started up the car and took off, heading in the direction of her apartment.

"You know, I've never had a boyfriend," she

said. "Is that kind of weird?"

"It's not weird at all. You were saving yourself for me." He took her hand, kissing her knuckles. He'd never been an overly affectionate guy, but with her, it would seem he was breaking every single kind of rule.

"You make me sound so sweet."

"You are sweet," he said. It was one of the reasons he liked her. She wasn't vicious or violent. There was no spoiled brat within her. She was the complete opposite of everything he was used to.

"How old are you?" she asked.

"I'm forty years old."

"I'll be twenty-two on my next birthday," she said.

"When is your birthday?" He already knew it was in two months, but he had to keep up the persona of only being the kind of guy who ran a bar.

She told him the date, and he smiled. "I'll have to make sure I prepare something extra special for you."

"I'd like that. Especially the part where you think we'll be together in a couple of months," she said.

"It would seem I've got a whole lot of surprises for you."

****

"Ouch!" Belle rubbed at her leg as she heard Diego wince.

"I can walk you around the apartment."

"It's fine. Honestly." She was determined to get this right. He had finally brought her back to his place after a week of visiting her at her apartment. She wasn't going to head home until she knew the complete layout by memory. He'd been surprised that she could function in her own place without a guide dog, which she had decided to call up for one when it was ready. She was nervous about having one after so long, especially as thinking back to her previous dog still pained her. Even thinking of his name hurt her. "I can do this. Besides, a little pain never hurt anyone." She let out a gasp as his arms snaked around her waist.

"A little pain never hurt anyone? I can think of all kinds of fun pains that will have you gasping for more."

"You're tempting me."

"And I can't bear to see you hurting yourself."

"It takes me a short time to memorize the place. Please, don't worry. I got this. I will always be able to handle this." She wrapped her arms around his neck, holding him. Touching his face, she felt where his lips were, and she kissed him. There had been a couple of occasions she'd kissed his nose, cheek, or top of his lips. He didn't seem to mind, and when he took control, sinking his fingers into her hair, and kissing her back with a passion, she was never going to mind that.

"I don't like seeing you in pain."

"I'm not in pain. It's just a little ouchy." She kissed him again. "Please, take me to the door."

He walked her to the door. Pressing her back flat against the surface, she walked the room, counting the steps in her head, until she remembered where the table was. Leaning down, she placed her hand on the hard surface, feeling along the edge. She circled the table several times, making sure she knew where it was. Then she chanced taking a seat. She stepped forward just as Diego let out a warning and something crashed down.

"I'm so sorry. I'm so sorry. Was it expensive? I can replace it. I promise."

"It's just a lamp."

"But if it's a lamp you like?"

He chuckled. "Don't worry about it. It's a lamp that can be replaced."

"I got tired of replacing lamps. It's why I don't

have any. I'm so sorry." It had been a long time since she felt angered by her ... blindness. She had never considered it a disability before, but now she did, and it pissed her off. "I'm so sorry."

She jumped a little as Diego wrapped his arms around her. "And I've told you to stop worrying about this. You are doing fine. I'm going to have to make some changes. Now, I have two other lamps in here, so I'm going to move you on to the dining room."

"Just how big is your apartment?"

"I like my space."

"Space? This is more than space." She loved it, really. "Describe it to me?"

When he did, it sounded more like a bachelor pad. Black, leather furniture, crisp white walls, all the up-to-date mod-cons, and everything that she could imagine him having, he had.

"It sounds like you."

"It does? My apartment sounds like me?"

"When we're together you're always in a suit. You're a businessman."

"I guess I am."

"What else do you do, besides running the club? Do you do anything else?" she asked. He walked her around the dining room, and she felt six chairs tucked under a table. The space really was incredible. Her father offered to rent her an apartment with more space, but she really wasn't interested.

She had picked her apartment for herself. Her father helped her as much as she would let him, but the point of moving was for her to be by herself. To learn to adapt on her own.

For the most part, she had succeeded.

"So, what would you like to eat?" he asked, moving them through to the kitchen.

"Pizza."

"I'll call now."

She ran her fingers over the counter. It was granite, and she smiled. She wondered if he cooked.

"Pizza is on the way."

"Do you cook?"

"Not even a little bit."

"Not even toast?"

"Nothing. I don't cook."

"Make coffee?" she asked.

"Nothing."

She felt how close he was. Reaching out, she touched him. He'd removed his jacket, but he still wore his shirt.

"White or black?"

"I always wear white shirts."

"A tie?"

"Rarely."

She slid her hand up his chest, touching the few open buttons. Again, she smiled, loving that about him. She began to open a few buttons, exposing his flesh. She pressed her lips against his skin, kissing him.

He ran his hands down her back, gripping her ass.

She tugged his shirt out of his pants, touching him. Stroking his flesh, she noticed a few old scars across his body.

"Were you in an accident?" she asked.

She felt him tense just a little beneath her touch, and she frowned. Why would he be tense?

"Yes."

"What's going on, Diego?"

"It's nothing. I was in a couple of fights when I was younger."

"Bad fights?"

"I wasn't a good boy, Belle."

"You weren't?"

"No, I was a bad boy."

She giggled as he growled out the "boy." Running her hands up his chest, she pushed the shirt from his body.

"I think I like that. My own little bad boy." She kissed down to his nipple, flicking the tip, and sliding her tongue across his chest, to his other one.

He let out a groan, and she wanted him again. He'd fucked her every single night that week, and each time was better than the last. Each second she spent with him seemed more magical than the last. They had both formed this kind of bubble around themselves, and she didn't want it to disappear or fade away.

As she kissed down his body, he didn't try to stop her. Whenever she had gone for his belt before, he always tried to stop her. Not this time.

She unbuckled his belt, waiting for the moment he'd tell her to stop. She didn't want to stop, and as he let her keep going, excitement built inside her.

"You know you're playing dangerously here?" he asked.

"I want to play with you, Diego." She kissed just above his brief line. She felt the edge of the fabric against her chin. "And I think you want me to play as well."

She pulled his boxer briefs down, and he took hold of her hand, wrapping it around his length.

"How about we spice things up a bit?"

"What do you have in mind?"

"Pizza is on its way. The time is ticking."

She smiled, working his length up and down, just the way he'd taught her. There was something incredibly sinful and dirty about having an older man teach her naughty things.

"I want you to make me come before that doorbell rings."

"I've never done this before," she said.

"Then let's see how well you do."

She gasped as he wrapped her hair around his fist, holding the length tight. Pressing her lips to the end of his cock, she felt him slick with pre-cum, and she teased him, licking him before taking the entire head into her mouth. Sucking him to the back of her throat, she pulled off until only the head remained before sliding back inside and moaning around his length. He tasted incredible, a little on the salty side, and she loved how hard yet soft he was. With each bob of her head, his grip seemed to tighten. It was at the point of the pain being a little more than she could handle, but she loved it. Her nipples felt so hard and her pussy wet with her juices.

She wanted this more than anything.

"Fuck, that feels good."

He thrust in her mouth, and she released his cock to grip his thighs, holding herself up, taking as much of him as she could She wished she could see him, watching him come apart. Instead, she listened, hearing his deep breaths, turning into pants. His cock seemed to get harder in her mouth, and saliva dripped down her chin. Diego held her head, rocking into her mouth.

She loved the possession as he held her, the control he exerted even when she was the one with his cock in her mouth.

She didn't succeed in making him come as the doorbell rang, interrupting them.

"Fuck!"

She pulled off his length, wiping the excess saliva with the back of her hand. "I failed."

He cupped her face. "You didn't fail, not even a little bit." He kissed her lips. "Stay here. Do you mind cold pizza?"

"Not at all."

"I'll be back, and we'll finish this."

She stayed perfectly still, trying to hear for when he came back. Anticipation ate away at her, but she stayed in position, waiting.

When he came back, she sensed ... something.

"What is it?" she asked.

"I've got to head out."

"You do?"

"Yes. Erm, I've got a few errands to run."

"Oh."

Silence fell between them.

"I can get a cab home. That's not a problem. You don't have to worry about me."

"It's not about the cab. I don't mind leaving you here. I just don't want you to be hurt."

"Diego, don't worry about it. If you're not here, I'd rather head home."

"I'll take you home."

She stepped toward the sound of him. Taking hold of his hands, she smiled. "Please, stop worrying so much about me."

He grabbed her ass, holding her close. "I'll always worry about you."

She kissed his lips, stepping back.

"I'm going to drop you off home, and no, I'm not going to hear any complaints about it either. You're too important to me to just abandon."

"I could come with you."

"Not tonight."

"You're not going to the club?"

"No. It's something else. Family stuff."

He rarely talked about his family.

"Whatever it is, I hope you get it sorted out."

"I will."

He helped her into her jacket. His impatience showed through, and she tried to rush. He didn't lose his temper with her or anything. She just knew he wanted to be somewhere else, and immediately. This was another one of those moments that pissed her off and where she wished she wasn't blind.

They made it to his car, and she quickly strapped in without taking her time.

Diego drove fast, and she realized she didn't know all that much about him. For a man who owned a club, something really important had come up.

When he came to a stop outside of her apartment, she jerked forward in her seat from the force.

Diego was already out of the car and opening her door.

It's fine. Everything is fine.

"You'd tell me if it was anything serious, wouldn't you?"

"Yes, of course. It's nothing."

"Are you sure?" She hated to pry, especially when he didn't want to tell her anything.

"It's nothing."

They went to her elevator, and she stayed tense at his side, wishing to be at home. He took the key from her, opening her door. He nudged her into her apartment, cupped her face, and kissed her hard.

"I would rather finish our bet than do this."

She held his arms. "It's fine. Honestly, it's fine."

"I'll be back as soon as I'm done."

Another kiss and then he was gone.

She went to the door, flicking the lock into place. The scent of his cologne still hung heavy in the air.

Reaching out for the door, she counted the steps as she took them toward her sitting room. Collapsing onto her sofa, she flung her head back, running a hand down her face.

Diego confused her.

Right now, she knew she should ask him more about his life and what he did, but at the same time, when she was with him, she felt so safe, so protected.

She'd given him her virginity.

"Get a grip, Belle. You're fine. This is fine."

She was just worrying for no reason at all. Her cell phone buzzed, alerting her to her father calling.

She instructed it to accept the call. "Hey, Dad," she said.

"Sweetheart. It has been too long since I heard from you."

She chuckled. "It has been a couple of days. Not that long."

"I miss you. Can I convince you to come home?"

"Not yet. Nothing bad has happened. I'm happy."

"You're still working in that restaurant?"

"Yes, and tutoring. Don't forget that." She loved teaching kids the piano. Hearing them improve and their true talent was precious to her.

"I don't like you working in a restaurant."

"Well, I don't like you eating lots of steak, but you still do it."

"Steak won't kill me," he said.

"Lots of steak will. I'm perfectly safe."

"I don't like it. I'm actually thinking of coming out for a visit soon."

"Has Melanie said something?" she asked.

She had confided to Melanie she'd met someone. She hadn't told her friend who it was because she was still a little pissed at her friend. Not once but twice now Melanie had left her. If it wasn't for Diego, she could have really hurt herself, but then, without Melanie, she wouldn't have met Diego.

No, she couldn't justify Melanie's abandonment.

"Why? What should she have told me?"

"Nothing. Nothing at all."

"Belle, you know I can see through your lies, right? You answer too quickly and your voice goes really high-pitched."

She groaned. "Okay, I may have met someone."

"Someone?"

"A guy? He owns a club. One Melanie abandoned me in." There, her father could focus on that.

"Hold on, abandoned? Met a guy? What the hell is going on?"

"It's nothing. You don't have to worry. I've got to go."

"Belle, if you hang up this phone, I will be there tomorrow morning and you will not be able to run away, remember that."

Taking a deep breath, she ran a hand down her face. "Okay, okay, fine." She told him everything. Her father was overprotective, and she loved that about him. Only, she didn't want her dad turning up.

This thing with Diego, it was new, so very new. A week kind of new. Meeting parents was strictly for stable relationships where people knew what was going to happen in the future. She didn't even know if she and Diego would last the month. He was her first boyfriend, and she didn't know what the whole protocol was.

There was silence across the line when she finished explaining all that had happened since she last talked to her dad. She did leave out the important detail of sleeping with Diego on his office desk. He really didn't need to know that.

"I'm going to want to meet this guy," he said.

"Dad, it's fine. Please, don't do the whole scary

dad routine. I like this guy."

"And if he likes you, he'll deal with me."

"I don't even know how serious this is. Could you at least give me a little time to figure out everything else?" she asked.

There was a short pause across the line before he agreed.

At least she had time to work out what it was they were doing with each other.

Chapter Five

A few days later, holding a bundle of roses, Diego made his way to Belle's apartment. His father had turned up at his apartment, demanding his presence at a business meeting. It was all the capos from different cities, and the head of the cartel. They wanted to start a new business venture, one that could help both of them with their drug trade. The cartel leader needed unlimited access through major cities, and well, he also needed the trade of guns.

The Boss had a week to think about it, and tomorrow night they would make their first deal with the cartel.

They had a mutual enemy in the Russians, and as they were now moving in on their turf, trying to sell them out of drugs, it was time to act quickly. With their connections to the cartel, it made them stronger, and in doing that, it made the Russians weaker. But this was only one part of his problem.

The other was Angelo.

He wanted the capo role, which meant he wanted Diego out. The only way to take a capo out was by death or proving they were working against The Boss. Seeing as Diego was neither working against The Boss, nor on his deathbed, Angelo was trying to find a way to take him out. Hiring a contract killer would be the easiest option, but it would easily be traced back to Angelo.

Diego also didn't know if Angelo had reached out to any of his men, and who he'd turned against him with the promise of more money and power, the two commodities that seemed to test a man's loyalty.

He was pissed, exceedingly pissed.

Not to mention he had to also keep his association with Belle a secret. No one could know.

Then, of course, he had to also keep up appearances with Charlotte Durante, his fiancée.

It helped that Charlotte didn't seem interested in him either. Time was ticking for him to marry her, but he couldn't find any enthusiasm to claim her since meeting Belle. The only woman who was on his mind, who he wanted, was on the other side of the door.

Knocking on the door, he waited.

The roses were to make him feel better. She deserved so much more than roses. He was a fucking pig.

Belle deserved someone she could love and trust. Not him.

She had no idea he was getting married, or that he was the mafia. She thought he owned a club and was a simple man.

There was nothing simple about his life.

His life was fucking dangerous.

"Who is it?" Belle asked.

He'd already talked to Richard. It seemed the guy with the agenda was the only man he could trust to put a guy to keep her safe. If Angelo ever found out about her, he'd kill her. He couldn't have that.

She didn't fit into his world, but he was determined to make it work.

"It's me, baby, open up."

He heard the lock click open, and she was at the door, a huge smile on her face. She reached out, touching his chest, and then flung herself into his arms, holding him tightly.

"I missed you."

This was not the welcome he hoped to receive. He'd left her, and she should be pissed at him.

She doesn't know the truth.

"Come on. I missed you. I just ordered pizza. It should be here any minute." She pulled him into her apartment, and he followed her, closing the door and flicking the lock into place. Her safety meant a great deal to him.

"I'm sorry I didn't call."

"Don't worry about it. I've missed you."

He watched her put her headphones away. She listened to a lot of audio books. She walked back toward him, and he noticed her counting, her lips moving just slightly.

She pushed him down on the sofa, and suddenly, she straddled him. It wasn't very smooth as she kneed him in the thigh, but he put her right and ran his hands up her thighs, moving around to her ass.

"Now this is a welcome I didn't expect."

She cupped the back of his head and took his lips in a hard kiss. "I missed you."

"You're not pissed at me?" he asked.

"Why would I be pissed at you? You've got things to do, and I can take care of myself. Don't become one of those guys that think I need you every single minute of every single day."

"Ouch, baby, that hurt," he said.

She giggled. "I know you're a busy guy. Is everything okay at the club?"

She thought whatever was wrong with him had to do with the club. He was a fucking asshole.

"Yes, everything is fine," he said, the lie falling easily from his lips.

"Good. I was worried about you."

"Next time, I'll call." He gripped her ass as she kissed him again. She bit down on his lip, and he groaned. His cock hardened, wanting inside her again.

Breaking from the kiss, he trailed his lips down her neck, sucking on the pulse. Her tits thrust out, and he quickly worked the oversized shirt over her head, throwing it to the floor. Her tits were covered by a plain white lace bra, and her dark nipples stood out in complete contrast against the fabric.

He fingered the strap as he took one of those nipples into his mouth, sucking hard on the bud.

She gasped, his name falling from her lips on a cry. He loved hearing her say his name, in any way she could. Most often it was filled with pleasure, and it drove him crazy. He'd never been addicted to anything in his life, but within a matter of days, he'd found his addiction in her, and he couldn't let her go.

Even when he knew he was bad for her. She deserved better, but he couldn't let her go. She was his reward for all the fucked-up shit he had to do.

Sinking his fingers into her hair, he tugged on the length, tilting her head back and arching those gorgeous tits toward his face. He licked them through the fabric, moving to the other breast to do the same.

Flicking the catch open, he pulled down her bra so he could get a good view of those babies. They were fucking amazing. So full. So perfect. They belonged to him.

Sliding his tongue across a nipple, he licked between the valley, going back to the other one.

Letting go of her hair, he ordered her to stay still. Pressing the tits together, he marveled at them before sucking and nipping at the flesh. He could gladly spend all day playing with her tits, but he needed inside her.

He helped her to her feet, and this time, he was the one to kneel before her. He helped her out of the jeans, putting her back to her feet and spreading her legs. He lifted her feet up, placing them on the edge of the sofa and spreading her legs wide. The lips of her pussy had already opened, and as he touched her, he slid a finger deep inside her to the knuckle, watching her take all of him. He added a second finger, pumping in deep.

She panted his name again.

He smiled. What better way to spend his day than with a woman crying out for him?

"You want my cock, baby?"

"Yes."

Removing his fingers from her pussy, he pressed his face between her thighs, licking at her clit. She tasted so fucking good. He'd been hungry for this cunt, wanting it for days, but holding himself back because he knew he couldn't have her.

Not yet, anyway.

She pressed up against his face, rocking her body for him. Gripping her hips, he held her in place as he licked and sucked at her pussy, drawing her closer to orgasm. He wanted her to come hard before he fucked her.

He wasn't going to wear a condom either. She wasn't on the pill, and he'd deal with all of that soon. For now, he just wanted to fuck her hard. To feel that heat wrapped around his length, and how wet she was.

Diego was used to getting what he wanted, and when it came to Belle, he wanted it all. Even as he thought about the other men in her life, and what she deserved, he couldn't bring himself to let her go. There was no way in hell he'd ever let another man touch her. She was his and his alone.

He would *make* this work with her.

She'd stumbled into his life, and now he couldn't give her back. He would do whatever it took to take her.

"I'm not going to last, Diego," she said.

"Come for me. Let me hear how good I make it for you."

She cried out, the sound echoing off the walls as she came hard.

He teased her clit, flicking his tongue repeatedly over her nub as she came.

The moment she started to come down from the peak, he pulled his cock from his pants and sat beside her, moving her to straddle his dick.

Holding himself at the base, he found her heat and lowered her onto his shaft, driving in deep and hearing her cry out.

With his hands on her hips, he controlled her motions, making her grind down on his length to take all of him. Every single inch was now inside her. He felt her pussy pulse with the ripples of her orgasm.

"I've missed you," she said.

"Me too." He *had* missed her. She was the first woman he'd ever thought about once he left her.

He moved one hand up to the back of her head, pulling her down for a kiss. Squeezing her ass with the other, he held perfectly still, feeling her body, hoping to memorize every single part of her for when he was away.

With Belle kissing him, he returned both of his hands to her hips and began to work her pussy over his length. He slid her up and down, slamming her the last inch or so. He swallowed all of her moans as he did this, wanting to keep them all to himself.

When it wasn't enough, and he had to go deeper, he moved her so she was lying on the sofa. Lifting one of her legs up along the back of the sofa, he held her open and watched his cock slide in and out of her. His length was covered in her cream, the evidence of how turned on she was by this.

"Touch your tits, baby."

She cupped those large beauties, and he pounded inside her, taking her harder as she grew wetter on his bare cock. Seeing her like this, all open and ready, he wanted to flood her with his cum, to make the final claiming of her.

He couldn't do that.

Whatever they had, it couldn't have children, at least not yet.

Staring at her, he wanted it fucking all. It was a feeling he'd never once experienced. This wasn't supposed to happen like this. There was no woman out there for him.

Pounding her pussy, he watched her, needing her, desperate for her, hungry for her. He felt the first stirrings of his orgasm, and for a split second, he wanted nothing more than to say to hell to the consequences and flood her pussy with all of him.

Only, reality set in and he had no choice but to pull out and cover her stomach with his release. It was unsatisfying, but he knew he had to at least protect her this way. He could keep her safe for now, but a baby would require him to move her, or something else.

Collapsing over her, he heard her giggle.

"We're going to need to shower."

He wrapped his arms around her. "We'll shower in a minute."

"Are you okay, Diego?"

"Yeah, I'm fine."

"You'd tell me if there was something wrong, right?"

"There's nothing wrong. I won't ever lie to you." He kissed the side of her breast, hating he had already lied to her. What was the problem with several more lies?

****

"You know what I realize?" Belle asked, a few days later. They were in her apartment. Diego hadn't taken her back to his, and she'd just finished her shift at the restaurant.

"No, what do you realize?"

"We rarely spend any time during the day together. I'm starting to think we're vampires." She did a little growl. She rested her chin on her hands, which were on his chest. It didn't matter to her what time of the day or night it was.

She did know the difference though. She liked working at night, and during the day, she loved to explore, when Melanie was available to.

Her friend hadn't exactly been around, and there currently wasn't a dog for her. Soon, she hoped. If her dad found out how she felt, he'd be here within the day. This was the only thing she missed about home, the freedom to go out and not worry about being attacked. In a big city it was a risk, not to mention all the different sounds, smells, and that she wasn't entirely acquainted with the big city. Melanie was supposed to help her but had proven to not be as good as her word.

"Do you want to go out more?" he asked.

"I don't know."

"You don't have to hide from me."

"Is it weird that I'd just really like to go for a walk?"

"It's not weird." He paused. "If I can arrange something, would you be willing to work with me?"

"This sounds a little mysterious."

"My garden is rather big. It's safe for you to go, but it's a couple of hours from here."

"You have a big house?"

"It's private. No one knows about it. I've been renovating it for a couple of years. I purchased it at a good price. Daylight robbery in truth, but I've been wanting to check on things. I could take you with me. It'll give you a chance to walk around."

"I like that." She kissed his chin, aiming for his lips. "You're so good to me." She stroked his chest. They had already made love twice and were currently waiting for Chinese to arrive. She stroked his chest. "How was work today?"

"It was the same. A lot of people partying."

"Have you seen Melanie at your club?" she asked. "I haven't seen her for a couple of days now, and she hasn't been in touch."

"This is the chick that left you high and dry?"

"Yes, we're still friends. I just don't trust her."

"There's a good reason for that."

She ignored that. "Have you seen her?"

"No, not at the club. The last time I saw her was when I found you on the floor."

"I'm really worried about her."

"You want me to check in on her? I can do that for you, if you want."

"You would?" she asked.

"Have you not realized there are a lot of things I'm willing to do for you?" He kissed her hard, and not only was there a flutter between her thighs, she felt it in her chest as well. Diego was so thoughtful and sweet.

"Thank you. I'm worried. She usually checks in by now, but I figured she felt a little guilty for abandoning me again. I can't be mad at her though, I got you this time."

"I'll go and find her. I'm going to give her shit, you know that, right?"

She moved over his body, feeling his cock start to harden against her stomach. "I don't have a problem with that. I just want to make sure she's okay."

She began to kiss her way down his body and was just at his cock when the doorbell rang.

"I'm starting to think the world is against you sucking my cock." He eased her back on the bed. She wrapped the sheet around her as he padded out of the room.

Pushing her hair off her face, she collapsed back on the bed. Everything was so amazing. She couldn't have expected this to happen for her.

Diego was everything she had ever wanted in a man and so much more.

She wanted all of him, all of the time. When he was around, she was filled with happiness, and she didn't want to lose that feeling, not even for a second.

The smell of food and the sound of him returning put a smile to her lips.

"I hope you're hungry. You want to eat in here or in the kitchen?"

"I'm happy to eat here. Will you grab a blanket to throw over the bed? I don't want to make a mess."

"Will do."

He placed the food on the bed, returning seconds later to place the blanket over the top. Once he did that, he handed her a carton of food, with some chopsticks. "You're good with this, right?"

"I'm good. Believe me, I can feed myself."

He kissed her lips, startling her.

"I'll never get bored of that, even if it does freak me out a little bit," she said.

"I never want to freak you out." He took her lips again. "I'm wondering if I should take the food away from you and have my way with you first."

Her stomach chose that moment to growl.

"On second thought, let's eat. I don't want you to eat me."

She gripped his arm, pulling him back. "You can eat me any time." She burst out laughing. "I'm so sorry. That sounded a lot sexier in my head."

He cupped her tit, his thumb stroking back and forth across her nipple. "I could eat you all day long, but

I'm also a gentleman. I need you to eat your food. We'll play after."

She didn't know when she got so lucky, but she had every intention of holding onto Diego, even if she didn't think she deserved him. He was such a good man.

Chapter Six

"There's decorating shit all over the place," Diego said, taking Belle's hand so she didn't trip and fall. He'd taken her to his private, secure country home on the outskirts of the city. He'd purchased the house many years ago, and it was the home where he'd killed his first wife.

Her death had put such a fucking stain on the house, he'd completely gutted the inside, tearing down walls and getting an architect in to help him rebuild from the inside. It had taken him several years as the project was top secret.

None of this was done in his real name.

He used a fake name as he didn't want his enemies to find this place. He had no intention of bringing Charlotte here to live.

He was torn between selling it or giving it to Belle.

She deserved so much more than a home where he killed his first wife.

"There are so many smells," she said.

"It's paint and varnish. The staircase was finished the other week."

"Tell me everything. What does it look like?" she asked.

He took her from room to room describing the work that had been done, allowing her to place her hands on surfaces to feel the smoothness or the carvings in the wood. This was his pride and joy. Watching her enjoyment, he couldn't help but feel a little guilty. She would never know the true history of this place.

He didn't want her to find out and was willing to do whatever it took for her to never know.

Running fingers through his hair, he glanced out

of the window. His life as capo always caught up to him in some way. His secret wouldn't stay that way for much longer, but until it did, he wanted to bask in all that she gave him. The way she looked at him. Even with her vacant eyes. She didn't see him, and yet she did. It was the craziest thing in the world. He loved it when she cupped his face, touching him, memorizing how he looked by touch alone. She thought he was handsome.

When he told her how beautiful he thought she was, she blushed, denying his words. She didn't think she was pretty, let alone beautiful. Her scar didn't bother him. Staring into her eyes, seeing the scar, he knew his woman was a fighter. He was so fucking enthralled by her. If his enemies ever caught the way he looked at her, they would hurt her.

He had to be more careful.

After the full tour of the house, he led her out into the garden. Not much had changed with this. The flowers still grew, and he employed a gardener to keep it neat and organized.

On the porch, Belle didn't move any further. She tilted her head up to the sky. The sun beamed down on the two of them.

If it was possible, she looked even more stunning in the light. Most often, he went to see her during the night, because of how much work he had to do. He tried to keep his nights for her, but there were a rare few when work got in the way.

"Come on, I've got a surprise for us."

"You have?"

"Yes. Stay there." He left her on the porch. Taking a single white rose, he removed all the thorns and checked for bugs. Returning to her, he slowly slid the rose into her hair. She'd bound her raven hair on top of her head. He wanted nothing more than to release it and run his fingers through the length. Instead, he put the rose into her hair.

"What is it?" she asked.

"A white rose."

"Thank you."

He took her hand, locking their fingers together, walking her back out to the garden. He'd stopped by before collecting her from her place to make sure everything was set up.

"You're being all mysterious, Diego."

"Can't I have a few mysteries?"

"Yes, you can. You're not taking me to kill me, are you?"

He pulled her in close, gripping her ass. "Never." He claimed her lips, moaning as she ground herself against him. "I'd miss you too much. No man in his right mind would leave this."

She chuckled. She opened her mouth and quickly closed it.

"What is it?" he asked.

"It's nothing. I'm hungry. Feed me." She pretended to bite him, and he laughed, wondering what she wanted to tell him.

He moved toward the patio in the center of the garden, pass all the rose bushes. A single table sat in the center, two chairs. Everything was ready for him to serve them lunch.

"Did you prepare a ... dinner for us?"

"Lunch, and then I'll take you for a walk so you can get accustomed to the garden." There was plenty of space for her, and he had more than enough time to help her get used to the space and where she could walk. Whenever they were here, she was protected and he always had time for her. Back in their real world, that wasn't the case.

Helping her into her chair, he opened up the basket and began to pull out fruit along with a couple of meats and cheese, which had been stored in a cooler.

Placing them on the table, he couldn't help but chance a look at her. The smile on her lips was infectious. He loved that he made her happy.

It's all lies, asshole.

Ignoring the pang of guilt, which seemed to come second nature to him around her, he took the seat opposite.

"First, a strawberry." He held the green stem and presented the juicy red fruit to her lips, which she took with relish. Some of the juice dribbled down her chin, but he dealt with that, leaning over and licking it off her chin.

She laughed.

"May I try?"

He handed her a fruit, and then guided her arm to his face. He took a bite out of the fruit.

"What do you think?" she asked.

"Not nearly as delicious as your pussy."

"Diego!"

"No one is here to hear what I've got to say. It's all for your ears only."

"Well in that case, you can say whatever you want."

"Does my woman like to hear sexy talk?" he asked.

"I'm your woman?"

"Of course you're my woman. Why wouldn't you be?" He took a bite of the fruit, stroking his fingers up her arm.

"I don't know. I don't actually know what all of this is between us. Forget I said anything."

He locked their fingers together when she tried to

pull away.

"Belle," he said. "Don't pull away from me now."

"I don't want to make this awkward, and I already have. What we're having is fun, and I don't want to spoil it."

"You're not going to spoil anything." He kissed the inside of her wrist. "I want you, Belle. You're mine, and no man will ever be able to take you from me. That's what I see when I look at you. You belong to me."

"I'm not a possession," she said on a whisper.

Her body betrayed her liking of being owned though. Her nipples were hard, pressing against the front of her shirt, and she was breathing in hard and deep.

"I didn't say you were." He got up from his seat and moved behind her, putting his hands on her shoulders, working out the knots that were there.

"I don't want a possession. I want a woman who is willing to take what she wants." He licked at her earlobe as he slowly moved his hands down her body, touching her tits, stroking the peak of her nipples, so she knew he could see how aroused she was, and it was all because of him.

He liked having this control over her body.

Moving down to her jeans, he cupped her pussy through the fabric, and she moaned. "This pussy is mine. You are mine, Belle. Always."

"We've only just met."

He flicked the catch of her jeans. No one was around for miles. This house was secured and locked down. He shoved his hand into her jeans, touching her over her panties.

"You don't want this with me." He teased her clit. Her panties were soaked, and he stroked over, pushing the fabric against her slit and hearing her cry out.

"What if someone sees?" she asked.

"No one will see you. I took your virginity, Belle. I have every single part of you, and I'm not giving it back." He sucked on her neck as he moved her panties out of the way, touching her wet, heated flesh.

Sliding a finger inside her, he heard her gasp, and he bit down over her pulse. She tilted her neck so he could lick and suck at her throat.

His cock throbbed, and he touched himself. The pants were too tight, so he opened the zipper, pulling his cock out and rubbing his dick as he teased her.

"Lift your top up. I want to see those tits."

She held her shirt up, and he got her to pull her bra down, exposing as much of her body as she could.

When she did, it was such a beautiful sight, one that made his balls ache. Stroking her clit, he let go of his dick to tease her nipples, watching them tighten and bud under his touch.

She was so sexy, and so far, no matter what he did, she responded to his touch as if she truly did belong to him.

He moved his fingers down to her pussy, feeling how wet she was. Drawing his finger back to her clit, he kept on stroking, bringing her close to orgasm. He didn't make her wait; he watched her come. Her head flung back, and she cried out his name. He was starting to get addicted to hearing "Diego" spill from her lips in a pleasured cry. It was enough to send him over the edge.

Diego continued to tease her pussy until she couldn't take it anymore. Pulling his hand from her pants, he sucked on his finger, tasting her, staring at her tits.

"Do you trust me, Belle?"

"Of course."

"Good."

He removed her shirt and bra, placing them on

the table. Next, he straddled her chair. Their height differences made this incredibly easy.

"Baby, suck on my cock. Get it nice and wet." Diego guided his length to her waiting mouth. She sucked on him without question, her saliva coating his length.

When he was completely covered, he moved to her tits, bending his knees and pressing those mounds together to create the perfect valley.

"What are you doing?"

"I'm fucking your tits." He took her hands, pressing them to her breasts. "Hold them together like this." He showed her what he wanted, and when it was at the right angle, he began to fuck her tits. Sliding in and out, he watched his cock appear at the top near her neck before withdrawing.

He was so close already, but feeling her breasts, watching her, he was a fucking doomed man. Each day he spent with her, he was becoming more and more enthralled by her with every passing second.

Her pussy was his. Her ass would soon belong to him, just like her mouth. Every single part of Belle was his, and he had no intention of giving it back. He wanted her all to himself, every single little part of her.

Driving his cock between her tits, he growled out her name as he came. His cum spilled out, coating her breasts and neck.

The best way to start an evening.

****

After nearly two months of being together, Belle learned many things. Diego had to vanish at odd hours during the day and night. He never allowed her to stay over at his apartment. His home was the only place of his they shared the night, and they were always alone. She had come to sense he was rarely alone. Someone was either following him, or calling him.

Also, did he have any friends?

Dating people usually met their good friends and their parents, right? Diego never once mentioned he had any friends or if he wanted her to meet them. Her father wanted to meet him though. She had told him she was seeing someone, and well, now it seemed like he wanted to get to know the guy that his daughter was dating.

Then of course, there was Melanie.

Diego told her he'd found her with a boyfriend, and she looked in a pretty rough state. He didn't want her talking to Melanie anymore, and well, that never sat well with her, which was why she had decided to head to a café near Melanie's place. It had taken her paying the cab driver double to help escort her inside.

She was in a part of the city she had never been. Everything felt different to her. Even the noise was overall louder than she was accustomed to. Her nerves were also shot because she didn't want to upset anyone by being here.

This was the first time she'd actually ignored Diego, but Melanie had once been her friend, an unreliable friend but one all the same.

Tucking her hair behind her ear, she stared down at the table, hoping Melanie would turn up soon.

Tapping her fingers on the table, she noticed some of the surface had been chipped.

When someone slumped down opposite her, she tried to conceal her worry, but Melanie's belch soon changed that.

"What do you want?" Melanie asked.

"I wanted to check on you."

"So, you're already disobeying your boyfriend?" She heard the smirk in Melanie voice.

"Melanie, what is going on?" she asked.

"Look, I don't have time for this. I really didn't want to have to deal with you coming to the city. I took care of you because your father was paying me. Now he's not and I'm only here because I need money, and your fat ass is going to need to move."

Belle was a little taken aback by Melanie's abrupt nature.

"What? I don't understand?"

"There's a lot you don't understand, sweetheart, and because I like my heart beating, I'm not going to enlighten you. You shouldn't be down in this part of town. It's dangerous for you. Now, how about a couple hundred bucks and I'll get you back to your apartment?"

"I thought we were friends."

"Oh, please, you think I want to spend my time with a woman who can't see? Half the time it's just plain old funny to watch you. Now, I'm bored. The money was good, but I've got a life to lead, and it's not playing dog to you."

"I've never treated you like a dog."

"I know. I wouldn't fucking let you."

Belle let out a gasp as she was suddenly pulled from the booth. It was a good thing she had decided to wear sneakers today because Melanie was not taking her time, and was pulling her out of the door.

"Melanie, please stop. I care about you. I don't understand what happened."

She was in the street. The ground was uneven, and Melanie growled. "I don't have time for this. You think I wanted to be your friend? I'm fucking hot, Belle. I can have any man I want and most often do. You've got way too much weight, and that scar on your face, it's fucking ugly. It used to help me get pity fucks, but now, it's just sad. I want my own life, and like I said, you're not paying me anymore, so let's get this show on the road, and stop pretending like we give a shit."

Melanie's words cut Belle to the core. Not the ones about her appearance as she couldn't see herself but had often assumed she wasn't particularly pretty.

"Are you going to cry?"

"No!" She reached into her purse, pulling out the notes. "That's all the money I have."

"Come on then, let's get you home."

"No. I don't need or want your help."

Melanie laughed. "For serious right now? You're going to think you're all independent. You can't fucking see."

"Leave me alone. I'm more than capable." She wasn't going to be around someone who only wanted money and had been forced to be with her. She didn't need Melanie, not anymore.

She would make it work. Her father had been the one to pay Melanie, and now, well, his plan had backfired for her to be with someone who cared. No one cared, not for her.

She wasn't going to cry, dammit.

Someone bumped into her, and she nearly fell on her ass.

"Watch where you're fucking going." She quickly moved out of the center of the pavement, or at least she hoped so. She touched a wall. Slowly, step by step, she walked down the street, only pausing when the brick would change to glass. She hated this.

There was no way she could look vulnerable in front of Melanie, not after her vile insults.

This was even more crazy of her though. She had no idea where she was, and she hadn't just called a cab.

This was stupid of her.

"Well, well, well, look who we have here," someone said.

Whoever it was stood a little too close as she smelled the bad breath on her face.

She tensed up. "Excuse me, please."

Someone waved something in front of her face. She felt the air change as they did this.

"Can't fucking see. A nice little blind piece of meat. I'd say the guys would have something to enjoy about this."

"Please leave me alone," she said.

Her heart was racing, and she was terrified. Nothing like this had ever happened to her before.

"No, I don't think that's going to be a problem."

She tried to cry out, but someone placed a hand over her mouth, and the next thing, she was being pulled down somewhere. She didn't know where she was or what was going on.

Fear covered her like a blanket, wrapping her up.

"I say we're going to have a lot of fun with this one, boys."

That was all she remembered as someone hit her hard across the head, and the world went completely blank.

Chapter Seven

"That's the second girl. You know if there's another one, you're going to feel the heat."

Diego handed back the photo Officer Jefferson had just given to him. The cop was on his personal payroll, and had helped him to get some heat off him a few times. The guy couldn't keep his dick in his pants and had not only a family of six, but also several children around the city with different women. He liked to party and fuck, and well, Diego liked to have a smooth, easy life.

It was a win-win for him.

Until situations like this that became a problem. A second girl had overdosed after buying drugs in his club. He didn't do drugs in the club. Any dealings with drugs were always far away from any establishment he or any capo owned. Their names were only ever rumored to be in different businesses, but right now, this was a lot of heat, especially as he took care of one drug-dealing barman.

Someone was dealing in his club, and that meant, he now had to catch him or her. Women were just as toxic as men, especially when they wanted an easy fix.

"I'll handle it."

"Please do. For now, you're safe. The girl was intoxicated and had said she'd moved from several clubs."

The only thing that brought Jefferson to him was the other girl had only been in this club. He knew. And now a second girl? A third, and he would have the cops here, possibly shutting him down.

"I'll take care of it." He opened up his desk, pulling out the envelope of hush money. Jefferson nodded his head and left. It was interesting because on the outside Jefferson was actually a good guy. When they first struck up their deal, he had him followed, and the evidence showed Jefferson was a good man, a family man. He just wasn't a one-woman kind of man.

Shaking his head, he got to work on the security footage. He allowed his facial recognition software to locate the woman. He kept security footage for a couple of weeks, so he had a lot to get through. His club was busy every single night.

The time he spent with Belle was the time he usually stayed at the club, to take care of everything.

This was a problem he could do without, especially as he'd planned a special getaway with Belle, only to have to redo his plans because he had family obligations with Charlotte. She had picked out a wedding dress. The cake was prepared and the flowers ordered. This weekend he now had to go and give his input on what location he wanted to get married.

He didn't want to get married. Not to fucking Charlotte Durante, that was for sure.

His cell phone started to ring, interrupting his thoughts. Not that they were good thoughts. Mostly he thought about killing Charlotte and making it look like an accident. Only, they would find another suitable daughter. If one wasn't ready yet, he'd have to wait for her to come of age, and then he'd marry, or the capo title would be handed to Angelo.

"Diego," he said, answering the call.

"Yeah, we've got a problem," Richard said.

This made Diego tense. "Has Angelo made his move?"

Since he'd teamed up with Richard, their mutual enemy being his good cousin Angelo, they had been gathering evidence so Diego could present it to The Boss. With hard proof of Angelo's deception and lack of loyalty, he'd be able to kill him without a single problem.

Only … Angelo had decided to play it safe for the past couple of weeks. There was no dirt on him, and he couldn't exactly charge him with fucking women as an offence.

It pissed Diego off, but he figured his cousin couldn't be entirely stupid, otherwise he'd have been caught out by now. His true self would have been shown.

They hadn't gotten this far in life by being stupid.

"Your girl was snatched by a couple of pimps two hours ago," Richard said. "My guy tracked them to a rundown block."

Diego laughed. "Nice try. Belle's at home. She was spending the day listening to her books."

"According to my guy, she left to meet a friend. A blonde that looked like she had seen better days. They got into a fight, the blonde left, and Belle started to make her way home. Only, she ended up in some guy's hands."

"You got the address?" Diego asked.

"Yes. Diego, these men, they're heavily armed, and they have got a whole block of women and johns."

"I don't give a fuck." He ended the call, grabbing his gun from the safe. Ignoring his men, as they would follow him anyway, he made his way down to his car, going to the trunk and pulling out his loaded weapon. Richard had already sent him the location where his woman was.

He was fucking pissed.

In his city, there was an operation of pimps, and this wasn't one that was paying them the rent.

That gave him an excuse to take them all out. Their lack of respect to his name. But what pissed him off was them thinking they could take his woman.

When he climbed behind the wheel, four of his men got into the car. He didn't have the time to argue with them, and besides, he would need all the help he could get.

Pulling away from the curb, he ignored the car that honked its horn as he pulled in front of it.

The place he was driving to was a rundown piece of shit. He knew of it, because he'd been tempted to purchase the land, demolish the crumbling building, and rebuild luxury apartments. The only problem was that the area had one of the highest crime rates and in all honesty, was a piece of shit. No matter how luxurious he'd make the apartments, no one would live there for an exorbitant price. Even he wouldn't do that, but he had found Melanie around that area.

She had been pissed but had also tried to blackmail him for money. She had been fucking high, and from the track marks in her arms at the time, she had been using hard. He didn't for a second believe Belle used drugs. Still, when he got back to her place after talking with Melanie, and warning her away from Belle, he'd inspected every single inch of her body and found nothing. Just a few scars from her accident all those years ago.

His woman was clean, but then, he hadn't expected anything else.

Coming to a stop at the building, he stared at the mess. Lights were on in odd rooms, and he saw a couple of semi-naked women on the outside. They looked a mess. There was nothing classy about them. Desperation and degradation clung to them, and seeing it, knowing his woman was in there, pissed him off.

Picking up his cell phone, he pocketed the thing and climbed out of the car. One of the men was smoking against the side of the building. He wore dirty jeans and had a chain hanging from the pocket.

Anger filled Diego.

He loaded his gun—being around Belle, he'd kept it unloaded—and fired, hitting the man in the head. The man went down, and the women started to scream.

He ignored them. No one would call the cops, not in this neighborhood. Or if they did, the cops never came.

He entered the building, saw another guy, and shot again.

Making his way up the stairs, he saw used condoms, needles, dirt, and shit. It was a fucking disease pit waiting to happen.

Taking the steps two at a time, he walked past rooms. The doors were still open, and he saw people fucking. Men with women. A gang of men with a woman.

Every detestable thing imaginable was happening, and it pissed him off.

He couldn't find Belle.

If one of these motherfuckers had touched her, he was going to make them wish they'd never even looked in her direction, let alone touched her.

His cell phone rang, and he picked it up, seeing Richard was the one calling.

"Where is she?" he asked. He had put a tracker in her bag and in some of her clothing, and of course in her cell phone. Richard was able to find her.

"They put her in the basement. The trackers are all there, Diego."

He hung up his cell phone. Richard was proving to be the guy he needed in this kind of situation. The guy was ace when it came to technology.

Turning on his heel, he made his way downstairs. When he was at the ground floor, he saw the door with the sign for basement above it.

Opening the door, he saw one guy about to shoot up. He pulled out his knife, as he didn't want to alert anyone else that was down there. Slitting the guy's throat was easy. He pulled him back, allowing him to bleed out. The shocked look in his eyes did not bother him.

Walking down the stairs, he heard a couple of guys calling out.

Shit!

He didn't want Belle to know who he was. This had put him in a fucking mess. Still, he wasn't going to walk away.

Not from this.

Holding his weapon, he rounded the corner to see, two guys, both with their pants on but without a shirt or shoes.

"Who the fuck are you?" one guy asked.

"Diego Leoni!" The moment he saw the fear in the guy's face, Diego smiled and fired his weapon, taking them both out with a bullet to the head.

Walking past their dead bodies, when he saw Belle, he wished he'd made them scream just a little.

They had chained her up in some rusty cuffs. She still had her clothes on, but they looked dirty and torn. She was cowering in the corner, crying.

There was something wet around her, and he knew they had pissed on her. The scent of urine was heavy in the air.

Removing his jacket, he got a little closer to her.

"Belle, baby, it's me."

She was crying, her hands covering her face.

He spoke to her again, then again, repeating the same words until she finally heard him.

"Diego?" she asked.

Her voice was croaky as if she'd been screaming.

"It's me. I'm coming toward you."

"How did you know?"

"Someone I know saw you. It's okay. I've got my

jacket."

"Diego, please, I'm scared."

"They're gone. They're not coming back," he said. He was pleased she was blind so she didn't see that he killed two people.

Placing the jacket over her shoulders, he gripped the cuffs. They were dirty and biting into her flesh.

"They chained me up like an animal. Are the police here?" she asked.

"Don't worry about that. Don't worry about anything right now. I'm just going to look for the key."

"Please, don't leave me. Please." She gripped his shirt, and he hated how scared she sounded.

Glancing behind him, he saw one of his men had at least followed him down.

"The key!" He mouthed the words for the man to do as he was bid.

After tonight he may have to kill all four men who had accompanied him.

"Who is that? Who is there?" Belle asked.

Her hearing was proving to be impeccable.

"It's a friend."

"I'm so scared."

"I know, baby." He grabbed the cuffs, giving them a tug as they were connected to the wall. Some of the brick looked like it had come away, and if he did give it a good tug, he may be able to get her out of there.

His guy came toward him with a key.

He took it from him, twisting the lock on each cuff. They had also put one around her neck as well, and the same key worked in that lock.

Anger consumed him, but he pushed it all down as he picked Belle up in his arms. Carrying her out of the basement, he met his other three men on the ground floor.

"Burn it," he said.

They nodded without saying a word. Leaving the building, he carried Belle closely against himself.

Richard had brought the truck into the main parking lot.

He opened the door, and Diego didn't give himself time to question him, just carried his woman into the back of the truck, holding her as she cried and wept.

Richard drove the truck, and he held his woman close, not wanting to let her go.

"Did they hurt her, Diego?" Richard asked.

"I don't know."

"We need to know."

"I know we fucking do." He was shaking with rage, but there was also something else.

He had his woman back, and he was so fucking thankful. She could have been killed. They could have just shot or killed her. Closing his eyes, he ignored the stench and simply held her, trying to calm his nerves.

"Diego!"

"Baby, I need to know if those men did anything else to you. Did they touch you? Rape you?"

"They didn't rape me," she said. "Please, Diego, I don't want to go to the hospital. I don't want anyone to know this."

He looked toward Richard as her sobs filled the air.

Diego didn't question where they were going. He didn't care. For now, he had four men who knew of Belle's existence. He had to keep her safe. Everything else could fucking wait.

When Richard pulled into an underground parking facility, Diego finally realized the other man hadn't dropped him at home, and he was somewhere he didn't recognize.

"What is this?" Diego asked.

"This is my home. Don't worry. You can't be tracked here. My home is an extension of my business and is locked up fucking tight. It could be used as a high security prison. I figured you'd want something private for a few days, if not a couple of hours."

Richard climbed out of the car, walking toward the side door of the van and sliding it open.

Diego didn't let Belle go. He carried her as he followed Richard through to his home. There were several security systems Richard had to get through, including voice recognition as well as fingerprint scanners. Once they got inside, the house looked like any regular house.

"I'll show you to your room," Richard said, walking up the stairs.

"I can walk, Diego," Belle said.

"No. I want to hold you."

She didn't speak again, and Richard showed him to a large bedroom with a four-poster bed. The space was incredible, and he walked toward a door that led into a massive en-suite bathroom.

"When I get bored, I build. This I what I do," Richard winked at him. "I'll be downstairs."

Richard left them alone, closing the door behind him. He didn't like trusting anyone, but he had no choice in this situation. Carrying Belle into the bathroom, he lowered her onto the toilet. He was about to step away to fill up the bath, but she caught his hand. "Please, don't go."

"I'm filling the bath. You want to get clean, don't you?"

"Yes." Her lips wobbled, and she stared down at her hands.

He took hold of her hands. "Look at me, baby."

He waited until she lifted her head. "You have nothing to be ashamed of. Nothing at all. This is not your fault. This has nothing to do with you."

She sniffled. "I … I…"

"It's fine, baby. I'm not going to leave you. I'm filling that tub so we can wash, and we can wash together if that will make you happy?"

"Yes. That will make me happy. Please. Yes."

He gripped her hand tightly. "Let me do this for you."

She let go of his hand. He stepped away, adding some salts to the water. He checked to make sure he wasn't making it too hot or too cold. When it was just right, he turned the taps off and went back to her.

"Come on. Let me help you." He helped her up, and slowly began to remove her clothing. He tried to ignore the bruising around her neck and wrists, but they seemed to be getting worse. He also noticed bruises on her face, including a busted lip.

When she was naked, he helped her into the water.

"I thought you said we were going to be taking this bath together?"

He heard the neediness and desperation within her voice. "I'm just getting naked now, baby."

Quickly removing his clothes, he joined her in the tub. When he wrapped his arms around her waist, she leaned back against him. He held her as close as he could, trying to offer her as much comfort and warmth as was possible.

She sniffled against his chest, and he stroked her hair.

"Let me get you cleaned up." He didn't want her covered in piss a moment longer.

Grabbing some soap and a sponge, he massaged it

to create some lather and then started to clean her body. She took the soap from his hands and washed her face. He got her as clean as possible before rinsing her hair.

He grabbed the shampoo and squirted a good amount on her hair. He'd never been the kind of guy to linger on washing a woman, so this was all new territory for him. Belle didn't try to take over, and she leaned back against him, letting him do all the work, which he didn't mind.

Tears fell from her eyes, but she didn't make a sound. Seeing her broken like this tore him apart as he didn't know what to do to make it up for her, or to make it better. He stayed silent, washing her hair, preparing her the best way he knew how.

"How did you know where to find me?" she asked.

"A friend."

"A friend?"

"He saw you. He knew we'd been out together, and he told me what he saw. I came and got you."

"I don't understand. What was the loud bang?"

"It was nothing. It was being taken care of."

There was a moment's pause and he finished rinsing her hair.

"You have a friend?" she asked.

He smiled. "I do."

"You've never mentioned having a friend before."

"I do."

"How many friends do you have?"

"I have one friend. It's his place we're in right now. He's going to help me take care of you." It was one of the safest places she could be. "Why were you in that part of the city?" he asked.

Belle only hesitated for a moment before she

spilled her secrets. The meeting she had with Melanie, what the other woman said. All of it came out, and the fact he was still in the bath rather than dealing with the problem, just went to prove to Diego how much this woman meant to him.

"I ... I feel like a fool. I knew we were having problems, you know. I just didn't realize how bad they were. I thought she at least liked me, but she only wanted money." She sniffled, and he held her close, kissing the top of her head.

"You're safe now, and I'm not going to let anything happen to you again." He stayed with her until the water turned cold.

Climbing out, he picked up a towel and helped her out of the water, drying her body. When he walked into the bedroom with Belle in his arms, he saw the clothes that had been left before him.

A pair of sweatpants and a shirt for him, boxer briefs and a large shirt for her. Richard had even put a name label on them.

Shaking his hand, he put her down on the floor, drying her body. He took care of her, wanting to protect her from all the bad shit in the world, so she knew there was nothing to be afraid of.

He dropped the towel, grabbing the boxers and instructing her to sit in them. She put her hands on his shoulders, and he noticed the bruises on her thighs. "You said they didn't rape you."

"They didn't."

"What are these bruises?"

"They ... stamped on me."

"You're safe now." He pulled up the shorts and next the shirt. Easing it over her head, he dropped the shirt, seeing how big it was in comparison to her curves. Tilting her head back, he sighed. "They hit you as well?"

"Yes."

"Pieces of shit," he said.

"I'm fine now."

"You shouldn't have to be fine."

He pulled back the covers and helped her into bed. "I want you to rest."

"You're not leaving, are you?"

Diego did have every intention of leaving, but seeing the forlorn on her face, he quickly pulled on his clothes and climbed in behind her. Wrapping his arms around her waist, he pressed his nose against her hair, kissing her neck.

"I've got you. I will always have you. Go to sleep. Rest. I'll always be here."

Diego didn't know how much time had passed until she fell asleep. When she did, he slowly eased out from the bed, giving her space. He stood for several minutes, watching her sleep.

Leaving the bedroom quietly, he found Richard eating out of a Chinese container and looking at something on his laptop.

"She okay?"

"She's out for the count. I've got to head out. Will you watch her for me?"

"Will do."

"Awesome."

"I have guns under secured in the third door along the corridor. I might also want to inform you that a couple of those perps have been seen with Angelo."

This made Diego stop.

"Come again?"

"My guy got a picture. I've been running it through recognition programs and ta-da, look what I found." Richard spun the laptop, and sure enough, there were surveillance images of those men with Angelo.

"They're on my turf. They had set up shop in my city," he said.

"Angelo has gone quiet in the past couple of weeks. Nothing new to report. He's going through all the same schedule and routine. He's not standing out."

"Then he knows we're onto him and we've got to pull back. This isn't enough to show The Boss. A meeting means nothing. There has to be more proof."

"We've come this far."

"I know, and now we've got to pull back. Otherwise we're all fucked. Angelo is still a cousin, and I need concrete evidence."

"Yeah, well, why don't I just put a bullet in his head and save you all the trouble?"

"If it was as simple as that, you would have done it. You know there are consequences for this bullshit. We can't ignore it, but we have to do this the right way. Are you good taking care of her until I get back?"

"She will be safe. She can't see shit, can she?"

"No, you know this. She is deadly with lamps. You might want to put away anything that is in her path. Stuff like that. She's usually fine, but this is a new place."

"No freaking out the girlfriend. Got it. Actually, she's your mistress, isn't she? Does she know she's the other woman?"

"Fuck off, Richard. You know she doesn't know the truth." He headed off to get some weapons. "And another thing, you can't scare her."

"She's blind?"

"She's got a hell of a perception. Her other senses are crazy good."

"Then she must be a bullshit reader because I would have a hell of a lot of questions for a guy who owns a club who was able to come and rescue me."

He was done with this conversation.

Chapter Eight

The moment Belle woke up, the entire events of the day before flooded back to her. The conversation with Melanie, being taken, the taunts. They had been so cruel to her. She knew they were only going to have their fun before they either put her to work, or used her for their own pleasure. They had gotten off on degrading her instead.

The sex would have happened soon.

But Diego had been there to stop them.

They hadn't raped her.

Sitting up, she reached for him, but wasn't surprised to find his side of the bed cold and empty. Gritting her teeth, she slid her feet out of the bed, pushing off the cover as she did so. Getting to her feet, she knew she wasn't in her apartment or Diego's. This was someplace new.

It smelled brand new, in a weird kind of way. She took a deep breath of the air, and tentatively took a step forward. She didn't encounter anything. Reaching her hands out, she tried to make sense of where she was.

Another step, and nothing.

Another, and she suddenly hit something hard. Crying out, she fell down, making so much noise as something fell on her. She gripped her leg, gasping at the pain.

The door opened.

"Shit! Diego said you had a thing for lamps."

For some crazy and bizarre reason, she found that utterly funny.

"You're okay, right?"

"Yeah, yeah, I'm fine. I'm a little embarrassed."

She sensed the guy, Diego's friend, move closer. He knelt in front of her, and she heard his clothing as he did this. He took the lamp from her leg.

"I didn't break it, did I?"

"No, this one is metal and is attached." He touched her thigh, and she tensed up. "But it looks like you're all fine. Just a little bruise. Nothing to worry about."

She rubbed her leg. "Where's Diego?"

"He had to go and take care of something. It's just you and me, kid. You want some help?"

"I need to use the bathroom."

"I'll help you inside, and give you some privacy, and then I'll lead you out to the sitting room and feed you."

"Thank you."

"No problem, kid."

"It's Belle. My name is Belle."

"It's a pretty name," he said.

"Erm, what's yours? Or would you like me to call you Diego's friend?"

"Oh, I see. I thought Diego told you."

"He might have done, but with everything, I've forgotten."

"No problem. It's Richard."

Silence fell between them.

"I'm holding my hand out for you to take."

"Oh, I'm so sorry." She tried to find his hand, and her face was getting hotter by the second. "I'm not usually like this."

"Don't worry about it. I'm going to put my hand on your hip and hold your hand to guide you. Is this okay?"

"Yes, yes, of course."

She still flinched as he touched her, but he made no comment on the action. He helped her into the bathroom, which she was thankful for. She really needed to go. He left her alone to pee, and when she finished, he returned. He didn't hold her hand but guided her to the sink so she could wash her hands and dry them.

When he was done there, they left the en-suite bathroom and went straight to the living room. At least that was what he said.

"You like Chinese food?"

"Yes."

"I'll be back. Don't move."

She wasn't going to risk any more lamps or potentially more damaging things. Keeping her hands to herself, she stayed perfectly seated.

"I've got a tray here for you. What do you like?"

"Anything. Lo mein, rice, I'm just hungry."

He chuckled. "You sound like my kind of girl."

She smiled as he put the carton in her hand and the fork.

"Do you need me to feed you?"

"No, I can manage on my own." She dipped the fork into the carton and brought the food to her lips. There wasn't much warmth left to it, but she didn't mind. Food was food, and she wasn't going to complain. At least she was getting fed.

"Have you known Diego long?"

"Not really. A couple of years if that? It may not be that long."

"Oh. Do you own a club as well?"

"No. I'm a security expert. It's what I do. I fixed Diego's club up real good. It's how he saw you. Shit."

"Saw me?"

"Can we not talk about it?"

"Diego saw me?"

"Yeah, on his security feed. He saw you'd been left alone and went to help."

"Oh."

"It's not as dirty or as crazy as it sounds."

She smiled. "It's fine. Really."

"You sure. He wasn't going all serial killer on you, I promise."

"It's really fine. I can handle it."

"I didn't expect him to date you though."

"You didn't?"

"Diego's an intense ... secretive kind of guy."

"You got that right. I didn't even know he had a friend."

"He doesn't talk about his life?"

"No. Nothing. He sometimes mentions the club, but we don't talk about our work for the most part." They did have sex a lot, not that she was complaining. The sex was more than incredible. Not that she had anyone to compare it to, nor did she want to. "So you work for him?"

"I've done a couple of jobs for him, but we're sort of in a joint venture at the moment."

"Do you like him?"

"He's an all right kind of guy. He has his demons like we all do."

"Thank you," she said. "For helping to save me."

"Diego did all the saving."

"Were the cops there?"

"The cops were notified, I'm sure."

He was speaking slowly.

She ate her food, realizing Richard was being careful around her, and she didn't know why.

"Would you like to drop me off back at my home?" she asked. "I don't want to intrude."

"You're not intruding."

She jumped as he touched her leg.

"Shit, sorry."

"Don't worry about it." That was all she seemed

to be saying at the moment.

"I've got to go and check on a few things. Enjoy your food."

Before she could stop him, he'd already gotten to his feet and moved away. Slumping down on the sofa, she was sad she'd forced him away.

What was she talking about that made him so nervous or for him to stop wanting to be near her? It made next to no sense at all.

As she ate her food, the sick feeling in her stomach slowly disappeared to be replaced with nerves. What was it Diego did exactly if it wasn't just the club?

****

Diego's first stop was to see his men, who were waiting for him at the club. All four of them were standing, and he was more than ready to end all of them. Stepping in front of the large men, he would kill each of them if they ever put Belle in danger.

He stared at each of the men. They were perfectly still, their hands in front of them, ready to take instructions. They were soldiers, these men. Their lives belonged to him as their capo, and they had to abide by his will.

"The block was destroyed, correct?" he asked.

"Yes, we stayed to see it burn to the ground." One of them spoke up.

"Did anyone make it out alive?"

"A couple of the whores and their clients, sir." This came from another.

He sat on his desk, gun in hand, ready.

"Do you remember what you pledged to me the day you worked for me?" he asked.

Their gazes were no longer staring straight ahead but at him.

"I pledged my life to yours." Each of them said

the exact same thing. They were like little sheep, only fueled by violence.

"The woman I saved tonight, she is … important to me. She is to be protected at all costs."

"Yes, sir."

"No one can know about her. I want to make myself perfectly clear here. Only you four know of her. If anyone finds out about her, it will be you four I hold responsible, and I will have my fun with your entrails, do I make myself clear?"

"Perfectly."

"Good. Now, if anyone asks, those men had set up a whorehouse in my area. They had done so without my permission, without my consent, and because of that, I dealt with it. It's the truth. You are not lying. You won't speak of the woman."

They all nodded.

"Get out," he said.

They all left him alone, and he sat back on his desk. It was a risk he was taking, but killing four of his closest men would also raise suspicion. He had to keep his fucking wits about him, or risk handing over his territory to Angelo. That shit wasn't happening, not on his watch.

Angelo would destroy everything he'd built, and nothing would make him hand over the keys of his kingdom to that sick, sadistic prick.

His men were dealt with; now he had to move on to another person.

Leaving his club, he took the back exit, so no one would see him. It wasn't often he walked around in sweatpants and a hoodie. The look didn't feel right for him, but at his next stop, he would certainly blend in.

He knew where Melanie lived because he'd been to see her. She was supposed to keep her distance, and well now, she had certainly overstayed her welcome.

Climbing out of his car, he made his way toward the building. It wasn't the worst one in the area, but it certainly wasn't the best.

With the drugs in his pocket, he made his way upstairs to her apartment. At first, he had every intention of knocking, but he needed to make sure she was free.

Melanie liked to fuck as if it was going out of fashion.

Opening the door, the stench of old food, stale sex, and dirt flooded his senses. He didn't know how she was able to look in any way presentable. Her home clearly wasn't kept.

"Oh, yes, oh fuck, that feels good. Your ass has seen a lot of cock, hasn't it, whore?"

Melanie's muffled response had Diego standing still. Looking around the corner, he saw the woman in question bent over the bed with a guy plowing into her ass. He had her ass cheeks spread and kept spitting down on his cock.

"Yeah, this is what it takes for some junk. You want to snort some happy powder, you got to pay the price."

He didn't have time to wait around for this shit to be over.

He withdrew the needle full of heroin, which he always kept on standby when he had to kill someone and make it look like an overdose.

Stepping up to the drug dealer, he plunged the needle into the man's neck, giving him a huge sweep of heroin into his blood.

The man staggered back, the good stuff hitting his blood, and he passed out, jerking and convulsing.

Melanie let out a scream, but Diego wrapped his fingers around her neck.

"You shouldn't have gone to her."

Fear flashed in her eyes. "I needed money."

"You will learn to do what I fucking say." He reached into his pocket. "You and I, we're going to have some fun with this."

"Please, Diego. I didn't tell her. I swear. She doesn't know, and neither does her dad. They don't know who you are or what it is you do."

He wasn't holding her tight enough to silence her. He didn't want to hear her voice.

"Come on, let's go and deal with this."

****

Diego left Melanie's home thirty minutes later.

The man who had been fucking her ass was dead from the heroin he'd injected, and Melanie was also gone. She finally snorted one too many lines for her own good. It would look like a drug deal gone bad, especially as Melanie already had the heroin that would look like she attacked her dealer for the coke.

He didn't know where she got the heroin from, but he'd find out. There were enough drugs in the city that it could have come from anywhere, any supplier at any time.

Back in his car, he saw he had a couple of missed calls from Richard.

He called him back, starting up the car.

"When are you going to be back?" Richard asked.

"I'm heading back now."

"Good. A guy still has to work to earn a living here."

"Oh, please, one look at your place and I know you're loaded and full of shit."

"There's a reason I'm loaded, and it's not to be taken the piss out of by you or anyone else I work for."

"I'll be there. I thought we were friends," he said,

smirking. Richard had been hanging around him, trying to make the connection. It had all been a ploy because of Angelo, but he actually liked the guy. He didn't talk incessantly, and he didn't brag about the women he'd fucked.

He wasn't so bad.

"Your mistress asks a lot of questions, and she makes it hard to lie to her."

"What?"

"Belle is up, and I got to say, she is a sweetheart, no doubt about that. Only problem with a sweetheart, they're like lie detectors. You want your secrets kept, you got to come and relieve me."

Richard hung up the phone, and Diego pressed his foot on the gas, running through a couple of red lights, and thanking his lucky stars no one was around to see him breaking every fucking law he could to get to Belle.

She was going to find out sooner rather than later. He just wanted it to be a whole lot later.

Why the fuck do you want this?
She's a blind chick.

You can have anyone you want. Why does it have to be her?

Diego didn't get it.

He'd tried to walk away several times, knowing he was only going to hurt her more, but each time he found himself back to her, never wanting to let her go.

Running fingers through his hair, he knew he couldn't let her go. But there was no way he could marry her, not with his future tied to Charlotte. He didn't want that woman. He hadn't even kissed her, or spent a single day with her. He sat beside her during dinners, started polite conversation, which was expected of him, but other than that, he didn't do anything else.

He stayed away from it all.

The wedding was going ahead.

If he called it off, bringing Belle into his world, he would hurt her.

He was fucked.

Totally, utterly fucked. He'd never been in this position with a woman. He used them and left them. It was the way he was brought up. They were good for bearing heirs, and getting his dick wet, that was all.

Belle was different in every single way.

She didn't look at him with disgust, nor did she consider it a duty to be with him. This was all because of he lies he'd spun, but they had worked.

He arrived at Richard's place, and the man himself was waiting at the main gate.

"You really do have this place locked up tight," Diego said when he got through the first security.

"You don't get this far without putting precautions in place."

Richard locked the gate, climbing in the car.

"Where's Belle?" he asked.

"I told her to stay at the table. I was going to play something with her, but she discovered I had a guitar and tuned it for me."

"You play guitar?"

"It relaxes me. I didn't say I was good at it."

"She teaches a lot," Diego said.

"You know she's too good for you, right? She's the kind of girl you're supposed to look at but not go near."

"You were the one that pointed her out to me," Diego said. "It's your fault I even approached her. Asshole."

"I told you to go and check to make sure she was okay, not start up a relationship with her. That is entirely different."

"I didn't intentionally start up a relationship with her."

Diego glanced over at Richard to see the other man staring at him. "You know that's fucking creepy, right? You've fallen for her?"

"I don't fall for any woman."

"Then let her go."

"Don't, man, don't fucking go there."

"If you can't even handle me suggesting you leave her alone, what do you think your family is going to think of you having a civilian like her? Or is that your intention?"

Diego didn't need this right now. He had the same thoughts moments ago.

"Richard, you are not my parents, my guardian, or any fucking relation to me. Keep your opinion to yourself and help me focus on bringing Angelo down. I don't need anything else from you."

With that, he parked the car and climbed out.

Richard didn't say a word as they entered his home. Diego didn't want to give Belle up, but he knew the risks he was facing by keeping her close.

"Who was it?" Belle asked.

"Your boyfriend," Richard said, heading for the kitchen.

"Diego?"

He moved into the dining room to see her getting out of her seat. He didn't want her moving around, so he pulled her into a hug.

"Where did you go?"

"I had a few errands to run. I expected you to be sleeping the day away."

"Richard's been keeping me company."

"He told me you tuned his guitar."

"I did. It sounds much better." She picked it up, strumming her fingers across the strings.

"I didn't know you could play."

"I can play most instruments. I love the piano most out of everything."

"Let me hear you play something," he said, taking a seat, feeling Richard's eyes in the back of his head.

"You want to hear something? Do you have a preference?" she asked, doing that lovely little nibble thing with her lip, showing her nerves.

"I don't. Just play me something."

He needed to hear and feel anything but the guilt. Looking at her face, seeing the cuts and bruises, knowing she was hurting, he had to keep her here for a couple of days. He'd already made a call to Angelo's Place, the restaurant where she worked. He had stolen the chef from Angelo, and opened up a restaurant just to taunt his cousin. The family believed it had been done in honor, but his cousin knew exactly why he'd done what he had.

Pushing thoughts of Angelo to the back of his mind, he watched Belle as she ran her fingers across the strings. The music that came out was soft, slow, beautiful. She stared ahead as she played.

Her strength, the music, he couldn't get enough of her as she brought the tune to a peak before sliding off. She placed her hand across the strings, silencing it all.

"That was beautiful," he said.

"Thank you. I love to play. It gives me something to do with my hands."

"You should play more often." He reached out, tucking some of her hair behind her ear.

"Erm, speaking of which, I need to get home. I've got to work, and I don't want to take too much time off."

"I've already spoken to your boss." Again, another lie. He was the main boss, and what he said, went. "You don't need to worry."

"What about the police? I was kidnapped and … hurt. Shouldn't I be telling them something?"

"No. It's all been taken care of."

She frowned. "I don't understand. How could it all be taken care of when I'm right here?"

He took her hands in his, slamming his lips down on hers.

"That's my cue to go," Richard said in the distance.

As he slid his tongue across her lips, she opened up to him and moaned as he kissed her back. She let go of him, to cup his cheek.

"We can't do this here."

"We can do whatever we want. Richard's gone. This is all ours."

She groaned. "I want to."

"Then do. I want you. I want to rid your mind of all the things those assholes did to you." He wasn't going to take no for an answer either. Reaching for her, he picked her up in his arms, carrying her back to the bedroom Richard had showed them. Kicking the door closed, he dropped her to the bed.

"There's something we should be doing," she said, moaning.

"I know what we should be doing."

"What?"

"Each other."

She burst out laughing, and he wrapped his arms around her, sliding the shirt off her head. He'd dressed her, and now he was getting her naked. He still hated to see the bruises, but he wasn't going to stop wanting her.

Sliding his fingers down her body, he sank his

hand beneath the band of the boxer briefs, cupping her pussy.

He slid his finger between her slit, finding her soaked.

"Please, please," she said.

"I love it when you beg me."

He gripped her hips, spinning her back to the bed and forcing her to bend over. Running his hands over her curvy ass, he spread her cheeks wide, seeing her cunt and asshole.

Her puckered anus was the only part of her he'd not possessed, but he intended to. He wanted to take her all the time, every single day.

Throwing his clothes to the floor, he got naked. His cock stood out, long and thick. He didn't have any condoms, but he wasn't going to not take her. Consequences be damned. He wanted her.

Sliding his cock between her wet folds, he wrapped her dark hair around his fist and slowly fed his cock into her greedy pussy. Sinking into her to the hilt, he closed his eyes, relishing the pulse of her around his length.

Nothing else on this planet could be as good. She was fucking magnificent to him. Slowly pulling out of her heat, he stared down at his length and saw how wet he was from her arousal. He wanted to feel her coming on his cock. He let go of her hip to slide his fingers between her thighs, touching her clit. Back and forth, he teased her, loving how she tightened around his length even more.

"Fuck, yeah, baby, come all over my cock. Let me have it all."

She cried out his name, and he teased her to an orgasm that nearly set off his own. He held himself perfectly still within her, allowing her time to come down from her orgasm before he gripped her hips and started to pound within her, filling her up, taking her hard. There was no way he could hold back his release, and as he came, he didn't pull out. Taking the chance, he slammed in deep, pulsing his cum deep inside her, flooding her womb.

No matter how selfish he knew he was being, he had no intention of ever stopping. She belonged to him, just as he belonged to her, and that was never going to change.

Chapter Nine

The days blended together. Belle got up and walked around Richard's home, guided either by him or by Diego. She'd eat, chill out, listen to movies, or just sit, waiting for the time to go by. She hadn't talked to her father in a long time. She had to tell him about Melanie and make sure the other woman, whom she would never call a friend again, didn't try to take more money from him.

As she sat, alone, listening to the complete silence, she couldn't help but wonder if she should return home. Life in the city was fun, and she had met Diego, but this wasn't her place. This wasn't her life. Look what happened the first time she was alone. She had gotten taken, and anything could have happened.

Tears spilled down her cheeks, and she pushed them away, not wanting to cry anymore. Crying was for babies. Tucking her hair behind her ears, she felt so incredibly alone. Diego didn't talk about what happened, and she knew something was going on. Whenever she stumbled into a room, Richard and Diego would go so silent even though they spoke in hushed whispers.

"Hey, beautiful," Diego said, kissing her neck.

"You're back." She had been so deep in thought she hadn't heard his return. The scent of his cologne was welcome to her. No matter how scared she felt, being near him always helped to calm her. Only, there was another scent in the air, one she wasn't acquainted with. It was feminine, sweet, and she'd never smelled it before.

"Were you with a woman?" she asked.

"What?"

"One of your errands. Were you seeing a woman?" She hated how judgmental she sounded.

"No, of course not."

"You were near a woman. Enough for the scent of her perfume to linger on you."

She got to her feet with the intention of storming away, only, if Diego hadn't caught her, she would have hit the coffee table, which she was sure had been moved since the last time she counted the steps.

"Jesus, Belle. No, I wasn't with a woman. I shared a ride with one, but that's it. I'm not seeing anyone."

"Oh," she said.

"Why would I lie to you?"

"I'm sorry." She took hold of his hands, blowing out a breath. "I've been doing some thinking lately, and I think we need to talk."

"What about?"

She nibbled her lip, suddenly incredibly nervous about what she was about to say. "I'm thinking I need to move back home. To be with my dad."

It wasn't an easy decision to make. In fact, it was one of the hardest she'd ever made in her life. She'd come out to the city, determined to prove she could make this work. With Melanie finally being honest about her feelings, it only made her feel trapped. If she went back home to her father, those feelings would soon disappear, which was what she was hoping for. The only problem she had was Diego.

Her feelings for him were not easily passed aside as if they meant nothing. He did, and leaving him, that was the part that was making this decision so much harder.

"You can't leave."

"Diego—"

"No, hear me out. I get that this is scary. Running away isn't going to stop this from happening."

"I'm not running away."

"Are you trying to break up with me?" he asked.

"No."

"It sounds like it to me. Have I done something wrong?"

"No, of course not." She took his hands. "Diego, look at me. I mean, really look at me. I'm ... not perfect. I'm not good enough for you."

"Who said?" He took her hands, kissing each of them in turn.

"I'm blind, Diego. I can't see. I wanted to storm off down the street, and instead I got taken. Don't you see this? I'm not good enough for you. You deserve someone who won't slow you down. Who'll be able to walk to you without being guided."

This was breaking her heart. She had fought all of her life against people who told her she couldn't do anything. There was no way she'd listen to someone who told her it wasn't possible.

She had sat at the piano for days at a time, practicing until her fingers hurt. No one would ever tell her she couldn't do something, and yet, here she was, running back home.

She sniffled, her heart breaking at the harsh reality of her situation.

Diego startled her as he pulled her into his lap, one of his hands going to her thigh as the other gripped her waist.

"You're not going," he said.

"But—"

"No buts. I like slowing down to help guide you down the street. It gives me an excuse to hold your hand as I do. All I want is to be close to you, Belle. I don't need to speed walk, or run through the park. None of that matters to me. Watching you smile, seeing how you are, that's what gives me purpose. I don't need you to leave me. I know I don't deserve you, but only because you should have someone a lot better than me."

"Diego, don't."

"I'm not going to have you talk bad about yourself. I happen to think you're incredible, and I'm not going to trade you for anyone or anything else." He kissed her cheek. "If I have to walk slower, it will give me time to appreciate the beauty around me. I'm not giving you up, Belle. You mean everything to me."

"You're sure?"

"I wouldn't be here arguing with you, if I wasn't sure. I mean every single word I say. I'm sticking around, no matter what."

She rested against him, calmed by his words. "Thank you."

"You don't need to thank me. I'm here because I want to be."

She laid her head on his shoulder. "I'm right where I want to be as well." He stroked her arm and thigh, and she found his touch relaxing. "I've still got to call my dad. He's going to be worried about me."

"You can call." He eased her off his lap, and they walked together into the sitting room. He helped her down onto the sofa, walking away.

Leaning back, she thought about what he'd said. He wanted to be around her. He didn't have a problem with her being blind. She had dreamed of finding a man like Diego for a long time now. It almost seemed a little surreal to finally have him within her grasp.

Especially like this.

Diego returned seconds later. "Do you remember his number?"

She told him the number and waited for it. He handed her the phone as soon as he pressed call. Taking the phone from him, she pressed it to her ear and waited.

She didn't have to wait long.

"Hello?"

"Dad, it's Belle."

"Belle, what the fuck, sweetheart? I've been worried sick. I've just landed. I'm waiting for a cab to take me to your place."

This made her sit up.

"Wait? What?"

"I didn't get an answer from you or from Melanie. You've not been at work, and the kids you teach were told you were sick. I got worried. I'm your father. I took the first plane this morning. I told you if I didn't hear from you for a short length of time, I was coming to check on you."

"Dad, you really don't need to worry."

"I'll be the judge of that. You've got a man in your life, and now you're not calling your father. See what the problem is here?"

She nibbled her lip. "Okay, fine. Fine. It's no problem."

"I know it's no problem. I'll see you soon, sweetie. We can catch up." He hung up.

"What is it?"

"My dad is heading to my place. I need to get home."

"What do you mean he's heading to your place?" Diego asked.

"I haven't called him, and he started to get worried. Shit. I'm so sorry."

"You've got nothing to be sorry about. We'll head out now." He stood up, and she lifted. His hands on her hips stopped her.

"No. You sit. You've already destroyed another lamp yesterday. Let's keep the damage to a minimum."

"What about my face? The bruises. He's going to

call the cops on you and think you're beating me up."

Diego cupped her face. "You need to stop panicking."

"I can't."

"We'll deal with everything when we get there. Just sit, stop stressing about something that may never happen, and let me take care of the rest."

She sat back down again, listening to Diego as he began to make some calls. This was good. She'd not hugged her dad in a long time, or been able to take him out to dinner. Also, he would get to see Diego.

Was it too soon for her boyfriend and father to meet?

This was the first time she had ever taken a boy home.

This was crazy.

She didn't know how much time had passed before Diego came back. He took her hand and led her out of the house. He eased her into the car and strapped her in.

"You know I can do that?"

"Yep, but I don't care. I like doing it." The back of his hand brushed across her breasts. "For that very reason."

"How far are we away from my place?" she asked.

"Not too far."

She didn't press for more information. She knew she probably should but right now, she was really trying not to freak out. Her father was coming to see her. This was the first time he'd flown out to her. She'd have to explain what happened with Melanie and for him to stop contacting her. Nothing good would ever come of it.

"What do we tell him about my bruises?" she asked.

"The truth. You had an argument with Melanie, and she left you there."

"She didn't really leave me there. I didn't want her help." Why would she want anyone's help after what she did? She didn't make a habit of forcing people to be around her.

"Come on, stop worrying. You still had an argument, and rather than see you to safety, Melanie left you high and dry. You were taken. I saved you. The end."

"He's going to want to talk to the cops. This is such a mess."

"I'll handle everything. You have nothing to worry about."

"It's easy for you to say. Your dad isn't like a war machine when he thinks his little girl is in danger."

"I'll prove to him that I've got everything under control, and believe me, I do."

She did believe him. If anyone had it all together it was Diego.

Forcing herself to relax, which was next to impossible, she listened to the world going by. Before her accident that claimed her sight, she had loved watching the world pass in a blur. There was something about driving, where everything sped up that always caught her attention. She remembered sitting in the back of the car, going nearly dizzy as she moved her head with each passing tree.

She did miss those moments.

Still, she remembered them so vividly.

The car came to a stop.

"Are we here?"

"Yeah, we're here."

"Oh, that really wasn't far at all."

"Richard is the kind of guy that likes his

protection no matter what." Diego unclipped his seatbelt before doing hers. She didn't open the car door. She had done that once many months ago and hit someone who was walking past.

Diego opened the door, and they made their way up to her apartment together.

Once inside, he still took control, ushering her toward the bathroom. She didn't put up a fight. They stepped under her small space, and she wanted nothing more than to explore him, but with her father coming, there was no time. Diego washed her body, then her hair, before doing his. He moved her out of the way of the water, and before she could climb out, he was already doing it, drying himself and then her.

His hands didn't linger as he touched her.

Next, they were in her bedroom, and he was helping her into a dress.

"Why a dress?"

"It looks lovely, and we don't have a clue when your dad is going to arrive. What should I order?"

"Pizza will be good, I think?" She really wasn't thinking clearly right now.

"Calm down. You have this. We have this."

"What if he doesn't like you?" she asked.

He chuckled. "The odds are, he's not going to like me. No dad in the world would ever like a man with their daughter. It's just the way it is. There's nothing I can do about it."

She sighed. "You're right. He pretty much hates you on principle, right?"

"You're his daughter, baby. He's not going to want to know that you're sleeping with me, or that his little girl is enjoying sex."

"Do you know this from experience?"

"No. I don't have any kids. I just know that if it

was my daughter, they're going to be fucked."

She burst out laughing. "They are?"

"Yes." He kissed her head. "I'm going to get dressed."

He stepped away from her, but she didn't immediately leave the room. "You want kids?"

"Yes."

"Oh."

"Do you?" he asked.

"I'm honestly not sure."

"Why not?"

"I don't know if I can have kids or if it would be responsible for me to have them."

"Do you want kids?"

"I think so. I mean, if I could, then yes."

"Then one day we're going to have kids," he said.

This made her heart leap. "We are?"

"Yes, we're going to have kids, and you're not going to stress or worry about taking care of them."

"I'd want to be there for my kids."

"And you will be. For our kids. I'll just make sure there is help. You need to understand, Belle. Where there is a will, there is always going to be a way, and, being the kind of guy I am, I'm going to always find it." He cupped her face, startling her. "Now, I'm just going to finish getting dressed, and then we're going to meet your father."

She nodded.

Diego had this magical away about him that always calmed her down. She hoped her father loved him, just like she did.

Hold on.

No.

She cared about Diego. Caring was different from love. She knew it was different. She didn't love him. It was way too soon to even think about that.

Pushing love and her feelings to one side, she listened to Diego as he changed. She didn't know how long he was from being done when her door was knocked at.

"It's showtime, baby. Don't worry about anything, okay?"

"You're right. I won't. I won't."

****

Belle wasn't good at hiding her nerves.

Diego stood behind her as she opened the door to her father.

"Pumpkin," he said, rushing into the room to hold her. Diego didn't like anyone touching her and certainly not her father. Still, he didn't set off a bad impression as he watched the two interact.

"Dad, I'd like you to meet someone—"

"What happened to your face?" he asked.

"Dad, we'll get to that. I'd really like you to meet—"

"Did you do this to my daughter, you fucking bastard?"

"Dad!"

"I've never raised a hand to your daughter," he said, finally speaking up.

"Dad, please, don't jump to conclusions. I'm fine. Diego would never hurt me." She stepped toward him, and Diego took her hand so she didn't bump into anything.

"It's a pleasure to meet you, sir."

"Diego?"

"Dad, I'd like you to meet Diego Leoni. My boyfriend."

Her cheeks went a beautiful pink as she said the last part.

"Your boyfriend who is not responsible for the bruises on your face "

"He's not. I promise you. He's the one that came to save me. He would never hurt me."

"I would never hurt her," he said.

"I'll be the judge of that."

Daddy didn't like him, not that Diego was surprised. Her father had already done his appraisal of him, and even if Diego was an upstanding citizen, earning billions in legit business, this man still wouldn't like him. Not that he had a problem with being this man's enemy. He wasn't giving Belle up. She belonged to him, and he was already working on the ways in order to keep her safe and in his life.

Selfish bastard that he was, he wanted it all.

He was going to get it as well.

"Dad, please, I don't want you to argue or to get into a fight. Let me tell you what happened. Diego is going to order pizza."

"You said your name was Leoni?" her father asked.

"Yes."

"Dad's name is James. James Johnson."

"It's a pleasure to meet you, sir." He held his hand out, very much aware that he wasn't much younger than the man in front of him. There were probably a couple of years that separated them, but that was about it. "I'll go and order that pizza," Diego said, making sure to kiss her temple before handing her back to her capable father, who was shooting daggers at him.

He grabbed his cell phone and moved to the kitchen, keeping them in his sights. James helped Belle sit down on the sofa, and he saw the other man wasn't happy with her at all, or with this current situation. When he finished ordering food, he moved toward them, taking a seat behind Belle as he did so. He wasn't going to create distance here, or give James any ammunition if he thought for even a second he could get rid of him. That shit wasn't happening. Not on his watch.

"So, how did you two meet?" James asked.

"I'll let Belle tell you."

He took her hand, locking their fingers together, and James stared down at their hands, again, not looking any the happier about it.

"So I've got Melanie to thank for a lot of things."

"Don't be angry with her, Dad. I'm really happy. Honestly. Diego is a good guy."

If looks could kill, Diego would be dead, so dead.

Another knock on the door, and Diego left to answer. Pulling out some money, he shoved it into the kid's hand, bringing in the pizza. He was getting hungry, and sensed a confrontation coming from her father.

James wouldn't do it in front of his daughter, but it was there, lingering around him like a fucking aura waiting to explode.

He ate his pizza, and Diego listened to them catch up. Belle didn't have a spare bedroom for her father, so he had to book a hotel room.

"I'm going to call a cab," James said, as it was getting late.

For a family visit, no one had died, and Diego considered that a plus.

"Nonsense. Diego, you'll drive my dad to his hotel, right?"

"Yes. I've got no problem with that." It would give them a chance to talk without her worrying, and if Diego had to shoot him and get rid of the body, he could also do that without getting caught as well.

"I wouldn't want to be a burden," James said.

"No burden," Diego said. "You're going to be

okay until I get back?"

"More than okay. This is my apartment. I know it by heart."

He took possession of her mouth before turning his attention to her father. Again, if looks had anything to do with his living, he'd be dead. He'd died a lot in this apartment just from James.

Taking the man's bags, they left her apartment, and he locked it from the outside so he would be sure she was safe.

He sent off a quick text to Richard to keep an extra eye on her. He didn't like leaving her, not even to help her father.

Richard responded with a thumbs up, and it was all he was going to get, so he took it.

Riding the elevator down to the ground floor, he left the apartment block, keeping an eye out for anyone nearby who might be acting suspicious. When he saw no one, he nodded for James to follow him. The older man did, and Diego shoved his suitcase into the back of the car. He spotted two of his men, waiting close by. To anyone looking, they were just two men reading a paper, but he knew who they were.

Climbing behind the wheel, he started the car as James got in. Neither of them had spoken to each other, and he ignored the tension brewing in the car.

He pulled out of the parking lot, which was behind the building. There was some parking at the front, but it was always full.

The moment they cleared the parking lot and joined traffic, James started talking.

"You need to stop seeing my daughter."

"Not happening."

"You think I don't know who you are, what it is you do?"

Diego smiled. "And what is it exactly you think I do?"

"Your family has been linked to the mafia. You've also been described as the capo of this city. You lost your first wife many years ago, and now you're getting married to your second. The one that's not my daughter. There was an announcement in the paper yesterday. My daughter doesn't like to read the news. She never did, but I fucking know who you are. You think you can take advantage of my girl?"

"I'm not taking advantage of Belle. I care about her."

"You're still getting married to another woman. You think Belle will like that? Being the mistress? The other woman?"

"She's not the other woman."

"She will be the moment you marry. Scrap that, she was the other woman the moment you were engaged to someone else."

"Charlotte is business, old man. You've got no right to meddle with this."

"Belle is my daughter. I love her very much, and she wanted her independence. I knew letting Melanie take care of her was a big mistake. I never liked that girl, but she'd never steered Belle wrong, until now."

"Your idea of taking care of her is laughable. She pulled Belle into my club not once but twice, and on both occasions, I took care of her."

"You had to."

"No, I didn't. I don't *have* to take care of anyone or anything. Belle, I took care of her because I wanted to."

"The life you live, Diego, it is not good for her. Look at her face."

"I'm not even responsible for that." Diego was

losing control of this conversation, and it pissed him off. His name had been printed many times. If they couldn't get to the press in time, they always passed the stories off as rumors, and hatred. Or the person writing the articles would be discovered to be an addict of some kind, and their storylines would never be remembered as truth but as the babbling writings of an addict waiting to get his next fix. "I'm not letting her go."

"You've got to tell her the truth."

"I don't have to do anything. Belle is mine, and if you want to stay a part of her life, you'll let me handle everything."

He glanced over at her father.

"Listen here, Diego. I don't give a flying fuck who you think you are or who you're connected to. You will tell my daughter exactly who you are, that you're getting married, and you will let me take her home with me. This is not an agreement. This is a fucking promise."

"Yeah, and why would I listen to you?" Diego laughed.

"Because if you loved her even a little bit, you'd let her go rather than hurt her. If my daughter is just a passing fancy for you, you won't care about her a year from now. I'm doing what is best for her."

"You know I could kill you right now. Tell her it was an accident."

"You're not going to do that," James said.

"Why not?"

"You think I didn't see the way you looked at her. How patient you are? I've been with Belle since the very beginning. When she was a baby. I remember her running around the neighborhood, screaming and laughing, and doing all the kinds of things kids do. Then the accident, and her sight was gone, vanished. I watched her struggle. I've seen her fight for everything, and I admire her for it. She has a spirit and a passion that I will never take away from her. When you look at her, you see her. You don't see that she's blind. You don't see that she's a burden. You see her, and I know you see an amazing woman. It's probably why you've broken every single rule you have. I don't know you, Diego. I know men like you. She has gotten you under her spell, and what is more, Belle doesn't even have a clue she's casting it. This is all new for her."

If it was anyone else, he would have killed them by now.

Just to keep The Boss safe, he should kill James.

The only problem? James was Belle's father, and what he was saying was right. He couldn't keep her as he would only break her heart more. He knew it, and he fucking hated it with every fiber of his being.

Keeping Belle to himself was the most selfish thing he'd done, but letting her go, he couldn't even think it, let alone do it.

"I've got to have some more time with her," Diego said. "Please."

"Did you even realize you were in love with her?"

Diego said nothing, simply staring at her father. He hated this fucker so much. There wasn't even a good reason as to why he felt this way, but he did. Especially in this moment. With Richard he didn't have to listen to his not-friend. With James, he was her father, and if anyone was going to take care of her better than him, it would be James.

"I need more time."

"You've got to the end of the week. Then I'm taking her home. I suggest you use that time wisely."

James got out of the car. He'd brought it to a stop outside the hotel. Diego waited as he got a key and disappeared inside his room before pulling away. He drove back to Belle's apartment with an overwhelming need to see her.

Parking up, he rushed inside her building, pulling out his key and entering her place within a matter of minutes.

He saw her on the sofa with some soft music playing.

"Diego?"

"Yeah, it's me."

He rushed to her side, taking her hand, and pulling her to her feet.

"What's the—"

Diego didn't give her a chance to stop. He slammed his lips down on hers, silencing any more words from her mouth. Sinking his fingers into her hair with one hand, with the other, he gripped her ass, moving her across the room, to her bedroom.

She didn't fight him, trusting him as he walked her back. Once they were in her bedroom, he made quick work of removing her pajamas. They were a cute pink pair, and he adored them, but he liked his woman naked and at his mercy.

Sitting her on the edge of the bed, he pulled and tugged at his own clothes until he was just as naked as she.

"Diego, what is going on?"

"Nothing. I just need to be inside you right now."

He nudged her back until she fell against the covers. Spreading her legs, he stared down at her pretty pink pussy.

The best pussy he'd ever eaten and been inside.

Opening the lips of her pussy, he slid his tongue between the silken folds, nipping and sucking at her bud.

She arched her back, crying out as he licked her.

Sliding across her clit, he nibbled on the bud before gliding down to plunge inside her. He began to fuck her with his tongue, making her take him, holding her legs wide, so he could eat her.

Her pleasured cries flooded the air, but he ignored them. This was about him tonight. He wanted to have his fill of her as much as he could before he let her go.

Inside he growled at the thought of letting her go, but he knew deep down her father was more that right. He had to do the right thing by her, even if he didn't want to. She deserved so much more, and being selfish with her, he couldn't do that.

He was getting married to another woman.

A woman who, at some point, would have to carry his child, even though he had no desire for any other woman but Belle. She had gotten beneath his skin, and there was no way he wanted to be with anyone else. Charlotte was nothing more than a duty. Belle, she was everything, the love, the pleasure, all of it.

"Diego," she said, crying out his name.

He wanted her so much.

Focusing on her clit, he teased her nub back and forth, getting her to the peak of orgasm before plunging her over the edge. As he did so, he didn't give her the chance to get accustomed to him.

He slid in deep, taking hold of her hands, locking their fingers together, and sliding in deep to the hilt.

Her cunt tightened around him, squeezing him. Pulling out, he slammed back inside, watching her as he did so. Her tits bounced with each thrust, and the bed banged against the wall from the force of his hard fucking.

He tried to get as deep as possible, to ruin her for any other man. He couldn't allow himself to think of her with anyone else.

Belle was his.

She belonged to him, and he wasn't going to let some asshole take her from him. Pounding inside her, he took her harder than he ever had before. Kissing her full lips, feeling her pussy flutter around him.

It was intense.

It was everything.

As he came, feeling Belle come with him as well, Diego didn't know how he was going to be able to let her go. Especially not at the end of the week.

Chapter Ten

Diego was having to run some errands, and her father walked her to the nearest coffee shop. Belle knew something had happened between the two men, but they both weren't saying a thing.

"A mocha latte?" James asked.

"Yes, please." She removed her jacket, placing it across her legs as she waited for her father to return. The coffee shop was busy, and she listened to all the noise around them. It was nice hearing people going about their day as if they didn't have a care in the world, and for most of them, they didn't.

Her father, though, he had an agenda. He'd been dropping hints of taking her back home, and she wasn't ready to leave.

Why would she want to leave when she had Diego and she wasn't willing to let him slip through her fingers?

"I'm back," James said. "So, one mocha latte, and I even got you a cinnamon roll."

"Yum."

"I know how much you like them." He put her hands near the plate so she would know where to touch.

Thanking him, she tore a bite and placed it in her mouth. The cinnamon sweetness exploded on her tongue, and she took another bite.

"Are you going to tell me what went on between you and Diego?" she asked.

"Nothing."

"Dad, I know you. I know you're not the kind of guy to keep your opinions to yourself. Just tell me. We're both adults here."

"I don't think he's good enough for you. There are a lot of reasons."

"Me being your daughter?"

"That is one of them. I want you to have a normal life. Diego, he can't offer you that."

"Why? Because he owns a club you think he doesn't have what it takes to take care of me?"

"Oh, I know he has what it takes. I know he's quite capable of taking care of you, but he can't give you a normal life. There are reasons and facts."

"Why are you being so secretive?" she asked. "You're not making sense."

"What exactly do you know about Diego?" he asked.

"I know a lot of things. I know that he's smart and kind." This made her father snort. "Dad, you don't know him. You're assessing him on one meeting. I've known him for weeks, and what I know, I like. Okay. I care about him." She nibbled her lip. "I, erm, I even think I might love him." She spoke so softly, merely a whisper.

"Belle?"

"No, please, don't judge me. I've never been with anyone else. Diego, we didn't just jump in this together, and it's not a mistake. He makes me laugh, and he makes me believe anything and everything is possible. Can't you see that?" she asked. "I really don't want to argue with you about this. Diego means a great deal to me, and so do you. Please, just … let's enjoy our coffee."

She didn't like feeling this way with her father. He was only trying to take care of her, and she got it, completely understood what he was trying to do. She just didn't like it. Not even a little bit.

Pressing her lips together, she tried to think of a million other things to talk about with her father, but came up blank.

"After we're done here, I'm going to go and check on Melanie."

"Dad?"

"No, I think that girl should be given a piece of my mind, and I'm going to be the one to tell her what I think of her ... annoyance. Stupid girl. I can't even believe she left you and she said all those things to you."

She smiled. This was easier for her to deal with. "Dad, you really don't have to worry about it. I know Diego was pissed at her."

"He was?"

"Yes. Don't pay her any more money, please. She doesn't deserve it."

"I'm reaching for your hand," he said. Belle held her hand open for him to take. "I care about you, a lot. I want to make sure you're happy at everything."

"Dad, I am happy. Honestly. I wasn't expecting Diego. I wasn't expecting any of this and I ... I did think Diego and I wouldn't work, but he is determined for us to make it work. I hope one day, you'll care about him just as much as I do."

He father gave her hand a little squeeze. "I love you, honey."

"I love you too. Tonight, I'm taking him to sing karaoke. Do you want to come?"

"You're taking Diego to sing?" James asked.

"Yes."

"Does he know?"

"Nope. That's the beauty of it. He doesn't have a clue, and I know he's going to love it."

"I don't know. Diego doesn't strike me as the kind of guy that loves to sing."

She chuckled. "You've got to give him a little more credit. He'll surprise you." She pulled out her cell phone and directed a call to Diego.

"Hey, baby, what's up?"

"I want you available tonight. I've got date

plans."

"Tonight?"

"No excuses. Please, Diego, I want you there. It'll be a lot of fun." Her father laughed.

"Why do I feel this could be torture?"

"That's just my dad. He thinks my plan for fun is totally wasted on you. Are you going to prove him right?" she asked.

"You know I can't do that. I'll meet you at eight, sound good?"

"Perfect."

She hung up the phone, sliding the device in her pocket.

"Belle, honey, I know you have feelings for him."

"Dad?"

"Hear me out. I'm your old man for a reason. I get to worry about you. Just take it easy. You don't know everything about him."

"Did you know everything about Mom?" she asked.

"I did. I knew everything about her. It's important to know the little things about a person. What makes them tick."

"It's not the same as when you and Mom were dating, Dad."

"I'm taking your hands," he said. She felt his touch and this time didn't flinch. "I would give everything to have her back for just a day. I loved your mother so much. I miss her each and every single day. I want that kind of love for you because I know it's out there."

"You know it's different with me." She let go of his hand to point at her eyes.

"No. True love. Real love, that's what counts. Everything else, it doesn't matter. When you meet the one, there is no fighting that love."

"Then, Dad, I have a feeling I may have met him, and I hope you can find it in your heart to accept that." She knew it was too soon, but everything he described was everything she felt.

****

Pocketing his cell phone, Diego joined the table where his father and his father's current fuck interest were waiting, along with Charlotte and her family.

"Is everything okay?" his father asked.

"Perfect." He'd been forced to come to this lunch at his father's request. All that he did was at either his father's or The Boss's request.

"The date of the wedding has been brought forward," Charlotte's mother said.

"Excuse me." Diego looked toward the woman who would be his future-mother-in-law. She looked like she sucked on lemons in her spare time.

"The wedding. The Boss wants to speed things up. He believes morale has been at an all-time low, and to help lift the darkness, he wants the wedding by the end of the month," his father said.

"Why wasn't I notified about this?" The end of the month was just over a week and a half away.

This wasn't what he wanted.

"We did send an email," Charlotte said.

"I didn't get it." He glared toward her mother. "Anything else I need to know about?"

"Yes, we hired the chef at Angelo's Place. We've been told it's where you like to eat."

This made Diego pause. "By who?"

"Angelo. He's been helping to contribute to the wedding."

Diego's hands clenched. It wouldn't do him any good to kill every single person at this table. The Boss would make him answer for the crimes, and none of them were worth it.

"There won't be a honeymoon immediately after the wedding, but in two months' time," her mother said.

The woman kept on talking even though he lost interest. The woman he wanted wasn't sitting at this table, and she shouldn't be.

"Well, it would seem you have everything planned out, and seeing as you've done well enough without me, I will leave you to continue the preparations." He got to his feet, throwing down some money before turning on his heel and walking out.

He should have known Angelo would be part of this in some way. That asshole had been playing with him for years.

Running a hand down his face, to clear the mess from his mind, he stood outside the restaurant, waiting for his car to be brought around.

"Diego?"

He looked toward the door to see Charlotte had followed him. Nodding in her direction, he stayed perfectly still.

"I know a lot is happening so fast," Charlotte said.

"It's not going to change what is happening though, is it? You'll be my wife, and whatever The Boss wants, he gets." He checked the time and saw it was a little after one. He needed to check in with Richard before he met up with Belle.

Shit, Belle. She wanted to take him out, and now he knew Angelo knew about Angelo's Place. Was it a taunt? A challenge? He needed to deal with his fucking wayward cousin once and for all. For too long he'd been in hiding, and it was time to seek him out.

"Do you want to get married?" Charlotte asked,

pulling him out of his thoughts.

"What?"

"In the past couple of weeks, you seem to have lost all interest when it comes to marriage with me," she said. "I understand. I'm not exactly the best pick."

"No, I don't want to get married to you, Charlotte. I don't love you. I don't care for you even a little bit. The idea of having to fuck you sickens me. Not because of who you are. I'm just not interested in you."

"You found someone else?" she asked.

"I'm not talking about this with you."

"I understand. Men in our world don't seem to think we understand anything, but we do. We understand love and loyalty and needing to do what is right. It's not easy for us."

"Are you telling me you're in love with someone else?"

This would make it easy for him, and a lot more interesting.

"No. I'm not in love with anyone. I don't even know if I've ever known what love is."

All he had to do was think about losing Belle, and he got a really good fucking idea.

"I know what love is."

"Is it worth it? The pain? The suffering?"

"For the right kind of person, anything is worth it," he said. "I'm going to ask you again, is there someone else?"

"No. There's no one else. I don't know how to help you get out of this wedding. If I refuse you, it'll cast me out even more. I can't do that."

"There is no way out, Charlotte. Don't you get that?"

"I'm sorry, Diego. I really am." She went to put her hand on his arm, but he pulled away. He had no desire for her to touch him at all.

"Goodbye, Charlotte."

His car arrived, and he moved away from her, with no interest in continuing a conversation.

Climbing behind the wheel, he pulled out of the restaurant, heading on the main road to Richard's headquarters. Belle's father making an appearance had screwed with his plans. He had no doubt that come the end of week deadline, he would tell Belle the truth. Diego didn't want that to happen. There was so fucking much he didn't want to happen.

Killing Charlotte wouldn't solve things, only escalate them. Marrying Belle, if she'd taken him, wouldn't work. Her family didn't offer the affluence that The Boss wanted.

Either way he looked at it, he was well and truly fucked.

His men joined him as he parked the car and made his way up to the top floor where Richard liked to look over the city. His building was complete with all the latest technology. He took the elevator, straightening the cuff of his jacket while he waited. The instant the elevator opened, he stepped off and found Richard in his office, staring down at a document.

Closing the door behind him, he stepped up to the desk.

"Am I interrupting something?"

"You don't have an appointment," Richard said.

"What the fuck is this? You were supposed to be helping me bring Angelo down."

"Yes, and in the process, we have absolutely nothing. The bastard has gone radio silent."

"Yeah, well, he's been stalking a little close to home."

"What makes you say that?"

"According to my soon to be mother-in-law, he recommended a chef at Angelo's Place. Need I remind you why I go to Angelo's Place?"

"We've got men guarding Belle and your establishments. He would have come up on the scanner."

"Not if your guys were sloppy or he has someone working with him. Check the security footage."

"You ever think you're being paranoid."

"No. Being paranoid keeps me alive and Belle breathing. Just seeing it as a coincidence is what gets people killed. Believe me, I've been in this business a long time to know when someone is fucking with me."

Richard grabbed his tablet with an over dramatic sigh. "How was the lunch with the fiancée?"

"Fuck off, Richard."

His not-friend started to laugh. "You really need to get a handle on that temper. What would Belle say?"

"I told you she's never going to find out."

"And I still think you're talking out of your ass, but what do I know?" Richard asked.

The main wall split open, revealing at least twenty different security monitors.

"Can you access all of the security feeds around the city?"

"I shouldn't be able to as they are protected, but it just takes a little time. You want me to have a play?"

"Another time. Focus on Angelo and the restaurant for now." He checked the time. He didn't want to miss his date with Belle.

He needed to take care of business first, even if he did find it more inconvenient to deal with.

"How far you want me to go back?" Richard asked.

"Start from yesterday and go back. You got that facial recognition thing?"

"Already running it, baby. Yeah, that sounded weird to me."

Diego shook his head, watching the screen. It showed Angelo's main security cameras outside and inside the building.

Checking the time stamp, he saw they went back at least two weeks.

"Wait, stop," he said, when something caught his attention.

"What is it?"

"Zoom in there. On that guy," Diego said.

"I'm zooming in, but I can't make out a face."

"Because the son of a bitch has it covered," Diego said. "He knew we were onto him. He's been laying low. No one walks into a restaurant wearing a scarf. Not in this heat. Fuck! Why wasn't I alerted to it?"

"Diego, you didn't put any warnings out to your restaurant. You thought it would alert them, remember?" Richard said.

"This means he knows about Belle. He's planning something."

Richard held his hands up in surrender. "Whoa, hold on a minute there. How do you make that giant leap? You can't just assume that because he's gone to eat in Angelo's something is about to go down."

"It's what I'd do," Diego said. "I want your men nearby tonight."

"Wait? Hold on a second, Diego. You're not making any sense at all right now."

"You want to get rid of Angelo, right?" Diego asked.

"I do, but I want facts. I don't want to jump to conclusions."

"I'm telling you right now, Angelo's about to make a move. It's perfect. He knows we've been following him, so he has laid low. He's even covered his tracks. Going to Angelo's with the pretense of talking to the chef."

"Diego, I really think this is a stretch. We don't know anything concrete. I can send the manpower, but what am I sending them to? We have nothing."

"Which is exactly what he wanted! Fuck." He yelled the word. "I've got a date tonight with Belle."

"Then go on your date."

"I can't. Especially not now. Knowing Angelo is out there."

"Diego, you've got this all wrong. I'm telling you. This is not what I've seen from Angelo before now."

"You're going to make a mistake with this, Richard. Get the men and be prepared."

"Go on your date. The dad already wants you gone. You're holding on by a thread. Take my advice and go and spend tonight with her. We can handle this in the morning when you're not completely stressing out about your wedding."

"How do you know about all that?" Diego asked.

"I've made it my business to know everything. I want Angelo dealt with. I want him gone. He's a toxin. A poison that shouldn't see the light of day, but when he's handled, your family and Boss will thank you for it."

Diego didn't agree. He knew Angelo. Had known him his entire life, and knew the little shit was up to something.

He couldn't convince Richard, and there was no way he could go to his father. The rivalry between them had been there since birth. He couldn't risk his capo title.

Leaving Richard's office, he made his way back to his car, with the intention of staying the night with Belle.

Chapter Eleven

A few hours later, Diego grimaced as he looked toward the stage. James was laughing, and Belle looked way too happy with herself.

"Karaoke?"

"Yes, isn't it great? I bet you haven't done anything like this before."

"Karaoke?" He looked around the bar. It was dark with a single light shining on the stage.

"You don't like it?"

"I'm going to go and find us a seat," James said.

"I love it."

"You're lying now," Belle said. "You really don't like to sing?"

"I can't sing, Belle. I don't do this kind of thing. It's fucking stupid."

"Wow, that is a huge leap from not liking it. Is there something I don't know about?" she asked.

"Yeah, I don't believe in getting up on stage and looking fucking stupid for people's amusement." He also didn't want to be on a date with James.

"Oh, well, I kind of put our names forward to sing. I'm going to head up onto the stage."

"Belle?" He held her close as he noticed someone come in close.

"I'm a regular here, Diego. Don't worry about it. Just sit back. Have a few drinks. I'll sing, and then we can leave."

Now he felt like a prick for upsetting her.

He watched the other man, who was the barman, walking her toward the stage. There was a seat, and he didn't like that someone else was helping her.

He found James in a small booth. He sat opposite the man who hated him.

"You could have handled that a lot better," James said.

"I didn't know she likes to sing."

"And she doesn't know you're part of a crime ring. I'd say you're even."

"I'm not part of a crime ring."

"Fine, mafia ring."

"You know, talking about it aloud can get you killed."

"I've had worse, believe me. I'm sure there's nothing you or your cronies could do to me."

"I wouldn't make offers like that. You'd be surprised."

"Watching your daughter go blind because of a driving accident, if that's not torture, then how about seeing the woman you love more than anything die before you? Only this isn't a bullet to the head. This is a disease eating her away bit by bit until there is nothing left. That is torture, and I've seen that."

"Belle's mother."

"Yep. I watched her die. I watched the vibrant, energetic woman slowly fade away until she was nothing more than a corpse. If you can still get up after that, then you can take on anything."

The person on stage finished their song, and Diego waited as Belle was moved onto the stage.

She looked a little sad, and he knew he was the one to put her in this mood.

"You know, Belle reminds me so much of her mother. They were both always so happy, so in love with life. Even Belle, no matter what difficulties she faces, she will always come out on top."

"I was drawn to her the moment I saw her," Diego admitted. It was hard for him to admit how quickly he fell for her, but she had worked her way into his heart. The moment she started singing though, her talent shone through

She could play instruments like a pro, and was absolutely stunning. He could listen to her play all day, but her singing, now that was something else entirely.

The passion in her voice filled the entire room. The flow of her voice enraptured him, taking him completely by surprise.

He loved this woman more than anyone else in the entire world.

"I know my life is not for her. I know it holds a lot of pain and death, but I can't let her go." He looked toward James. "I know you want me to. I can't do it."

"You're not going to give her the life she deserves. She will always be the other woman." James shook his head. "I'm going to tell her the truth, and when she finds out from me, and not from you, it'll break her heart."

"Then don't tell her. You know I love her. You know I want to do right by her."

"But you're still going to marry another woman. You'll still keep her as a secret."

"I don't want to keep her as a secret."

"Diego, we all have to make choices we don't want." James slammed his hand on the table. "You're not a child. She's not a child. She's not a piece of property. She's my daughter, and I want what is best for her, and it's not you."

Diego laughed. "You know, I would have killed a man who insulted me for less. I'm in love with your daughter, James. You can try to fight me all you want, but I will stop you at every turn."

With that, he got to his feet, approaching the stage.

He got onto the stage, and as he touched her hip,

she stopped singing. Flicking through the options, he picked a well-known song.

"What are you doing?" she asked.

"I don't like to sing. I don't like to be on center stage, but for you, Belle, I'm willing to do a whole lot more."

Picking up the mic, he held her hand, and sang his heart out when it was needed. He sounded awful, and Belle sounded amazing. He would have to get her to sing to him more often.

By the time they were done, the crowd clapped, showing their approval. He held Belle's hand up, allowing her to get all the praise. He adored this woman.

No, he loved this woman so damn much.

He didn't even know how it was possible for him to love her this much, but it was. It so was much more than anything he'd ever felt before, and it consumed him.

Walking her back to their booth, he made his way to the bar to grab a round of drinks. He kept to a soda for himself.

Several people slapped him on the back as he passed. The temptation to threaten them was strong, but he knew he wasn't in his world at the moment. This was Belle's.

"You two totally rocked the stage," James said.

"Dad said he's staying for another couple of weeks," Belle said.

"He did?"

"Yep. Isn't that great?"

"Brilliant." He looked at James, who had a brow raised. Diego had no doubt James was sticking around to keep an eye on him. He hadn't told her yet, so that was a plus on his side.

If he had his wish, Belle would never know the truth about his situation. Men were able to live double lives, and some never got caught.

You don't want to live a double life.

He pushed that thought to the back of his mind.

It didn't matter what he did or didn't want it to happen. The fact still remained that it was going to happen eventually.

Would it break her?

Would it stop her looking at him the way she did?

Damn it. He didn't want James to be right about this. He loved her, and he didn't want to lose her. He'd never had to make a decision this challenging before.

They finished off their drinks, and Belle declared she was starving and wanted to take her dad to Mary's. All he wanted to do was take her home where he knew it was safe.

Instead, he made sure to put his jacket around Belle as they headed on out.

The night was so busy as they got onto the street. He looked left and right, keeping Belle by his side. He still had a sneaking suspicion about Angelo, and he was rarely ever wrong.

Just as they crossed the road, the sound of tires squealing followed by gunshots filled the air.

Screams, cries, and yells erupted all around him, and he quickly tried to push Belle to the ground. In the rush, she'd been pulled from his arms, and he moved to her side. Diego didn't get to see who was shooting, but as they took off, he saw his men following in pursuit.

"Diego? Dad?"

Hearing his name, he quickly walked to Belle's side, helping her to her feet.

"Are you okay?"

"I don't know. I think so. Where's my dad?" she asked.

He quickly checked her over to make sure there

were no marks or shots, before glancing down the street.

Several people were crying, and there were bodies on the ground.

"Shit!" He spotted James, blood seeping out of his chest.

"What is it? What's wrong?"

"Your dad's been hit. It's okay, James." Removing the jacket he'd placed around Belle, he put some pressure to the wound.

"Dad's been shot. Daddy?"

Belle knelt on the ground as James took a breath.

"How bad is it? What's going on? Diego, what's happening?"

"Someone, call an ambulance." The cry came down the street.

Diego kept the pressure on the wound, knowing his time was coming to an end. It wouldn't be long now before he had to tell her something.

"Diego, please, talk to me?" She sniffled.

He looked up to see the woman he loved looking distraught. She couldn't see what was happening. Her hands were shaking. She was going into shock. He had to take control of everything, and he didn't want to hurt her.

"I'm so sorry, baby."

With that, he placed his hand over her face, holding her close, stopping her from fighting him, until she passed out cold. He couldn't do what was needed of him with her distracting him.

One day, she'd forgive him. It just wouldn't be any day soon.

****

Belle came to ... somewhere. There was no smell, and as she sat up, she felt something around her wrist. Touching the metal, she knew she'd been cuffed to something. Touching the space around her, she realized she was on the bed.

Alone.

There was no other scent.

Everything was a little hazy, and then she recalled the screaming.

The gunshots, and little by little, it came back to her in a nightmare of sounds and darkness.

Her father.

"Help," she said.

Getting to her feet, she took a step to side, trying to find the wall. After three steps, she found nothing, so she went in the opposite direction, finding the wall.

The chain on her wrist was embarrassing and not what she wanted to have done to herself.

"Is anyone there?"

No sound.

Silence.

Her mouth was incredibly dry.

Stroking her fingers along the wall, she tried to think of anything she could say to make someone hear her.

Nothing came to mind.

"Hello. Can someone help me?" She turned and the cuff on her wrist had gone as far as it would let her.

She had no choice but to stop.

Moving in the other direction, she came to a stop at the bed. Moving around it, she tried again, getting to nowhere.

The room had to be large, or she was taking really tiny steps.

Finally, giving up on her useless exploring, she sat back on the bed, crossing her legs, wrapping her arms around herself, and trying not to freak out about what was going on around her.

What the hell happened?

What happened to her dad?

Why was she locked in a room?

Rubbing at her head, she tried to make sense of it.

The sound of a door opening had her scrambling to sit up.

She couldn't make out anything, no scent, no distinct sound. Nothing.

"Hello," she said.

"I see you're awake."

She didn't recognize the voice. "Who are you? Why am I here?"

"I bet you have a whole lot of questions, and well, my son, he'll be down to answer most of them, I believe. You've just got to give him time."

She frowned. "Your son?"

"Diego."

"You're Diego's father."

"Yes, I'm Diego's father, and you, my dear, have been taken for a fool."

"What?"

"You really think he was just a lonely guy who owned a bar?"

"He's not?"

"I have to say I thought his distraction would have been for someone more ... interesting. I guess he has a thing for women who can't see him."

She sensed the man coming closer, and she took a step back.

"You do know when you're in danger. It's a shame those same instincts didn't kick in around my son."

"I want to see Diego."

"It's good to want things in life. It doesn't mean we'll always get them." She flinched as he touched her hair. It wasn't aggressive. He merely tucked some of her hair behind her ear. "Beautiful. Maybe I do see a certain charm, but it's still not enough to put all that we had built in jeopardy."

"I don't understand."

"Of course you don't. Why would you understand? You've been kept in the dark. To not be able to see what is right in front of you. Diego has been lying to you. My son is capo of this city. He rules this place, and he took my place because I was ready to step down."

"Capo?"

"Yes, and I also want you to know, he's engaged to be married. There is no strength unless there is wealth and power, and the woman he is going to marry will provide all that."

Diego was engaged to be married to another woman.

He wasn't just a bar owner but a capo.

She pressed a hand to her chest. Everything was caving in on her, and she couldn't breathe.

"Calm down, dear. You're going to give yourself a heart attack."

She heard the door slam closed, making her jump.

"Wait, wait. What about my dad?" She walked too fast and the chain pulled her back, but she kept trying to move, ending up on the floor, trying to crawl. The metal cut into her flesh, and she screamed, begging for them to let her know what was happening with her father.

This couldn't be happening to her.

Diego had told her so many lies.

What the hell was she going to do? The man she thought he was, he didn't exist. He'd not even been real. Everything she had with Diego had been a lie. Giving him her virginity, believing she was falling in love with him. It had all been a trick.

A vicious, nasty lie.

Crawling back on the floor, she rested against the wall, drawing her knees up. They had chained her to the bed like she was some kind of animal.

Where was her dad?

What was she going to do?

Were they going to kill her?

She didn't want to die.

But what else did she have to live for? Resting her head against the wall, she took a deep breath.

In and out.

She did it slowly, trying to stop herself from panicking. It wouldn't help her in this situation.

She had to think, to be ready.

Covering her face, she allowed herself a few moments to completely break down, crying for everything that could have been.

Chapter Twelve

"It's not looking good," the doctor said. "If he makes it through the night, we'll see. For now, we've got to take it one moment at a time."

Diego looked down at James. He had no choice but to come back to the hospital. Belle had been out for the count, and he'd given her to his father and told him to take care of her until he returned.

This had been one of five attacks. The other four attacks had been at his places of business, including the bar and Angelo's. Two other attacks had taken place on another capo's land. For his own part, he had three attacks on his turf. Cops were everywhere, and he didn't want Belle drawing any more attention than was needed. He'd already called Richard, and wanted him here.

"You'll call me if there's any change?" Diego asked.

"The daughter is down as next of kin."

"I'm with Belle. She's already stressed out by everything that has happened. I don't want to worry her. I will also supply a huge donation to your ward for you to forward all messages."

"That won't be necessary," the doctor said.

"I insist. I will also be supplying two guards for him. I don't want him to be at risk."

The doctor didn't put up an argument as he wrote out a check.

"There will be more for you to pay extra attention to him."

The doctor nodded before leaving.

He had to make this right for Belle. The only reason James got hit was because they were coming for him. Someone had been able to tail him, and he'd not even seen it. That meant, someone was that good, or one of his men had given away his location, which pissed him off.

Leaving the hospital, he found Richard already waiting for him.

"Her father's in the hospital?"

"Yeah, and it doesn't look good."

"I'm sorry, man," he said.

"Yeah, well, I'm sorry too." He rubbed at his eyes, fucking exhausted with the whole thing. There was just no way he could have stopped this. He knew something was going to happen; he just didn't know what and when.

"I'm sorry I didn't listen to you."

"Let's not go there, man, none of us know what could have happened."

"Yeah, well, I can't help but wonder if I could have helped you stop this."

"It doesn't matter now. Angelo made his move, and I wasn't ready."

"You can't blame yourself for this," Richard said.

"My woman's dad is in the hospital. He warned me about something like this, and I didn't listen. I thought I knew everything, and look at what is happening. He's in a coma right now. He may never get out of that. Not to mention my dad has Belle. I couldn't leave her alone. Fuck! When did everything get screwed up?"

"Around the time you started dating Belle."

"Shut up, Richard. I really don't need to hear you talk about all this bullshit right now."

Richard shrugged. "This was your call to make with Belle."

"I don't want to talk about it. Not now, not ever. I told you to keep an eye on Angelo, and you wouldn't fucking listen. Let's keep the blame to a minimum tonight." He was tired and all he wanted to do was lie down and go to sleep. Before he could do that, he needed to go and see Belle, and then of course, it was a meeting of all the capos, with the boss, to deal with this shit show.

"Angelo *was* being watched, Diego. These attacks didn't include him, which mean he has men acting on his behalf. I'm watching Angelo, not every fucker that he comes into contact with. I don't have that kind of resources." Richard turned and walked away.

He would know more of what happened as soon as he attended the meeting. Until then, he was in the dark.

Richard drove him to his home, and Diego didn't even invite him in, assuming the not-friend would do that himself.

His father was in his office, enjoying a glass of brandy when he entered.

"Where's Belle?" he asked.

"She's in one of the rooms, secured. You don't have to worry about her," his father said.

"Secured?"

His father picked up a remote and turned the television on.

"You fucking bastard!" The television showed Belle chained up in a room. There was no furniture other than a bed. She was huddled in the corner, looking terrified.

"So this is the reason you ran out at lunch? This is the reason your priorities have been affected? This blind fucking slut?"

"You be careful."

"You are my son."

"And I'm your capo. That girl is mine. You insult her, you insult me. Dad or not, I will take you down."

"You'd face consequences."

"In case you didn't get the memo, I don't give a shit about them. I'll deal with whatever is thrown my way." He stepped up to his father.

"You always were a piece of shit. Always thought you had what it took."

"What's the matter, Dad? Does it bug you that I've taken over and shown The Boss what a real man can do?"

His father drew his fist back as if to hit him. For years he took the hits without fighting back. No more. He was a strong man, independent, and there was no way he was going to let him speak out about his woman.

Slamming his fist into his father's face, he felt immense joy at the sound of shattered bones, and his scream.

"Stay away from her. If I hear you've even looked in her direction, I'll fucking kill you." With that, he turned on his heel, heading toward Belle. Richard was lurking close. "Stay with him. Make sure he doesn't do anything stupid. If he tries to hurt you, kill him."

"You're giving me permission to kill him?"

"Why not? I seem to be on a roll tonight." He also didn't want an audience when he saw Belle.

The cuffs on her irritated him, and as he made his way to the room, he felt … nervous. He was Diego Leoni. He didn't get nervous.

Turning the door handle, he entered the room.

"Belle?" He closed the door, moving toward the bed where he saw her on the security footage. She was still kneeling in the corner, and seeing her like this broke his heart.

"Diego," she said.

"Yes, it's me." He took a step toward her, but she threw her hand up.

"No. I don't want you to come a step closer."

"Belle, don't do this."

"Capo? You're not just a nightclub owner, are you? Capo is something related to the mafia, isn't it?"

"Belle—"

"Isn't it!" she screamed at him, getting to her feet. Her gaze was off in the distance, but he saw through her blank stare. She was hurting, and it was all because of him.

He stayed silent, resting his hands on his hips. "I don't want to argue with you."

"Who are you?"

"I'm Diego Leoni."

"What are you?"

"I'm just a man."

"You're not just an ordinary man. Stop lying to me. Stop with all the bullshit and tell me the truth."

He didn't want her to know the truth, but she already knew so much. There was no way he'd be able to let her go. If he didn't keep her now, she would be killed.

"I'm capo of the city," he said, opening up and telling her everything. He told her who he was, and what he did, not leaving anything out, including tonight. "You and your father got caught in the crossfire."

"Where is my dad? Did he know? Is he okay? Please tell me he's okay?"

He went to her, reaching for her arms, but she screamed at him.

"Don't touch me."

She slammed his hands off her. Diego wasn't going to be pushed aside. Pulling her into his arms, he didn't allow her to say no for an answer. She screamed at him, trying to get away. He wasn't letting her go.

Holding onto her, he collapsed onto the bed, with her in his lap, holding her tight against his body so she didn't move, so she didn't fight against him. Slowly her wiggling stopped, and he didn't let up, knowing she was a fighter and would do everything in her power to hold him off.

"You lied to me," she said, whispering the words.

"I didn't tell you the whole truth."

"You're not who I thought you were, and you're engaged."

Diego gritted his teeth.

"Please, Diego, let me go."

"Not happening."

"You can't keep me here."

"I can't let you go either. You've seen too much. You know too much."

She began to cry, sobbing against his chest. "What happened to my father?"

"He's in a coma. I've paid for all the best kind of care money can buy. He will be protected and safe."

"He knew about you?"

"Yes. He recognized me and my name."

"I don't watch the news," she said. "I stopped a long time ago."

He stroked his fingers through her hair, holding her, wanting to take her pain away, but not seeing any way he could do that.

"I never wanted to lie to you, but knowing how you were with me, you didn't treat me any differently, and I liked it. I shouldn't have pursued you. I even tried to stop, but every single time I did, you were always there, waiting."

"I want to go back home," she said. "I won't say anything. I don't know anything."

He sighed, slowly lowering her to the bed. Her hands were clenched at her sides, and she had already done a lot of damage with those claws. He felt the scratch along his cheek, but if it made her feel better, he took the pain. "You're not going home."

In his need to see her, he'd forgotten the key to the cuff. He was going to have to keep her locked in this room for a considerable time, so she didn't hurt herself. It wasn't what he wanted to do, but until she came around to who he was and that she wasn't leaving, he was going to have to keep her in this prison.

Getting to his feet, he walked toward the door. "I'll be back with some food." He saw the tray his father had left in the corner, and it pissed him off.

"I won't say anything about who you are, or what you do. I don't know anything."

"We were attacked tonight, Belle. My enemies found where we were, and your father got caught in the crossfire. It wasn't what I wanted to happen, but it did, and now I've got to fix it. If I let you leave, you'll be killed. I'm taking care of your dad. If you leave, I will remove all security around your father that I've put in place."

"My father can afford it."

"Yes, and your father is in a coma unable to take care of his own needs."

"I can take care of him."

"You're willing to take that risk rather than stay here."

"I don't want to be near a liar. A liar and a cheat. What kind of woman would marry you?"

He laughed. "The kind that is doing her duty. My fiancée is not someone I would pick. She's who has been picked for me, and I can promise you, I have never touched her. I have no intention of touching her."

"You were still going to continue seeing me?"

"I had every intention of building a life with you." He put the tray he'd picked up on the edge of the bed and sat down beside Belle. Placing his hand on her stomach, he stared at her. "My baby could be here right now, Belle. You and me could have made a boy or a girl."

"What?"

"I came inside you, and as I did, I knew I wasn't going to let you go. You're mine. You will always be mine, and there's no getting away from that."

"No."

"Yes. There is a chance you could be pregnant, but I guess we'll find out soon enough."

Before she could shove his hand away, he left, picking up the tray. At the door, he turned back to look at her. "For what it's worth, I do actually love you, Belle."

He closed the door, not giving her time to dispute his claim. He had hoped to tell her in a more romantic and humble setting, but that decision had been taken from him.

Carrying the tray through to the kitchen, he tossed the soup or porridge, or vomit, he didn't know what, into the trash. Cleaning up the dishes, he opened the fridge and got to work making her a sandwich.

As he was spreading the bread with some olive butter, he paused as he noticed his hands were shaking.

He'd never been the kind of guy to shake.

Staring down at him, he thought about Belle, and he clenched his teeth together. Throwing the knife across the kitchen, he turned and slammed his fist into the glass cabinet, before throwing the blender off the counter as well.

Gripping the edge of the granite worktop, he took several deep breaths. The rage continued to flood his veins, and his temples pounded with it.

Calm down.

He had to remain calm. Making any decisions now would ruin everything. After another deep breath, he stepped over the glass, tossed the bread, which could have shards of glass, into the trash, and started again, away from the mess he'd created. He wrapped his cut and bleeding knuckles in a towel so he didn't ruin more of Belle's food.

"You okay?" Richard asked.

"You're supposed to be keeping an eye on my father."

"Already done. He's out for the count. I'm going to ask again, are you okay?"

"Yep. Absolutely nothing wrong." He cut the bread into little triangles before turning toward his not-friend. "Do you know what happened?"

He had intended to come and talk to his father, but after his little spat with Belle, he knew it was useless. He'd only kill him.

"It was Angelo. He attacked with the Russians. The rest of the capos and The Boss know. You have a meeting tomorrow night once they can do some damage control."

"Right, of course."

"Also, your father has made The Boss and the Durantes aware of Belle's presence."

Diego burst out laughing, and once he started, he couldn't seem to stop himself.

"I don't think any of this is funny."

"That's because you're not me. Ignore me." He bent forward, laughing so hard his stomach hurt. "Everything is so fucked."

"Will they kill her?"

"No, they won't. Believe it or not, the mafia don't shy away from a mistress. Only when that mistress gets a little too big for her boots, if you know what I mean." He didn't want Belle to be his mistress.

"Do you want me to take that upstairs to her?"

Richard asked.

"No. I will be handling all of Belle's care. No one else."

He left Richard alone in the kitchen. For now, he couldn't give a fuck if it was protocol to have a civilian or an outsider in his home. Let him explore. Let him find shit. He couldn't give two fucks right about now. Entering her room, he closed the door, noticing there was no lock on the inside. *Great, just fucking great.*

"Who is there?"

"It's me," he said.

She relaxed a little but tensed up immediately after.

"I don't want you to be here."

"Tough. Your dad wouldn't approve of me starving you, and I don't approve of such methods. You will eat this sandwich or I will feed you."

His knuckles hadn't bled through the towel, so he considered that a good thing.

"I don't want to eat it."

"Belle, don't piss me off. Not right now. You hate me, I get it, but do you think your father when he gets out of his coma is going to be able to cope knowing you're sick?" He didn't like playing the dad card, but he was more than happy to do so if it got him the results he needed.

"I hate you."

"No, you don't. If you hated me, you'd be able to deal with this a whole lot more. You love me, and that is what kills you."

"You don't even know what love is."

"I know what love is. I've just never felt it before until you."

She flinched as he touched her cheek.

"Eat." He put the small triangle into her hand and

waited. He expected her to throw it at him, but she clearly had gotten past the childish stage as she handed him the bread.

"I don't love you."

"I know."

He wasn't going to argue with her.

"I think what you did was unfair," she said.

"Baby, what I did was fucking awful, but I still did it and it got me you. I'd do it again in a heartbeat. Eat your sandwich, and then I'll take you for a shower."

"I don't want you to touch me."

"I won't. I said I'll take you for a shower, not fuck you." Anyone else, he'd have killed by now because of the effort. With Belle, it was so much different. Running a hand down his face, he ignored his own hunger to watch her eat.

"You need to eat something," she said, taking the second triangle of sandwich. "Please, share this with me."

"I made it for you."

"And you're not eating."

"You're going to take care of me."

"I don't want you to starve. I'm not a monster here."

"I know. I'm the fucking monster." He took the triangle and shoved it in his mouth, chewing on the food. There was no taste. He didn't want to eat anything because he felt sick to his stomach.

He'd nearly lost Belle today, and that was enough to send him over the edge.

Stroking his fingers down her arm, he ignored the flinch, and touched her pulse. Still alive. Still breathing.

He couldn't ask for more.

****

Belle sensed a change within Diego. The way he

touched her, it was like he was checking she was still alive. His touch was so gentle. She wanted to know her father was okay, and above all else, regardless of everything, she wanted Diego to throw his arms around her and hug her tight.

What kind of person did that make her? She wanted to be held by the very man who had lied to her. Who was seeing someone else.

"Did you eat the other part of the sandwich?" There was no way she could eat anything else, not after what they'd been through.

"It's all gone." He slid off the bed. "It's time for your shower."

"I don't want to take a shower."

"I didn't ask you, Belle. I'm telling you. I'll be back in a moment." She heard the door close behind him, leaving her alone.

Rubbing at her temple, she thought about what he said. Was it possible for her to be pregnant? She knew it only took one time, but could she be that unlucky?

No.

There's no way she could be pregnant.

Or could she?

With her hand on her stomach, she couldn't feel anything. There was no baby, but then, she wasn't a pregnancy test.

How had her life gotten so fucked?

Again, Melanie.

If she'd not been in that stupid club, she wouldn't be here now, and wouldn't be at Diego's mercy.

He returned to the room, without saying a word. His cologne was heavy in the air. She flinched as he touched her arms, and twisted the key in the lock. When they gave, she felt huge relief. She didn't try to make a run for it. Knowing her luck, she would fall down the stairs and break her neck, which wasn't in her plans any time soon.

Diego helped her off the bed and with his hands on her hips, led her out of the bedroom. He stood directly behind her.

"Where are we going?"

"My room."

"Your room?"

"Yes. Don't get any ideas of trying to run away. You'll never get away in time."

"I had no intention of running. It's pointless. I know you'd stop me."

"Damn right. We're about to walk up some stairs." His grip tightened on her hips, halting her. "Step. Step. Step." He kept on doing this for ten more steps before walking her down a short corridor, or at least, she thought it was. He stopped her again and leaned around her to open the door.

She was moved inside, and she heard him close the door and flick the lock into place. Her heart rate picked up.

"We're not in my room. I can't give you a tour. I've got to get you ready for a shower. You smell."

Again, she didn't bite. He was baiting her, and she didn't understand why, but she wasn't going to give him the satisfaction of showing she even cared. He took her into his bathroom.

She heard him turn on the shower and the distinctive sound of him removing his clothes. Next, he was touching her. This time, she anticipated his touch and didn't flinch. After everything that had happened to them, she felt off balance and so alone.

Once she was naked, Diego stood behind her once again, guiding her into the shower. The water wasn't cold as she stepped inside, the warmth a welcome against the cool of the night.

"I don't like your dad," she said.

"Neither do I. There's a lot you don't know about me, Belle. It's all the bad stuff you don't need to know."

"I've never lied to you."

"I know. It's what makes you a good person, when I'm not."

"You can be a good person as well," she said.

He took her hand, placing it over his chest. His heart raced beneath her touch. "You've felt every single one of my scars. They weren't from accidents. They were from fights, from training. From killing people."

She went to pull her hand away, but he circled her wrist, stopping her from going anywhere. "Diego, why are you telling me all this stuff now?"

"You have a right to know. There's no reason to keep secrets from you. You know everything else. You know who I am."

"Wait, you've killed people?"

"Yes."

"Why aren't you in jail?"

"I kill bad people."

"What gives you the right to decide that?"

"I'm the judge, jury, and executioner in my city, Belle. The men that shot at us, who put your father in the hospital, the justice system won't make them pay. If the evidence is not there, it'll get thrown out. I won't take that chance with your safety. I don't answer to the law. I make my own."

"Is there anything else I need to know?" she asked.

He was overloading her with information, so why not completely bombard her?

"Melanie won't be giving you trouble any time soon."

"What?"

"She overdosed."

"How do you know this?"

"I made sure she did."

"What?" She pulled away from him, but he caught her arms.

"I took care of the bitch. She was a slut. I walked in on her being fucked in the ass by her dealer so she could score more drugs, Belle. The world is not full of fairy tales. You can't rely on anyone or expect to get anything done."

"You don't know that. You don't know anything. You're filling it up with your toxic interpretations."

"Melanie left you not once but twice to go and get her fix. Her arms were covered with track marks, and she was doing the hard drugs. She left you. You nearly got raped and killed. I'm not taking that chance." He cupped her face, tilting her head back. "You can hate me all you want, Belle. I accept it, but you are going to realize that you belong to me. I take care of what's mine, and you are mine."

"You don't get to make that choice."

His lips slammed down on hers, startling her. At first, she didn't respond to his kiss, but then, her body betrayed her, wanting him so much.

He is a liar.

A cheat.

You're his other woman.

She pushed him away, trying not to react to his touch, but it was impossible. She wanted him, even after knowing the truth.

"I get to make that choice. The moment I took your virginity on my office desk, Belle. You became mine."

"I'm not the first virgin you had, Diego. You

can't make the claim that I'm special."

"I can, and I will. You are fucking special because you're the only virgin I want." With that, he kissed her again.

At first, she fought him, but in truth it wasn't a real fight. She wanted him, even after everything. Groaning into his mouth, she wrapped her arms around his neck, his body pressing against hers. The hardness of his cock dug into her stomach, letting her know he wanted to be here just as much as she did.

She wanted him inside her so badly.

Belle hated herself for her weakness. It wasn't fair, nor was it right for her to want this man. He was a killer, but he was still Diego. Still *her* Diego.

He drove her crazy as he suddenly spun her away from him. He pressed her hands against the tile, sucking on her neck, right over her pulse. His hands tilted her body forward, and he kicked open her thighs, exposing her.

She cried out as his fingers moved between her spread legs, touching her pussy. Two fingers teased over her clit before sliding down to penetrate inside her.

He removed his fingers as he bit her ear. "You can hate me all you want, but your body doesn't lie. It wants me, Belle. It wants my cock inside you."

"Please," she said.

"Tell me you want me."

She whimpered.

"If you want to come on my cock, tell me you want me. Tell me you want this." He cupped her tits, pinching the peaks as he did.

"Please, Diego."

"Tell me." He growled the words against her skin.

"Fuck me, Diego. Please, I need you inside me."

He pushed her forward, spreading the cheeks of her ass. She gasped as he slammed to the hilt inside her. From this angle he felt thicker, fuller. He pulled out of her, only to slam back inside. His grip went to her hips, holding her tightly as he pounded inside her, over and over.

She screamed his name, not wanting him to stop. To keep on claiming her. To fuck her. To own her.

He let go of her hip long enough to tease her clit. The touch was all she needed to throw herself into orgasm. She pushed back against his pounding cock. Diego wasn't done with her though. He kept on stroking her, clearly wanting her to find a second release.

She didn't think it was possible to have a second one, not after everything they had experienced together in a matter of hours, but once again, Diego proved her wrong.

The second orgasm took her by surprise and completely shook her to the core as he fucked her hard. Her pussy tightened around him, wanting more of what he could give, desperate and hungry for it.

"Yes, please, yes," she said.

"Fuck, Belle, I love you so much. There's no way I could ever stop this. I don't want to."

He slammed in deep as he came, his cock pulsing his cum inside her.

"You didn't pull out," she said.

"I'll never pull out, and I won't ever use a rubber between us again." He stroked her back.

"You're going to make sure I can't leave."

"Belle, you need to understand, you're never leaving. You belong to me, and there's no way I'm going to let you go."

He pulled out of her, and she stood up. She didn't move as he washed her body. He didn't use a sponge, but his hands as he soaped her body. Next, he took care of her hair. She was relieved he didn't use another woman's washing gel. That would have been a huge insult.

"What is your fiancée like?" she asked.

He paused in washing her body. She had taken him by surprise. *Good.* She was tired of being the only one who was surprised.

"You don't need to worry about Charlotte."

"Her name's Charlotte?"

"Yes."

"It's a pretty name."

"I have no desire to talk about her, Belle, and neither should you."

"Why not? She's going to be a big part of your life, right? Isn't that the point of all marriages?"

He turned off the water. "I know what you're trying to do. It's not going to work."

"What? I'm trying to figure out more information on my boyfriend's fiancée."

"No, what you're trying to do is create a distance between us. It's not going to work. You can hate me all you want, I'll accept it. I don't love Charlotte. I don't want her as my wife. I want you."

"Me?"

"Yes, and until I can figure out how to have you, I've got to continue on with this farce of a wedding."

"You think I'd marry you?" She gasped as he cupped her face, tilting her head back.

"In a heartbeat. You're angry. You're saying stuff you don't really mean. It's why it hurts so much. You want to take back all the angry things you've said." He kissed her. "Don't worry about it. I'm not angry with you. I can take whatever you throw at me, because I know you're doing it because you love me."

"Love shouldn't make you angry."

"Love makes you do crazy fucking things like lie to the girl so she doesn't know who you are. Love makes you keep up the false pretense because you couldn't stand to have her know the truth. I didn't ask for this life, Belle. I was fucking born into it. There's no way out for me, but you have given me a glimpse of everything I missed out on. I will never stop loving you."

He helped her out of the shower, and he was gentle as he dried her skin.

His attention and love were breaking her heart.

"I wish you hadn't lied to me."

"I know."

"I don't think I can ever forgive you."

"You will."

She sighed. There was no talking to him, when he was so determined to see his own needs before her own.

Chapter Thirteen

"You brought a civilian into our lives. Have you gone completely mad?" Durante asked.

Diego looked toward his future father-in-law and contemplated killing the bastard. Durante was in fact a good man. A good capo. He had loyalty amongst his ranks, and he made sure men were willing to die to save him and his family. Mostly his family. Durante was one of the few men who didn't have a mistress. He had no use for one because he was completely besotted with his wife.

"I did what I had to do," Diego said. "None of you were aware of Angelo's manipulations and influence. I was, and so was Richard. He's a security expert, and he had kept an eye on Angelo."

"Forgive me," The Boss said. "Why was he keeping an eye on Angelo? I think it's good I now know the truth of the betrayal, but I wasn't born yesterday. There's always a reason why you take a sudden interest in someone. What this man wants is revenge. I want to know why."

Diego looked toward Richard. "This is for you. I brought you here, the rest is on you."

Richard shrugged. "Angelo is responsible for the rape and murder of my sister. She was fifteen years old. Minding her own business when Angelo took her."

"How can we trust this … person? He has a clear disliking of Angelo."

"I've got a disliking of all self-righteous pricks who think they're above the law." Richard pointed his remote at the screen. He'd connected his laptop to the main screen, and the moment he clicked the button, feminine screams filled the air, begs and pleas.

Diego hadn't seen this footage, and what he saw

sickened him.

Angelo, along with three other men, were raping a girl. One by one, they were taking her, changing places. They were laughing about it.

"Turn it off," Angelo's father said.

"What? You think that's all I've got? I found this video along with fifteen others of him raping girls. Now, I'm no expert. I always trust software." The video came to a stop on a close up. Richard zoomed in to the neck of one of the men. "But that, my friends, is a Russian ownership ink. Every single video I have, more of these men are there. Some of the girls are underage. Some of them aren't."

"Angelo's just lost his way."

"With all due respect, your son can stay fucking lost. He attacked five of our places, and nearly killed Diego."

"Yes, let's go back to Diego," Angelo's father said. "His little exploits have been brought to our attention. What do you have to say about that, Durante? He's supposed to be marrying your daughter."

"Belle Johnson and her father, James," The Boss said.

"The father is in the hospital in a coma. It's unclear if he'll ever wake up. The girl is in our care," his father said, surprising Diego by standing up for him. "With regards to the Durante girl, the wedding is still going ahead as planned."

"She doesn't cause a problem?" Angelo's father asked.

"Not as big a one as your son. Belle can be taken care of and handled by Diego. Your son, however, has turned his loyalty, and last time I checked, he knew some of our secrets," his father said. "At your insistence he could be trusted."

"Diego has failed to provide an heir. He should be forced to step down. My son should take his rightful place as capo," Angelo's father said.

Diego snorted. "Please, as if that is going to happen. I may not have produced an heir, but Belle could be carrying my child. My first wife was a fucking traitor. You want to keep throwing that in my face? If I recall, it was you that suggested that union, not me."

Angelo's father's face went bright red. "This is outrageous."

"And now I'm bored." The Boss clicked his fingers, and Angelo's father was seized. "I cannot guarantee you are not working for your son. You are defending him at every single turn, and because of that, I cannot trust you. You'll be held until we get Angelo back. Until then, you should get your things in order."

The man screamed as he was pulled out of the meeting.

Diego watched him go.

"Richard, you must leave," The Boss said. "I have seen all the necessary evidence, but you are neither capo nor a made man. Be thankful you are leaving with your head intact."

Diego waited as Richard left the room. He had no doubt he was going to his home and would bitch at him. His not-friend liked to bitch like a woman.

"For the rest of you, Angelo needs to be seized. We cannot risk him making a deal that could affect all of us."

"I warned you about letting him in on private business," Diego said.

"Be careful," The Boss said. "You still have not provided an heir, and at forty years old, your position is not secured. Be glad I haven't demanded your girl's life or that of her father."

"I won't kill them," Diego said.

"*You* won't, but I will find someone who will. I want as many men as possible you all can spare. Angelo knows all of our cities. He knows our setup. He can hide in plain sight, or he can skip all of us and go to the law. I don't want the Feds breathing down my fucking neck any time soon. Do you understand?" They all agreed, and The Boss hit his hand on the table. "Get the fuck out of my house."

Diego left the room, heading straight for his car. His father was hot on his tracks.

"Why did you stick up for me in there?" Diego asked.

His father smirked. "You think you're the only one to make a mistake in your life? You won't be the only one, and it won't be this one time either. We all have our secrets. Angelo has been a problem for some time. You brought his connections to our attention, and we ignored you. That was our mistake."

"I can't give up on Belle."

"You know, some men can have their cake and eat it."

"I don't want to marry Charlotte," he said.

His father sighed. "Right now, you need to focus on finding Angelo and making sure your girl stays quiet."

"And if she's pregnant with my child?"

"Let's do this in the car." His father looked past his shoulder, and Diego saw Durante waiting. "Go and talk to him."

He didn't like it when his father was the fucking voice of reason in his life. He'd been capo for some time now.

Stepping away from the car, he approached Durante.

"You care about this girl?" Durante asked, getting right down to the point.

"I don't have to say anything."

"Look, I'm asking man to man. Not capo to capo. You think I've not been in your position with a decision like this. Do you think you're the only one that has to make this choice?"

"I mean no disrespect with regards to Charlotte."

"My daughter has no wish to marry you either. We must do what we can in our life. If your girl is pregnant, we'll come up with an alternative to our arrangement."

Diego stared at Durante. He was a few years older than Diego himself. "Why would you bend on this?"

"I'm a simple man, Diego. Just because I'm capo, doesn't mean I can't be ... lenient. I love my family. I want to see them happy. I will do what is necessary for our Boss. Not everything in life has to be done through marriage. There are other means." Durante slapped him on the back before turning on his heel to leave.

Diego didn't have a clue what was going on, but it was something.

Heading back to the car, he climbed behind the wheel and pulled out of the driveway, taking off toward their home.

"Are you going to tell me what is going on?" Diego asked.

"Durante is not an easy man to please, but he's an easy man to piss off. If he hears anyone talking about his girl being an outsider, he deals with them the only way he knows how. If Belle is pregnant, you can keep her as your mistress."

"No."

"It's a solution. I don't see you making any other

agreement with Durante that will make The Boss happy. There are always sacrifices to be made. You know this. You've been aware of them for a long time. You can't have everything you want in life without consequences. For now, I think you should focus on dealing with Angelo. He's our main problem. Then you can deal with whatever problem Belle gives you."

Diego didn't say another word. He wanted Belle to be pregnant. If she was, he'd find a way to make it work.

****

"I want to go and see my dad," Belle said the moment Diego made his presence known. She was in his bedroom, and she had tried to explore her surroundings. A lamp had paid, along with a few pictures she believed. She wasn't entirely sure, but she had tried to be as careful as possible.

Even though it was mind-numbingly boring, she had sat on his bed, waiting for his return. She missed the freedom of being in her apartment, listening to her books or at the very least, movies.

"It can't happen. Not yet."

"He's my dad. Please, why can't I go and see him?" The bed dipped beside her. Diego took her hands.

"I can't trust you."

"You can't trust me? I'm not the one that lied to you."

"I'm talking about the cops and your new potential allies."

"I wouldn't try to talk to the cops. Please, Diego. I just want to know my dad is fine."

"He is."

"Ugh!" She pulled her hand away, sliding as far as the bed would allow. "This isn't fair. I've done nothing to you, and yet you're keeping me as a prisoner."

"You could have died on me."

"My dad still could die, and I don't even get to hold his hand."

"The doctor told me is stable. He's not out of the danger zone, but he's holding his own."

She released a breath, slowly.

"I can't deal with this right now. I can't even think. You've got me trapped in here. I can't do anything. I can't even move. I made a mess of your room."

"I see you took the life of my lamp."

"I don't want to be here. I promise you I won't say anything. I just want to go back to living life without you." For a split second she had hoped she'd gotten through, but no such luck.

"Not happening. You want to go for a walk, we can do that."

The bed moved again, letting her know he was up on his feet.

"What are you doing?"

"I've got men posted all around the house. You're not going out naked, and you do need some fresh air." She gasped as he pulled her to her feet. He started to put clothes on her, making her step into a pair of shorts, lifting her head up to put a large top on her. "I'm going to need to buy you some clothes. There's just no way to stop your tits from looking incredible." He stroked a finger against the side of her breast, and he chuckled as she went to swat him away. He was the one in charge, not her. Each time she tried to take that power away, he showed her just how far she was under his spell.

She found it really freaking annoying.

With his hands on her hips, he stood directly behind her as he walked her out of the bedroom. This time, as they were going downstairs, he actually stood in front of her and told her to get up.

"What? You're going to give me a piggyback?"

"Why not? I've never done one. It could be fun."

"Hell, no. I'm not doing that. What if we fall? What if you drop me?"

"At this rate it'll be time to go to bed so it doesn't really matter. Come on, Belle, live dangerously. Stop being such a scaredy-cat."

"I'm not scared."

"Prove it. Jump on up and prove me wrong."

She gritted her teeth, wanting nothing more than to push him downstairs. Instead, she gripped his shoulders, not wanting to hurt him or cause him any real damage. She let out a squeal as he lifted her up, his arms resting beneath her knees.

"What the hell?" she asked.

"How do you feel?"

"Like you should put me down." She screamed as he nudged her up.

"Just checking to make sure you're secure."

"How old are you?" she asked.

"Forty years old. You?"

"You know how old I am. Right now, you're acting like a child."

"Come on, baby, this is a lot of fun." He began to move downstairs, and she wrapped her arms around him, not wanting him to let her go. She couldn't stand for him to do that. "You're going to need to learn that I'm not going to drop you or let you go."

"This is so crazy."

"It's not crazy. You need to get downstairs, and I want to hold you. Simple as. I love that you rely on me."

There he went talking about the love word, a word she couldn't trust coming out of his mouth.

"I really wish you'd stop saying that."

"Love? I love you. I want to be with you. I want to love you for the rest of my days."

"What about your fiancée?"

"I don't love her. I don't want to marry her. I want her gone, and I want to be with you. Only you. Always, you."

"You're infuriating."

"I think, Belle, you're not used to having someone tell you that they love you."

"I believe, Diego, you're saying it a little too much. I don't think you love me at all. I think you *think* you love me."

"That's a lot of thinking."

"Where are we?" She had been so focused on the conversation she hadn't been paying attention to where they were going.

"We're about to enter the kitchen. No one is here. The cook left early as she always does. Food is already in the oven, waiting to be eaten. Now, we're outside."

She didn't need for him to tell her the last part. The slight breeze on her face felt incredible.

"What time is it?"

"It's four in the afternoon."

"How long have I been with you?"

"A couple of days. Not too long." He took several steps into the garden.

"Is this the same place you took me to before?"

"No. Don't talk about that place. I don't make a habit of sharing where all of my places are." He continued to walk down a straight path.

"You can put me down. I'd like to walk."

"I will. There's too many rocks around. The garden has a lot of features. Once I pass the maze, I'll put you down."

"You have a maze?"

"Yes. It was a design feature my mom liked."

"Oh. You live with your dad?"

"I don't live with him. We share a place, that's it."

"So, he was capo before you?"

"Yes."

"And you took over from him."

"He handed it down to me. It's my duty to keep this city belonging to The Boss, and as head capo, all decisions come to me."

"So why do you need to get married?" she asked.

"I'm getting older. I have to have a male heir to take over from me."

"What if you get a girl?"

"She will either marry who I decide or marry who she chooses."

"She can't take over from you?"

"No. Only men take over."

"Sexist."

He chuckled. "It is what it is."

"And women are only good for marrying and baby making."

"You have many additional qualities. In my world, they are just not as important as the men."

"I don't like your world," she said.

"It's one of the many reasons why I tried to keep it from you."

"You didn't succeed."

"No, it would seem when it comes to you, I do nothing but fail."

"I'm sorry."

"Don't be. The time we've shared before you knew the truth was the best time of my life."

Belle gripped him a little tighter. "It was?"

"Yes."

"You didn't find it a joke?"

"Why would I find it a joke? I enjoyed being near you. I enjoyed doing the same things normal people do. It's why I kept so much of who I am a secret from you. I didn't want to spoil what we'd made with each other. I would have continued with it as well, if I could have."

"Nothing ever lasts forever."

"I like to believe everything lasts forever so long as you're willing to give it a try."

"You're an optimist."

He burst out laughing. "No, not even close. Before you, I didn't believe in happy ever after or miracles. I believe in you and in what we have."

He came to a stop and lowered her down until her feet hit the ground. He helped to steady her with his hands on hers.

"What we had was based on lies, Diego. How can we have … anything?"

She heard his heavy sigh, and it upset her to know she was the cause.

"I didn't intentionally lie to you, Belle. I omitted the truth of who I was."

"You're going to try and defend your lies now?"

"No. I'm telling you that I didn't want to lie to you." He stroked her cheek. "I would never do anything to hurt you."

"I don't think I can talk about this right now." Her thoughts and emotions were confused. He'd messed with her head. Their time together wasn't just special to him, but meant a great deal to her. However, it was now tainted with the lies he spilled. She didn't know what was truth and what wasn't. How could she know? He's completely abused that kind of trust.

"One day, I know you're going to find it in your heart to forgive me."

"And if I don't?"

"You will, one day. I'm a patient guy."

"You're persistent."

"That I am too. See, we're on the same page."

"I don't think agreeing to patience and persistence is the same thing."

"It's close. Come on, let's not argue for another moment. Can we just find some common ground? Some peace?" He kissed each of her inner wrists. The action was so sweet that it took her by surprise.

He had this way about him that was always taking her by surprise.

"I don't want to argue anymore."

"Good, neither do I."

"I don't want to be kept from my father, Diego." She heard him sigh again. "I know you're tired of me asking about this, but he is my father and I love him so much. If he'd not come to see me, he wouldn't have gotten hurt."

"It's not your fault he's hurt."

"Yes, it is. If I'd stayed at home and just accepted I needed help, none of this would have happened."

He let her go but only so he could hold her face. He was so close she felt his breath fan across her face.

"I'm not going to let you go. You should know that. Having you in my life, that is what I want."

She was talking to a deaf man. Whatever she said to him, he wasn't taking notice. There was no way they could be together, but he seemed determined to make it work. She chose not to argue with him.

Everything he spoke about, she wanted just as much, and it hurt her to know she would never have it. Another woman would be with him. Someone else would get to have his baby, wear his ring, and call herself Mrs. Leoni.

Pushing her pain aside, she held his arm, walking across the smooth grass. The feel of it beneath her feet helped to relax her.

Diego didn't speak, and she didn't try to start an argument. Neither of them needed the added stress, and nothing good could possibly come from arguing.

"After dinner, I've got to head out," he said.

"Where are you going?

"I've got to hunt for Angelo. He's out there, and while he's a risk, he needs to be taken care of."

"Angelo? Like the restaurant?"

"Oh, Belle, I own the restaurant where you work."

"You do?"

"Yes, I'm the boss. It's why Tanya didn't have a problem with me sitting next to you."

"Oh."

"Yeah, oh."

"So, you own a lot of businesses?"

"I have to."

"Do you own everything?"

"Not everything."

"There are actually things you don't own?"

"Yes."

"Great," she said. This was just another element of his control.

"Don't be angry about this."

"Why should I be angry? I'm finally learning the truth. I don't always like it, but it's the truth, nonetheless." She rubbed at her temples, and her stomach started to growl. "I'm hungry. Can we go and eat?"

"Sure."

Diego picked her back up and carried her back to the house. She wanted to demand he put her down, but she just wanted some food and space. If she was eating, they weren't talking. Their biggest problem seemed to be the moment they started to talk. When they entered the dining room, Diego let her know that his father and Richard were already sitting down eating.

"Do you really think she should be eating with us?" his father said.

"She's not a prisoner."

"Chained up is the best way to deal with her. She will try to escape."

"She's not going to escape."

"I'm not going to stop her if she does. It would serve her right getting run down, and doing us all a favor."

She jumped as someone slammed their fist down hard on the table. Her heart raced, and she didn't know what was going on.

"Enough," Diego said.

"I've lost my appetite."

"I don't want to cause a problem. I can eat another time," she said.

"You will both eat, and he will fucking deal with this. You're not going to be chained up in a room like an animal. You're a human being."

"Anyone want to scream tension," Richard said.

No one else spoke as the table went silent. She ate as much as she could stomach, but with her nerves, that turned out to be very little.

"Do you want me to take you back up to my room?" Diego asked.

"Yes, if that's okay?"

He helped her out of the dining room and she said her goodnights to the room. No one spoke back, but she didn't expect them to.

"I don't want you to get into an argument with your father over me," she said.

"He thinks he knows what is best. He doesn't, otherwise he'd still be capo."

"He loves you." Diego snorted. "You're his son."

"I'm a commodity to him. We're not people in this world. We're things to be used as they see fit."

"I don't think that's entirely fair," she said.

"Then you don't get it, and you never will." He pressed a kiss to her lips. "Try to get some rest. I'll be back as soon as I can."

Much to her surprise, she heard the door close but not the actual lock flicking into place.

She was free to roam around. He didn't want her feeling like a caged animal. This was crazy.

Stepping up to the door, she placed her hand on the wood. Slowly, running her fingers across it, she found the door handle and waited as patiently as possible. Diego wouldn't linger at his home. He had too much work to do in finding his cousin.

Opening the door, she stepped out, closing it as quietly as possible behind her. Heart racing, hands clammy, she knew she was going to fuck this up, but still, she kept on moving. With both of her hands and her chest pressed to the door, she took a side step, then another. Her pace was slow, but she knew she had to change walls because of where the stairs opened up.

Keeping her back to the wall, she reached out her hands and took a couple of steps, finding the other wall. She continued her journey toward the stairs. When her hands finally found the corner of the wall, she took a deep breath.

Freedom was just a couple of steps, and possibly death away. She didn't know who he would have on watch keeping an eye on her, but she was more than willing to take that chance.

Gripping the banister, she slid her foot across the

carpet until she found the edge of the step.

She moved down, and did the same, keeping a death grip on the banister as she did this. Another step down, and she started to gain a little more confidence. By the last step, she ran out of banister and there was nothing but air. Halting her steps, she clenched her hands into fists. She couldn't turn back now.

Not after getting this far.

She took a step, holding out her arms, and when she found the wall, she ran her hands down until she felt the banister. Taking it a step at a time, she came back to air. The ticking of the clock let her know she was at the bottom of the staircase, and there was no current risk of breaking her neck during a fall.

"You got this, Belle. You can do this."

She walked slowly forward until she reached the front door. With her hand finally on the handle she was about to twist it when she heard someone clear their throat.

It wasn't Diego.

"Leaving so soon?" his father asked.

"I'm just admiring this woodwork."

"You're a terrible liar."

She didn't like having her back to him, and even though she couldn't see him, she wanted him to know she wasn't afraid.

In fact, she was really fucking terrified, but she kept her cool, refusing to give in to the fear of his presence alone. If she was afraid now, how would she feel if she saw him?

"I want to go and see my dad."

"It doesn't matter what you want. When my son is able, he'll take you."

"He's not the boss of me."

His father burst out laughing. "Girl, every single

woman has a boss. They just don't realize it yet."

"No, we don't."

"You're a stubborn one, aren't you? Can't see and yet you still think you've got power here."

"You can't make me do something I don't want."

"I could have come up those stairs and pushed you down them. I didn't. You're not as weak as I assumed you were."

"I didn't ask for Diego to want me," she said. "I didn't know the truth."

"Are you telling me that if you did know what he was capable of, you'd have left him?"

She opened her mouth to confirm it, but no words came out.

His father laughed even harder.

"Well, well, well, the goody little blind girl has gone and fallen in love with the big old bad wolf."

"Let me go."

"No. I don't always agree with my son, but I'm not going to fuck this up for him. I never wanted Angelo to take his place. His first wife was a traitorous whore, and believe me, he paid the price for that. I'm sure you've felt the scars on his body. He got away from the men who had hoped to kill him. No one has ever been able to fool my son."

"You sound proud."

"I am, but I must test him in all things. I'm going to approach you now. I'm not going to hurt you. I won't even put you back in your room with the cuffs. I'll take you back to Diego's room, where he left you, safe and sound."

"Why? Why not just kill me?"

Again, he burst out laughing. "You're the first woman to ever wonder why I'm not going to kill you. Are you wired right?"

"I'm starting to think not." She hated being vulnerable. What she didn't want was to be lulled into a false sense of security only to be betrayed.

"How about we stop with the fear of the threats, I take you back to your room, and you stop trying to cause trouble? Diego will take you to your father when you're ready. He's still in a coma. It's not like you're going to be any help to him. Far from it in fact."

Without putting up a fight, Belle walked with Diego's father back to the room, wondering what the hell she was supposed to do.

Chapter Fourteen

It took James several days to come out of the coma. The moment Diego got the notification of James being awake, he went to confirm the news himself. With the potential of Belle being pregnant with his baby Durante had postponed the wedding for a couple of weeks, until they could confirm. During this time, he was working with the other capos and Richard to find Angelo.

His slippery little cousin had gone into hiding, but he had no doubt he'd find him. Angelo liked the attention a little too much, and the moment he thought no one was looking, he'd pop up. After years of dealing with Angelo, Diego was hoping his cousin hadn't suddenly gone shy.

Entering the hospital room, he saw James laughing with the nurse. The smile vanished the moment he looked toward him.

"I will leave you two alone."

"Thank you," James said.

"You look good," Diego said, closing the door. He pulled a chair up toward the bed, staring at James, looking for any signs of sickness or problems.

"Where's my daughter, Diego?"

"You remember everything?"

"I remember enough to know that I'll kick your ass if you keep her from me."

Diego laughed. "Your daughter has been giving me enough trouble."

"She didn't get shot?"

"No. She's healthy."

"Where is she? The doctor said she hasn't come to see me. Are you keeping me from my own little girl?"

Diego held his hands up in surrender. "I've got to keep her safe. The shootings were caused by my cousin.

He's switched sides and is working with our enemies."

"There's a surprise."

"The hit was supposed to be on me. You took a bullet for me," Diego said.

"I took a bullet for my daughter, Diego. Nothing more. Don't read anything else into this. I love Belle, and I want to make sure she has as happy and fulfilling a life as possible."

"You still don't think that's with me."

"You're marrying another woman."

"Not if Belle's pregnant."

"Pregnant?"

"I'm setting up a deal. I have no wish to marry this woman. If she's not Belle, I don't want her."

"You're determined to see this through."

"I'm determined to show the woman I love that I'm going to go all the way."

"Diego, Belle's blind. She's never going to have a normal life. She's never going to see danger coming. The life you're offering her, it's not a good one. She will be in the way."

Diego ran a hand down his face. "Is that how you see her? In the way?"

"No, of course not."

"I know Belle. I know her better than she knows herself. She's strong. She doesn't need either one of us to survive. She'll never be in the way. She'll never be a problem. I love her, Mr. Johnson. I love her more than anything. So much so I'm working my ass off to come up with an alternative deal. You're not getting rid of me, and I'm not going to let you take Belle from me." He got to his feet.

"This isn't going to end well," James said. "Belle will listen to me eventually. She'll know what a mistake she is making."

Diego was at the door. Glancing back at James, he shook his head. "No father will ever agree with the man who wants to marry their daughter. I'm not most men, James. I will not hurt your daughter again, but she will never listen to you."

With that, he left James, making a point to the doctor to keep him in and safe. He didn't want the other man messing up his plans.

Once he was outside the hospital, he made a call to Richard.

"Tell me what you've got." He was still on Angelo's trail, and it was starting to wear thin.

"Not a lot. There hasn't been a sighting since the shootout. The club is still closed."

"Good. I don't want any heat on me." He'd already had to deal with two women that had overdosed. Right now, he had one focus and that was getting Angelo. "Has there been any other sighting at his apartment?"

"Nothing."

"I'm heading there now." He'd not gone to Angelo's apartment for the sole reason of lulling his cousin into a false sense of security. He was bored of trying to wait.

"You need backup."

"No. I've got my men. What I need is for you to keep an eye on everything else." He hung up his cell phone before climbing into the back of his car. He told his men where he wanted to go.

For now, until Angelo was caught, he had no choice but to take the extra protection. It pissed him off, but there wasn't anything he could do about it. The rules had to be followed, and he had to make sure he stayed alive. Resting his head back against the seat, he closed his eyes. His thoughts, as always, returned to Belle.

He had broken her trust, and he knew she was bored staying at his home. He needed to stop by her apartment and get her some of her books that she loved to listen to. Between dealing with the cops, hunting Angelo, and trying to come up with a deal for Durante, he'd put all of his energies elsewhere. At night, he often collapsed in bed. Belle was always sleeping so never knew when he was there.

In her sleep, she would still curl up against him. The few moments where there was no anger or resentment, he'd bask in them, stroking her hair, loving her the only way he knew how.

It was never enough though.

Nothing with her was ever enough, and it fucking destroyed him.

"We're here."

Pulling out of his thoughts, he stared at the luxury building where his cousin usually lived. Climbing out of the car, he made his way inside, taking the stairs to the correct floor. Considering Angelo was afraid of heights, he ironically lived on the top floor, looking out over the city.

He didn't have a key, so gripping the doorknob, he slammed his body weight against the door.

Once, twice, and a third time with the help of his men, and the door flung open.

The apartment hadn't been touched, or at least, it looked pristine.

He didn't linger or take his time. He was here on a mission, and it was simple what he had to do.

Opening each door in turn, he checked to see if there was anything out of the ordinary.

Nothing stood out. The apartment looked like it wasn't lived in. He moved from the sitting room, to the kitchen. He checked in the fridge to see the milk had spoiled. Closing it up, he looked in each bedroom.

When that didn't show anything, as a final straw, he opened the last door, which was supposed to be a closet.

He couldn't make anything out, and he grabbed the switch on the light, flicking it on.

"Bingo." The closet was covered in pictures, notes, and plans. He saw images of himself leaving the club, his home, and even Belle's apartment. There were pictures of her, and of the capos.

They never stuck to a strict schedule as it helped them stop the chance of getting hurt. Seeing all the evidence before him, he dialed The Boss.

"You need to get the hell out of there now. They're coming for you."

"Diego?"

"Get the fuck out now. There's going to be an attack." Closing his cell phone, he rushed out of the apartment. "We've got to go. The Boss needs us."

Angelo's real target had been The Boss. Once he took him out, the entire outfit would spin out of control, and there wouldn't be able to fend off every single attack. He'd underestimated Angelo. He only hoped he could fucking fix this before it got worse.

****

For fun and boredom, Belle put her head on the floor and began to lift her body up, flinging her legs back until they rested on the bed. She lifted up, and rolled over, falling over the other side of the bed. She turned, and did this again.

She couldn't recall a time in her life when she'd ever been so bored. If she wanted to, she could try to explore the house, but she'd already killed Diego's other lamp, and well, she didn't want to bump into his father.

The older man ... unnerved her.

She didn't know what he wanted from her exactly, but it always left her with a twisting in the pit of her stomach. He was a man of few words, but his presence always made her want to be elsewhere.

When there was a knock at the door, she frowned. Diego always entered letting her know it was him. His father entered, and rarely spoke. Richard never did.

"Who is it?"

"It's, erm, it's Charlotte Durante."

This made Belle tense up.

The woman who was supposed to marry Diego.

"I don't think you should be here," she said.

"I think we should talk."

"I don't think we should." There was no way she could sit with the other woman. She was going to be married to Diego, while she was the other woman. The mistress. Even thinking it pissed her off.

The door still opened.

Charlotte didn't respect boundaries. Why wasn't she surprised by that?

Belle waited for the other woman to speak.

"I'm sorry for ignoring you."

"I don't think we should meet. I don't think it's what Diego would want."

"I, erm, my dad told me what happened. You're Belle Johnson."

"I am. You're Charlotte Durante."

"Yes."

"You're engaged to be married to Diego." It didn't stop hurting no matter how many times she kept on saying it.

"The wedding has been postponed for a couple of weeks."

"I'm sorry." Inside she was jumping for joy. Why are you happy? He lied, and he was more than willing to cheat. Asshole.

"Can I approach? I know you can't see. I don't want to scare you."

"Have you come here to kill me?"

"No. I just wanted to see you. Maybe talk to you. I don't think having all this information dumped in your lap is fun."

"No, it really isn't. I'm still waiting to find out what happened with my dad." She clasped her hands together, feeling the bed dip close beside her.

This isn't weird.

Just a fiancée checking in with her fiancé's girlfriend.

Belle tried not to wince at her own thoughts. "I didn't know he was engaged. He doesn't wear a ring. I would have checked."

"How would you have checked? You're blind."

"My hands. I'd have felt a ring or at least an indentation of where a ring lies. He wouldn't have been able to lie about that."

"Oh, I'm sorry. Our engagement has been rather sudden. It was arranged. What they think is best for the capo."

"Do you want to get married to him?" Belle asked. This conversation would be a lot easier if Charlotte was a bitch.

"I can't answer that."

"There's only two of us here. It's not like I can run to the cops."

"That's not funny," Charlotte said.

"I'm not laughing. I'm just being honest with you. You're here. How crazy is this? The fiancée coming to see the girlfriend. I didn't want this."

"I don't want to get married," Charlotte said. "I wanted to continue my education. I'd love to be a teacher one day."

"Why can't you do that? Pursue what you want?"

"I'm a Durante. My obligation is to my capo, my father, and The Boss."

"This boss guy is sounding like an asshole." Belle jumped as Charlotte grabbed her hand.

"Be careful of the insults you throw around. It's not good to call him names."

"He's just a guy."

"He's more than just a guy. You wouldn't understand."

Belle took a deep breath. "Then enlighten me."

"I didn't come here to tell you about The Boss, or our way of life. I just wanted to tell you that I don't mind you and Diego being together."

"Wait, what? How is that even possible?" she asked. There was no way she would be happy if she was in Charlotte's shoes.

"I don't love Diego. If this wedding goes through, I don't mind you being part of his life."

Belle shook her head. "It's not going to happen."

"You will have my blessing to be together. A lot of men have a woman they truly care about."

Belle pulled away from Charlotte, suddenly needing space. "No, you don't understand. I'm not going to be the other woman. I'm not going to share him with you. I don't want that for myself or for any child we may have." She stood up and then sat down. "I'm sorry. I'm not wired that way. I couldn't handle the nights wondering if he was in your bed. I don't share."

"I don't love him," Charlotte said. "It would be an obligation."

"Then you shouldn't get married."

"We're going around in circles here."

"You should leave," she said. "I'm not trying to

be a bitch here, Charlotte. What you want, I cannot give you. I'm sorry. You seem like a nice person, you really do. I hope you and Diego have a wonderful life."

She waited, but Charlotte made no move to leave.

"I've upset you," Charlotte said. "It wasn't my intention, I promise you."

"Why did you come?"

"I wanted to see you. When I heard about you, I know how cold Diego can be. We've been engaged for a short time, and he's never so much as held my hand."

"What? He hasn't held your hand? Kissed you?"

"Nope. Not even a hug."

"Oh."

"I take it from that look you're giving, Diego has done far more with you."

Belle didn't say anything. What was the point? There was a chance she was carrying his baby, and also, he spent that much time with her. He held her hand, pulled her in close, and always kissed her. Diego was in fact, a really affectionate man, only, he didn't share those affections with just anyone.

Did that mean he truly loved her?

She wasn't some kind of possession for him to keep from others.

The bedroom door opened again, and Belle lifted her head.

"What are you doing with her?" Diego asked.

"I just wanted to come and see her. Give her some company."

"Leave."

"Diego?" Belle asked.

"I didn't invite her here. She shouldn't be here, and I don't want her anywhere near you. Leave, now."

Belle listened as the other woman left the room. She flinched as the door slammed closed.

"Are you still here?"

"I'm still here. I'm sorry she came. I had no idea she would come see you." He grabbed her hands, making her once again jump.

"It's fine. I think she was trying to make peace."

"I don't care what kind of peace she was making. She shouldn't be here. I don't want her near you."

"Am I such a bad person?"

"No, you know this." He stroked her cheek, right down where the scar was. "I don't want you upset. I don't want to marry her."

"Yeah, Charlotte was giving me a thorough explanation. She said she didn't have a problem with you and me being together while you're married to her." She snorted.

"She did?"

"Yes. In a weird way, I think your fiancée is actually really nice." She shook her head, pulling away from him. She stood up and stayed close to the bed so she could round it.

"What's the matter?" he asked.

"It's nothing."

"I know you, Belle. Tell me what is going on."

"I can't do it," she said. "You want the truth? Well, here it is. I don't want to share you. Ever. I don't want to be the other woman. When you're with someone you're not supposed to think about anyone else."

"Belle, I don't want her."

"But if I'm not pregnant with your baby, you're going to her. That's why we've had sex so much, right? You want to make me pregnant?" She shook her head. "I can't talk about this. I'm so confused."

"I want to keep you."

"Diego, we can't always have what we want."

"I don't believe that."

She chuckled. "Of course you don't."

"Your father is awake."

The sudden shift of conversation startled her. "He is?"

"Yes. He's stable. Talking. He told me I needed to let you go. Everyone is telling me to let you go, and yet no one is listening. I can't." He moved toward her. She heard his voice get louder with each passing step. "I can't lose you. You think it has to do with my desire to keep you. Why can't you see it's because I love you? I love you more than anything, and I'm willing to fight for this, for us." He kissed her hard, and she couldn't resist him. Wrapping her arms around his neck, she held onto him, not wanting to let go, hungry for him.

Diego lifted her up, placing her gently on the bed as he did.

He never kisses Charlotte.

He never holds Charlotte.

He's always tender with me.

She cried out as his lips traveled down her neck. He pulled down the shorts she was wearing, which were her clothing of choice nowadays. He kissed down her body, lifting the shirt she wore to kiss each of her nipples in turn. She arched up, begging for more, needing his lips on every single part of her. He was burning her alive with his touch, and she didn't want him to stop.

Diego moved between her thighs, his lips above her pussy, and as his tongue slid across her slit, she cried out.

"There's no way I could give up this pretty pussy. You're all mine, Belle. The pleasure I can give you, I want to be the only man you go to. The only man you trust."

"I do, Diego." She gasped as his tongue dipped down inside her, sliding back up to circle her bud, and down to fuck her with his tongue. The pleasure was instant and intense, making her beg for more of him, wanting him more than she had ever wanted anyone else. She begged him to make her come, but he didn't let her fall over the edge.

He stopped her just as she was at the peak, ready to plunge into orgasm. Diego slid his cock in deep, taking her breath away as he rocked inside her. She felt each inch of him as he slid inside, going to the hilt before pulling out.

"You think I want to give this up? That the only reason I want you is to keep you as a toy? Feel this, Belle. Feel me inside you. Feel what I do to you. What you do to me. There is no one else I want. When I close my eyes, all I see is you. You're the only woman I want. Since the moment I met you, there hasn't been anyone else. Just you. You're the one I want more than anything else."

She cried out as he slammed in hard, the bed hitting the wall with each repeated thrust. He didn't stop in his thrusts as he reached between her thighs, stroking her pussy, teasing her clit as he did so.

Belle came hard, screaming his name, begging for him not to stop. Not to let her go. She didn't want to leave him or to stop feeling this. He drove her wild and crazy, and she didn't know of any other person she would ever want. Diego was the love of her life. As he slid in deep, she felt him reach his own orgasm, panting in her ear as he filled her pussy. Each pulse made her gasp until he finally collapsed against her.

Chapter Fifteen

Diego stroked Belle's shoulder. He'd made love to her more than once since he returned from saving The Boss. The hit Angelo organized, with the help of the Russians, didn't go off as smoothly as Angelo had hoped.

The Boss had all the capos on high alert, so there were more soldiers to keep him safe. There was no way The Boss would try to run, not in a fight. It wasn't part of who he was. He'd stay and fight to protect his family no matter the danger. When Diego and the other capos arrived, they had been able to take the Russians from behind. No one stood a chance, but Angelo, the slimy fucker, was nowhere to be found. Diego had gathered all the information he needed though, and Richard was currently working through it.

His father had told him Charlotte was paying Belle a visit, and it pissed him off. He didn't want her anywhere near Belle. In fact, he didn't want any of his family around her. How the fuck was he going to be able to keep her when he wanted everyone else to stay as far away from her as humanly possible? He was never going to be able to achieve that. What he wanted was a fucking miracle.

"What are you thinking about?" Belle asked. Her fingers stroked his face. "You've got frown lines." She touched his forehead before going to his eyes. "Are you okay?"

"I'm fine. I'm just thinking about all the shit I've got to deal with."

"Is it bad?"

"Angelo took a hit out on The Boss, and even as we had them surrounded, he snuck away."

"You can't blame yourself. Angelo sounds like a coward."

"He is." He thought of all the times he'd beaten him as a kid. Whenever they were alone, Angelo would always use the element of surprise to get his attention. Maybe that was what he was missing. Angelo was constantly surprising them. What if he turned the tables on him? Surprised *him.* He'd have to locate him, but what if Angel was actually watching him, waiting for him to be vulnerable? There could be a way for him to lure Angelo into his own trap. "You ... are ... a ... genius."

She laughed as he kissed her between each word she spoke.

"Now that you're in a good mood, and I've helped you solve whatever your problem is, I want to go and see my dad."

"Belle?"

"No, please, Diego. I know you think I'm going to run off." She grabbed his hand, placing it across her stomach. "I'm not going to cause anything that means if I am pregnant I'm raising this baby alone. I also don't want to hear that you got arrested either. I'm not going to say anything. I'll be good. Wow, that sounds rather strange. I won't say anything. I want to ... do this. I nearly lost my father. He's awake, and I want to talk to him."

He took her hands. "I'll go and see if I can arrange it."

"You will?"

"Yes. Belle, if you break your promise, I will have no choice but to kill you."

He saw the sadness on her face. "I'm not going to do anything to make you hurt me. I just want to see my dad. That's all."

"Fine." He kissed her lips. "I'll be back. Stay here."

He left her on the bed as he made his way into his father's office. Paperwork was on every single surface, and several images were pinned up.

"You really worked through all of this mess?" Diego asked.

"It wasn't hard to do. Everyone has an order, and well, Angelo's is based on each hit he's taken." Richard stood. "These are the first hits that were organized. Not the shootings. Angelo or one of his men were responsible for the drug overdosing coming from your club."

"I took out that barman," Diego said. "You saw him on the security footage dealing out his drugs."

"Yes, and we're figuring he was replaced by someone within the club. It's not exactly hard to do. Drug dealers come in all shapes, sizes, and sexes. Moving on, we're not here to figure out who sold the drugs. These are the hits that were taken in the five different locations, which ended with your shooting."

"How the fuck did he know where I was going to be?" Diego asked.

"He didn't. It's why he's got a picture of you."

"You were tailed," his father said. "That's how he was able to do this. He watched your movements. Either that, or your girl is in on it."

"Belle's not in on it."

"She's not," Richard said. "As part of my arrangement with Diego, I was asked to keep an eye on her. The only person who was connected to Angelo and Belle was Melanie. She was getting the drugs from him and helping to distribute them." Richard pointed at another wall. "I may have mixed mine and Angelo's information to help us pin him down."

"Whatever it takes."

"Belle is an innocent in this. She's just a woman who is trying to make a life for herself."

"As I knew she was," Diego said. Belle couldn't hurt anyone. She had hit him when she found out the truth, but he also knew that was because of the pain he'd caused her.

"So, then we move back to Angelo's next hit. The Boss. He's not wanting to take your job, Diego. He's wanting absolute power, and he's using the Russians to get it. Now, this is the problem. Moving onto the next hit which would be the consigliere and the underboss. They are who he's going after next. However, this was all based on The Boss being taken out."

Looking over the evidence, Diego frowned. "So we don't know who he is taking out next?"

"No. He messed up his last hit. Where would he go from there?"

Diego looked at the work, and glanced through everything he saw.

"It's Angelo. He'll continue on," Diego said.

"But that's not what he has planned."

"I know this guy. I know what he's capable of. Failing to kill The Boss is not a mission fail for him. He'll come back. He'll see it as a postponement. He's going to go after the consigliere and the underboss. Take them out, he'll weaken us."

"Not if you give him a better target. One he wants."

"What?" Diego asked.

"You. Angelo had three attacks of the five happen in your domain. One of them was designed to get you. I'd say you'd be a pretty big fucking lure for him. You don't always have your guards with you."

"That was before the attack, Richard. There's no way he'd fall for it. He's stupid, but he'd see a trap like that."

"Not if you're going to Belle's apartment and he

thinks you're going alone. She's the one place that isn't targeted. The one place you have the illusion of being safe and the one place where he could attack you, thinking you're alone."

Diego stared at Richard. The plan ... could work. "That's the best plan you got?"

"I don't see *you* coming up with anything else. He takes out the consigliere and the underboss, it'll be the capos next. The hits that took place were designed to weaken and separate. With that, he could pick you off one by one until there is nothing and no one left."

"Then we take the fight to him. I'm not going to sit around waiting for shit to happen. Find him. You know where his hideouts are. There is enough evidence here for you to at least narrow down the search."

"What about the Russians?" Richard asked.

"We'll deal with them as well. We don't fuck around with shit like this. Find Angelo. I'll take care of him. His ass-whooping has been long overdue." He turned to look at his father. "I'm taking Belle to see her father."

"That's not a good idea."

"I know my woman, Dad. She needs to go and see him, and I trust her."

"And if she can't keep her fucking mouth closed? You've got what it takes to kill her, son?"

"I've got what it takes to deal with her. I trust her. The next time you send Charlotte to go and talk to her, I kill *her*, understand?" He turned on his heel and left the room. Richard could find Angelo at any time so now he had to work fast.

Belle was still on the bed.

"Are we still going to see him?"

"Yes, but we've got to make this trip quick. Richard's looking for Angelo as we speak." He grabbed some of his spare clothes.

He needed to get some clothes from Belle's apartment. He'd been dressing her in his stuff. He liked seeing her walking around in his shorts and shirt.

As he grabbed a shirt, he paused.

This had to work. He had to deal with Angelo before his cousin hurt Belle. Anyone else he didn't give a fuck about, but Belle was his responsibility and he needed to take care of her. He wasn't entirely convinced of Richard's plan, but it was the best one they had, and seeing as they had no other way of finding Angelo, he had to be used as the bait.

Dressing Belle quickly, he threw on a suit. He made her lift up on his back. It was going to be faster than actually guiding her.

He left his home, placing her in the car and climbing behind the wheel. His men were already climbing into the spare car to follow him. He didn't give them any other direction. Pulling out of the driveway, he began the journey toward the hospital.

"I hate hospitals."

"You do?"

"Yeah, when my mom got sick, her last days were spent in the hospital. She had a private room, and I know my dad tried to make it like home, but it wasn't the same. You could see her fading with every passing second. Have you been in a lot of hospitals?"

"No."

"What happens when you get hurt?"

"We pay a doctor to come and tend our wounds."

"But if it's serious?"

"If it's serious and you're important, you'll go to the hospital. Otherwise, you'll deal with the pain."

"That sounds awful."

"It's fine."

"Diego, what happens if I don't get pregnant?" she asked.

"I'm not going to marry Charlotte. I want you, and there's no way I would put what we have at risk for a deal."

"A deal?"

"This arranged marriage brings the family closer."

"Why not do a business deal then? Like a merger. Is there something you and her father have that you could both compromise on?" Belle asked.

"You don't want to share me either?"

"No, I don't want to share you. I'm still pissed that you lied to me, and I'm not happy about it. If I can help ... keep you, I will."

"Are you trying to tell me you love me?" he asked.

Belle was silent, and he glanced over at her. Her head was facing him, but he knew she couldn't see him. Her teeth were nibbling on her lip. "Yes."

"I didn't hear that."

She burst out laughing. "You dork. You did hear that, and you know I do. I love you. It's what made finding out about Charlotte so much harder. She also seems really nice."

"She is in fact nice."

"You don't want her?"

"No. When it comes to Charlotte, I don't feel anything for her."

"She told me you didn't even hold her hand."

"I told you plenty of times. There's no one else I want other than you. I don't want to hold Charlotte's hand or kiss her cheek, or have anything more to do with her than is necessary. I fell hard for you, Belle Johnson, and you have ruined me for all other women."

She had this glorious smile on her face. "I'm not going to complain about that. I rather like that I ruined you."

"I bet you do."

She put her hand on his thigh. "Please tell me I'm holding your leg?"

"You are."

"Good. Good. I didn't want you to think of it as a come on."

"It's not?"

"We're on the way to see my dad. I don't want you to be hard when we walk into the room."

"It's probably the most action he's ever seen."

"Hey, don't be mean. He's never really gotten over my mom. He loved her so much, and when he spoke his vows of being with her forever, he meant them. Every single word."

"You want him to be happy though, right?"

"Of course. I've even encouraged him to date. To sign up for those dating sites, but he won't have any of it. Maybe after this, I can convince him that he needs to find someone."

"I don't imagine it would be that easy."

"Why?"

"I know if I lost you, I'd take down every single person who stole you from me until someone finally killed me so I could be with you."

"Diego?"

"You know, I'm a fucking killer. I've taken lives without even blinking. It's what I've been trained to do. It's what I know, and yet with you, I turn into a fucking pussy. It's ridiculous. If my men saw me with you, heard me, they'd all laugh at me."

She laughed, and he glanced over at her. "I love that you're like this with me. It means a whole lot more to me knowing I'm the only one you want."

"You *are* the only one I want." He gripped her hand as he navigated the traffic. They weren't too far from the hospital.

His men were following behind him, and he didn't see any signs of being tailed or impending danger.

Belle stayed silent as he got them to the hospital, parking the car.

He climbed out and paid for parking before coming back to help her out.

"Do you want me to piggyback you?" he asked.

"Dad would be real thrilled with that. I'm happy to just walk."

He held her hand, locking their fingers together, and walked her across the parking lot. It was still busy even though it was early morning now. He'd take her for breakfast after they saw her father.

The days were blending together during his search for Angelo.

Diego opted for the elevator so she didn't hurt herself anymore and for speed. His men entered along with them, and he moved her so they had their backs to the wall.

"It's a little crowded."

"They're my men," he said. "You don't have to worry about whispering."

"Oh, hey, guys," she said.

None of them spoke back. "She's talking to you."

"Hello, Belle," they all said together.

"They're not used to anyone wanting to talk to them."

"Did I break some kind of 'don't speak' code?" she asked.

"No, they are more seen and not heard."

"That sucks. I don't want them to be around me

unless they're willing to talk. It's bad enough I can't see them. The least they can do is say hello."

Diego looked at his men, and he saw them all smiling. It wasn't in sarcasm either or mocking her. They liked her, and for him, he was more than happy with that.

She had this way about her that made people like her. Melanie was the one person who didn't seem to get her charm.

The elevator doors opened up, and his men created a path for them. No one was in James's room. He opened the door, and Belle stepped in.

"Belle."

"Dad?"

He helped her go toward the bed, and when she was safe, he let her go, standing back to give them both some space.

"I missed you "

"I missed you too. I was so worried about you. I didn't want anything to happen to you." Belle touched his face. "How are you? What has the doctor said? When can you leave?"

"Wait a minute. Let me look at you. You look beautiful, Belle. You're being treated well."

"Diego treats me well."

"That's good to know. I'd still kick his ass when I get out of this bed."

Belle sat beside her father, holding his hands.

"You'll do no such thing. You're going to have to rest and take care of yourself. I'm not going to let you do anything that could take you from me."

"One day I will go, Belle."

"That day is not today. Besides, you want to be around for grandkids one day, right?"

Diego watched her. She was something else entirely. The love he felt for her, he'd never experienced this kind of feeling before in his life. She made him want so many different things.

He hoped she was pregnant and not just for his sake but because he wanted a family with her.

If he fought hard enough, he knew he could make this work with them. He had no intention of being shared though. Durante wanted something from him, as otherwise he wouldn't have given him the choice between Charlotte and Belle.

There was a way out of the marriage; he just had to find it.

Rather than invade their moment, Diego stepped outside the room, closing the door behind him. He trusted Belle, and now was the time to show her just how much he did.

****

"What was that?" Belle asked.

"Diego has just walked out, closing the door, giving us some privacy."

"He has?"

"Yes."

She smiled. "He trusts me."

"Yes, and now is your chance to leave."

"To leave?"

"I can be ready to go in a matter of minutes."

"Dad?"

"We need to get you away from him."

She reached out, hoping she didn't touch any wires or anything that were connected to him. "Dad, you need to stop."

"What I need to do is protect you."

"I don't need protecting." She held onto his hands tightly, not wanting to let him go. "Diego's not going to hurt me."

Her father grabbed her wrists. "This? This is the

kind of not hurt you're talking about?"

"They're bruised?"

"Yes, Belle. It looks like you were chained up like some kind of animal."

"I was." She winced. "This had nothing to do with Diego though. I promise you."

"You promise me that Diego had nothing to do with chaining my daughter up?"

"No, he didn't." This wasn't going to sound any better. "His dad did."

"What?"

"Look, long story short. Diego was helping you and he gave me to his father to take care of. Because I'm blind, he chained me up in a bedroom with only one bed. It was fine. The cuffs weren't, but when Diego got home, he was able to help me."

"Are you even listening to yourself? You're justifying his actions."

"No, I'm justifying his father's, but I don't want to run away, Dad. Where would we go?"

"Back home."

"You think Diego wouldn't find us at home?"

"I can have protection in place. I can keep you safe."

"I'm not in any danger with him. Diego loves me, Dad." She placed her hands on her stomach. "I may also be carrying his child. I don't want to run from this or away from him. I want to see this head-on. I love him."

"No."

"Yes. Dad, please, don't do this because if you make a scene or you cause trouble, I can't stop what will happen. You know who he is. You know what he's capable of. What his family are capable of. I don't want anything to happen to you, but I love him. I love him so much, and he doesn't care about this." She pointed at her face. "He loves me, and I wish you could feel it. When I'm with him, the way he is with me, it's magical."

"I see the way he looks at you, Belle. I know Diego loves you."

"He does, and I love him so much."

"You're willing to be the other woman? A mistress?"

"I'm not going to be the other woman, Dad. He's going to figure this out. I just need you to be my dad and to love me and to tell me everything is going to be okay."

She waited, listening for any change in her father.

"I love you, honey. I love you so much, and everything is going to be okay. I won't let him hurt you, and I'll be here if he ever lets you down."

She smiled. "See, that wasn't so bad, was it?"

"It wasn't."

The door opened once again.

"I don't want to ruin this moment, but I've got to take her back home," Diego said.

Her father sighed. "You could leave her here with me."

"Not going to happen. I don't know how safe this hospital is, but I will put extra men on your door."

"Shouldn't he come back with me?" Belle asked.

"When he's better. They're still monitoring him. Besides, I bet he'd kill my dad if given the chance," Diego said.

"Damn straight. He and I have an issue to deal with."

"Dad?"

"No man puts my girl in cuffs. You know that."

She laughed. "I better go."

Her father held her close. His arms went around her, and she closed her eyes, feeling safe. "Everything is going to be okay, Belle. I know it is."

"I love you, Dad."

"I love you too, sweetheart."

Diego took her hand and led her out of the hospital room. By the time they got back in the car, her stomach was growling.

"I'll take you for breakfast, and then I'm taking you back home."

"What's the rush?"

"I've got a hunch to work through, and I think it'll pay off."

"A hunch?"

"Yes."

"Okay."

They went to Mary's for breakfast, and Belle ordered as much fat and carbohydrates as she could think of, without caring what Diego thought of her. He ordered exactly the same.

"Thank you for taking me to see my dad," she said, sipping at the coffee Mary had brought her. Mary always gave her coffee in a takeaway mug, and placed her fingers on the top where she was to put her lips. It was the odd kindness of others that always gave Belle hope.

"I wanted to take you the first time you asked, but there are rules in place for all of us."

"I get it. I do. It's just, I don't like them."

He laughed. "No one likes rules."

"I do, most of the time. They're always there for a reason. You know, having fire exits in buildings, fixing broken pavement. I've tripped over a couple of those. Never falling in love with a mafia man."

"I'm going to touch your hand."

She didn't flinch when he did.

"Falling in love with a mafia man? Let me guess, this guy is sexy as hell."

"I don't know. I've never seen him. He feels sexy. He's got a few scars and at times a really bad attitude, but I like him. He's not for everyone. Even if he *did* lie at the start of our relationship."

He squeezed her hand a little tighter. "I didn't know what to do."

"You're going to admit that."

"Yes. I've got nothing to lose, and, Belle, you have always had a way with me that makes me want to speak the truth."

"I'm a truth serum. Just what every girl wants to hear."

"I want you to marry me," he said.

"Diego, you can't ask that. Not yet."

"I can. Regardless if you're pregnant or not. I'm marrying you. I'm claiming you as mine."

"I don't want you to get in trouble."

"I'll figure something out. Either way, I won't be marrying another woman. I won't betray you, ever. You're my future, Belle. You're everything I ever want."

"You know, you shouldn't be proposing in my favorite place."

"This is the perfect place, and you know it. Over breakfast." He rubbed her fingers. "I already have a ring for you."

"You do?"

"I had every intention of marrying you." He pressed a kiss to her fingers. "I just didn't completely anticipate how much I was going to fall in love with you."

"You're saying so many amazing things, Diego."

"Just the truth. With you, it's always the truth."

"I held off bringing you lovebirds breakfast, but I don't want it to be cold," Mary said.

Belle laughed. "It smells amazing."

"Of course it does. I cooked it especially for you guys. It's not often I get to see love bloom in here, but I see it with you two. Enjoy. You both deserve it."

Chapter Sixteen

Arriving back home, Diego wasn't prepared to see Charlotte. He didn't want the other woman in his home, but she seemed determined to stick around.

"What do you want?" he asked.

"I wanted to spend some time with Belle. I'm only here as a friend, I promise."

"Diego, who is it?" Belle asked.

"Charlotte's here."

"Hi," Belle said.

Diego held Belle's arm and moved her toward the library. He put her on the sofa. "I'll be back in a minute."

Belle caught his hand before he could leave. "Don't be mean."

"That woman shouldn't be here, and I'm not going to allow her to hurt you."

"She's not going to hurt me, but think about it. You're supposed to marry her."

"I'm not marrying her. Now, let me go and deal with this."

He pulled his hand from hers and found Charlotte standing in the main reception near the front door.

"What do you want?"

She held her hands up. "I'm here as a friend. I'm not looking for anything. I promise."

"Why? If she's pregnant it means we don't get married."

"I know. Can I be honest with you?"

"Yes." He rubbed at his temples. He didn't have time for this.

"I don't want to marry you."

This made him lower his hands. "You don't?"

"No. I don't love you. I don't want to be married to anyone. I've got plans and I was hoping that if Belle's pregnant and you marry her, you can in some way help me?" she asked.

Everyone always had an agenda. He wasn't surprised. "What do you want?"

"I want to teach. I want to go back to college and get a degree and be able to teach. It's my dream. I'm hoping that if you're agreeable, you'll talk to my father. Maybe even help me. If you have kids with Belle, it would come in handy. I'd be their teacher."

He frowned at her, completely blown away by her wishes.

"A teacher?"

She nodded. "I'd make a good one. I love learning, and I love teaching. I know you're probably thinking it's laughable."

"I'm not. I've got a few ideas that could expand my businesses with your father. Is there any area he's hoping to develop with me?"

"The clubs," she said after a moment's pause.

"The clubs?"

"I overheard a conversation … if it will help. Our clubs are not making enough money to break even. I know from research that you know a thing or two about running a successful nightclub. It's small, but it's something. A business venture together. Some solid ground."

"You know you could be killed for telling me this?"

"We're all sharing the same problem. I don't see why asking for help will be an issue." She shrugged. "I just want to have my own life. I don't want to cause a fuss."

He stared at her for several moments and nodded. "I've got some business to take care of. Then I'll deal with your father."

"Can I hang out with her? She seems really nice, and I'd really like a friend."

"You are being open and honest about all of this."

"I've got nothing to lose and everything to gain. I'm not a horrible person. I promise."

He also knew that as an outcast, she didn't have any friends.

"Sure, you can hang out with her." He knew for a fact she wasn't anything like Melanie.

Entering the library with Charlotte close to him, he knelt in front of Belle.

"What's going on?" she asked.

"Charlotte wants to hang out with you. Do you want her around?"

"Why would she want to do that?" Belle asked.

"She's looking for a friend. Like you are."

"I don't know," Belle said. "Why would she want to be friends with a woman who stole her fiancé?"

"I don't really want him. You've done me a favor," Charlotte said.

"We've got a plan to put in place, and I need to go and take care of some business. I'll be taking Richard with me. I can leave you alone with my dad—"

"Charlotte's fine."

He chuckled. Grabbing her face, he slammed his lips down on hers. "I love you, and I'll be back as soon as I can." Getting to his feet he looked at Charlotte. "Anything happens to her, I'll hold you personally responsible."

"You can't go around threatening people," Belle said.

"I can do whatever the hell I want. I'll be back. Try not to get into trouble."

"I'm not a child."

He laughed, leaving Belle and Charlotte alone.

He found Richard in the main dining room.

"How do you feel about killing Angelo?"

"It's on my list of things to achieve before I turn fifty," Richard said.

"I want to deal with him now. I am done with all of this waiting."

"Angelo will follow you wherever you go, Diego. You want to deal with him now, at Belle's apartment. I can do that. You can't take any bodyguards with you. You've got to go alone."

"That's why I want you to come with me."

"I'm coming with you, regardless. I blend into the crowd, and he won't even have a clue I'm there," Richard said.

"We can't draw attention."

Richard leaned back in his chair. "We won't. He'll come to Belle's apartment. I can guarantee you he will. He's probably already set a trap there for you. You'll be walking in blind. It's the one place you're going to need to go that you haven't."

"I don't care. I've always won against Angelo. There's nothing he can try that I don't already know. Question is, do you trust me?"

"You've not given me any reason to doubt you. It's why I'm still here. Let's go." Richard disconnected his laptop, bringing it along with him.

"Do you carry that thing everywhere?"

"Yep. You never know when you might need to hack into something."

Diego informed his head of security what he intended to do and ordered them to keep their distance, not to draw attention, and to listen for his signal if he even gave one.

Climbing into the car, he pulled out of the driveway, hoping he wasn't making a mistake leaving

Charlotte and Belle alone.

"What's your plan?" Richard asked, opening up his laptop. "You've got to be ready in case Angelo strikes."

"I'm sneaking into Belle's apartment. If he's there, he's going to expect me to come through the front door, not the back door."

He glanced over when Richard didn't respond. "That actually sounds logical. Angelo will be alone."

"How do you know?"

"Simple, too many men will alert you. The idea is to be ready for you." Richard opened up his laptop and started doing some clicking. Diego found it really irritating. "I can confirm our boy has been making random visits to Belle's apartment."

"He has?" Diego's rage went up a notch. He had to get himself under control before he completely lost it.

"We checked all his usual hideouts, and I kept surveillance on Belle's place, just in case he decided to check it out. He's been there only a couple of times, always waiting and checking for you. When he gets bored, he leaves. This is the one place he's going to best you. By thinking he has the element of surprise. He knows you're in love with Belle. What better place to hide than the apartment he thinks you won't be cautious over?"

"It sounds stupid, but it would explain why we can't find him."

"He's probably been hiding out with the Russians, Diego. There's no way I can get into any of their safe houses or places."

"Angelo likes to think that he's smart. He's really not, and this just proves it. He doesn't think I'd suspect Belle's apartment because I'm too busy taking care of her, even though that's where I planned to go first, but I got distracted and busy. He's an asshole, not smart. Either way, it's the only place he could go where he thinks he has a chance of besting me."

"I've got your back, Diego. He won't win this. I promise."

"I believe you. I imagine Angelo's reputation is holding on by a thread with how fucking stupid he's looked, thinking he can take us all on without any consequences. He's only good at hiding. Deep down, Angelo's a big coward."

"You think he's actually done a deal with the Russians where he hands over the boss and he gets power? Like he believes that will happen?"

"That I do."

"How would that work? It's not like they'd give him a position amongst their ranks, and surely, he knows that. It's the Russians. They would put one of their own above him in any position of power."

"Unless during the process of a takeover, we killed plenty of his enemy so he only has to deal with a couple. He gets rid of them, takes The Boss's place, he has his own kingdom all of a sudden. It's Angelo. It doesn't have to make sense."

"I'm a simple man at heart. I love my computers and being the boss in my world, but this goes far above anything I've ever thought about. You men with wanting to rule the world."

"I don't want to rule the world. I'd rather be the one in charge than leave things to Angelo. He's a bastard and a first-class fucking prick. He'd tear this city apart before he ever rebuilt it."

"Still, he went to a lot of hard work to get this. It's got to mean something."

"Yeah, it means he wants power. He wants it all. That's never a good quality in a leader." He pulled up a few blocks from Belle's apartment. "We're going to have to walk from here."

"Cool, we get to exercise."

"You need to leave the computer. You'll stand out, and I don't know if Angelo's keeping an eye on the street."

"Let's go then."

He'd parked the car and quickly approached the car with his men, giving them the details of where to go and to stay out of sight.

Walking side by side with Richard, they headed down the street toward the building.

"Do you want to go through the front door?"

"No. We're going up the fire escape."

"Are you fucking shitting me?"

"No. What's wrong?"

"Nothing. I would have worn my bad suit."

He rolled his eyes, not in the mood to deal with his not-friend.

"When all of this is over," Richard said as Diego began to climb the fire escape at the side of the building, "we should grab a beer."

"When all this is over, I'm taking Belle away for a couple of weeks."

"You want company?"

"Nope."

"You know I'll be your best man, right?"

Diego paused, glancing down at Richard. "No, you won't."

"I've been watching you, Diego. You've got no friends of your own. I'm your best choice."

"You do know we're not friends."

"And you do know we are. You're just fighting against it, but that's okay with me. You keep on fighting, and I'm going to keep on winning."

He got to the floor where Belle's apartment was. Stepping around the building, he was careful as he looked into the main window. The curtains were drawn, and with the sun casting shadows, he was able to walk past, going to the bedroom window. Much to his surprise, the curtain was open, and the window partially lifted.

Being careful and quiet, Diego lifted up the window. The bedroom door was closed, and he thanked Belle for not having too much furniture.

Climbing into the window, he helped Richard and lowered it down again.

Belle had nice, thick carpets, and he stood at the door, placing his ear against the wood. In the other room he heard muffled conversation, but he could only make out one person.

"Be careful."

"I will."

Gripping the door handle, he twisted it. The metal seemed to creak as he did so, and click loudly as he opened the door.

There were no gunshots, and he gritted his teeth, taking his time.

Come on. Come on.

With the door released, he stepped out of her room. Grabbing his gun from the inside of his jacket, he grabbed the silencer and slid it into place on the gun. In an ideal world, he would want to take Angelo back home to his family. This wasn't an ideal world. This was his fucking world, and he didn't always get what he wanted.

Just as he rounded the corner, wood exploded to his left. Richard went down on the floor and Diego rolled, firing his weapon in the right direction.

More gunshots hit around him but didn't actually get him.

"You're still a shit fucking shot," Diego said.

He moved out of the way as Angelo shot at him.

Richard got up, rushing out from his cover, firing his gun, but Angelo shot him. The hit landed in Richard's thigh.

Getting to his feet, Diego held the gun trained on Angelo's head.

In one of Angelo's hands was a gun, in the other a cell phone.

"You shoot me, your girl is going to die," Angelo said.

"Put the gun down."

"Fuck you. You think I was born yesterday? I know what a good shot you are. I know you could kill me right there. I'm not lowering my weapon. Drop yours if you love your woman."

"Not going to happen."

"You don't love Belle? Please, I've seen the pictures. You're so fucking in love with her it makes me sick. I don't know how they could put a weak asshole in my place."

"The only one weak here is you," Diego said. "Your time is up, Angelo. The Boss knows everything. We know what you were planning."

"You're really willing to risk your girlfriend? Maybe I should keep her alive. Make her suck my dick over your dead body."

"That's never going to happen," Diego said.

"No, you're right. I've got my guy trained on her right now." Angelo put the phone to his ear. "She's wearing a sexy little bikini and sitting relaxing, reading a book. She looks sexy as fuck."

"Who is with her?"

"Your girl is on her own."

Diego was done playing games. He fired the gun,

shooting Angelo in the fucking head. He watched his cousin go down.

"What the fuck? What about Belle? You've got to get some guys over there."

"I don't need to."

"Were your feelings for her a fucking lie?"

"No. Belle is safe. Angelo didn't have eyes on her."

"How the fuck could you know?"

"Three reasons. One, my woman would never wear a bikini, believe me. Two, she listens to books because she doesn't like reading braille. She says it gives her a headache." He lifted up the audio CD of one of her books for Richard to see. "And third, Charlotte's with her. She's not alone, and I doubt she's even sunbathing. She wouldn't do something like that with Charlotte until she felt comfortable with her. At the moment, it's still weird."

"Yeah, Charlotte is your fiancée?"

"No, she's not. Not for much longer. I've got a plan I'm working on." He walked back to Richard, spreading open the guy's shirt. "This looks bad. We're going to need to get you to the hospital."

"I'll be fine. Let me bleed out. Leave me with the asshole."

"Not going to happen," Diego said, helping Richard to his feet.

"And why is that not going to happen?"

"You're my not-friend."

Richard laughed and groaned. "Shit, I shouldn't laugh. This is going to fucking kill me."

Diego called his men to come and take care of the body. He also texted The Boss to say it had been taken care of. Now, he had to get Richard to the hospital so he didn't die on him.

He didn't consider him a friend, but he also didn't see him as his enemy either, and he wasn't going to allow him to bleed out on Belle's carpet.

****

After taking Richard to the hospital, and staying to make sure he'd survive, Diego had another stop to make to Durante. After dealing with Angelo, he didn't want to wait around for Belle to take a pregnancy test. All of his problems he wanted to be dealt with now, so he could focus all of his energies on his woman.

One of Durante's men opened the door, showing him to a sitting room. He knew he wasn't welcome. As capo, they rarely had unscheduled visits so this was breaking rules and code, but for now, he didn't see a reason why he couldn't.

"Diego, I wasn't expecting you."

"I'm sure you've heard the news. Angelo is no longer a threat."

"Yes, The Boss is already planning an attack on the Russians. It's going to be a bloodbath but one we can win now that our secrets are safe."

"Speaking of secrets, I have a proposition for you."

"You do?"

"I don't want to marry your daughter. I have no intention of doing so, but I have a feeling we could negotiate a compromise that will bind us together better than marriage. With a marriage, betrayals can still happen. Enemies still grow stronger, but in business, our only focus is bringing in the wealth and allowing our clubs to thrive."

"Clubs?"

"I've been made aware that your nightclubs are costing you money. They haven't been bringing home a profit for some time."

"Charlotte," Durante said, through gritted teeth.

"She has no wish to marry either, Durante. You told me you were a good man. I'm hoping that you're willing to go into business with me, as partners, not as a son-in-law."

"You think you have what it takes to help my clubs to thrive? All of them?"

"Yes. With an expansion within my city, it will spread for us, and we'll be able to rule out the competition. People want fun. They want excitement. That's everything I give them and more."

"And in return, you don't want to marry Charlotte?"

"Correct. I don't want to make you my enemy. I want to make you my business partner."

"That is … compelling."

"We'd have to go to The Boss to change the arrangements."

"There is where our problems lie, Diego. I want to go into business with you. I never liked Angelo. He was too much of a hothead, but you've got a firm head on your shoulders. You know how to do business, and that's what we need."

"Then we come up with a good enough plan and business model to prove to The Boss that a wedding is not what is needed. There is also something else."

Durante chuckled. "Isn't there always?"

"Your daughter. She doesn't want to get married. She wants to go to school. She wants to learn to teach."

"And you're here to fight for her cause?"

"I'm here to suggest that if Belle's pregnant, I wouldn't mind her being around to help teach my kids. It could be good in the long term. It's something to consider."

"You're just all full of the ideas today," Durante

said.

"I'm fighting for my future, so I'm willing to take as many risks as I can." Especially if it meant being with his woman at the end of the day.

****

"Do I make you nervous?" Charlotte asked.

"Yes. No. Maybe. I don't know."

Charlotte chuckled.

"It's not a bad thing, you know, but this is kind of strange."

"I know. When I was told about you, I felt nothing. I know my mom and the women who were around were going crazy and saying some pretty mean things." They were walking the garden. Charlotte had her arm through hers, and she knew there was also a guard close to them as well. Belle listened to the other woman, who had loosened up around her as the time passed. "They kept looking at me and gossiping about you. Saying all these things."

"Let me guess, whore, slut, bitch, that kind of thing?"

"A lot more as well."

"Fun times."

"Anyway, I'm not trying to insult you."

Belle laughed. "Totally not insulted. I may even agree with them."

"As I was listening and they were getting angry for me, and I just thought, this woman is doing me a favor. I've got a chance to get out of this arrangement. Planning my wedding has been exhausting, not to mention boring. We had to go on this cake test thing, and oh my, I think if I was to even look at cake right now, I'd vomit."

"What cake did you decide on?" Belle asked.

"There was lemon, chocolate, strawberry, orange,

and a fruit one. Those were our options with different buttercreams."

"Chocolate with salted caramel buttercream is my favorite," Belle said.

Charlotte stopped walking, causing Belle to jolt back.

"What?" she asked.

"That's the same cake Diego enjoyed. He wanted that one, but I couldn't stand it. I loved the orange one. He hated it."

"Liking the same cake doesn't mean anything."

"You're just being stubborn. This means you are both supposed to be together. You and Diego. See, it's fate."

"I didn't think you'd be the kind of girl who believed in that?" Belle asked.

"I don't usually, but seeing as my future is kind of hanging in the balance on all of this, I'm taking anything."

"What's it like with the other women?" If she was to end up marrying Diego and having a child with him, she needed to be prepared for what was to come.

"You don't want to know."

"That bad?"

"Worse. I'm considered a social outcast."

"Why?"

"My mom is not part of the family. My dad went against his family and married my mother. Something happened that still made him capo. Since then, my mother has never been accepted, and neither have I."

"So being an outcast is what I've got to look forward to." She shrugged. "I've never needed the approval of anyone else anyway."

"See, that is the way to totally see it. To ignore all those haters. Besides, you're going to have me. We're going to be best friends."

"Why?"

"I like you, Belle. You need to have a little faith."

"You don't know me."

"You're sleeping with my ex-fiancé and I love you for it. How about we go from there?"

Belle wanted to argue, but instead, she didn't see a reason to do it. Spending time with Charlotte was a lot of fun. They walked for hours in the garden before having dinner together. Diego's father was nowhere to be found, and for Belle, she was welcome to him not being around.

After dinner, Charlotte helped her up to Diego's room, letting her shower. Charlotte didn't leave even when she had gotten dressed.

Sitting on the bed, she waited for the other woman to finish in the shower and Charlotte helped her downstairs so they could go and watch a movie.

"I don't have to put it on."

"It's fine. I like to listen anyway."

She snuggled behind a pillow as Charlotte put on some shark movie. It sounded rather good, and Belle was able to imagine what was going on. If she was on her own, she would have clicked for extra description, but that could irritate others and she really liked being with Charlotte.

The night wore on, and she closed her eyes, feeling sleep finally claim her after a really long day.

Chapter Seventeen

Diego entered the movie room to see Belle and Charlotte curled up on the sofa together. They looked like the best of friends. He didn't want to wake them, but it was also nine in the morning and he had news.

When he clapped his hands, both women let out a scream. Charlotte ended up on the floor while Belle scrambled to her feet.

"It's fine. It's me," Diego said.

"Did you really have to make that sound?" Belle asked.

"Yes, I did."

"You scared me," Charlotte said.

"You do realize you could have slept in beds, right?"

"Of course we did. We fell asleep," Belle said.

"I don't care. Sit. Sit," he said, urging Charlotte to sit down.

"What is it?" Belle asked.

"I've got news."

"Good news?" Charlotte asked.

"Yes, don't keep interrupting," he said. "Angelo has been dealt with. He won't be a problem anymore."

"That's good," Belle said. "Right? He was a problem?"

"Yes. He tried to set a trap for me in your apartment."

Belle placed a hand to her chest. "My apartment?"

"Yes."

"Asshole," she said.

"I also spoke with Durante," he said.

Charlotte leaned forward.

"We're not getting married."

Charlotte threw her arms up, letting out a cheer. "Yes, yes, I knew you could do it."

"We're going into business together. We drafted up an agreement, shared it with The Boss, and it means our wedding won't be taking place."

"I'm so happy right now," Charlotte said, holding Belle close and hugging her tight.

"Yeah, I still need to breathe. Why do I feel there's a catch coming on? You've given us all the good news. There is always a catch. Always something bad."

Charlotte looked to him.

"There is. The first, you can continue your education, but your father has agreed on one condition."

"What?" Charlotte asked.

"He picks the college."

Charlotte groaned. "He's going to pick one I hate."

"But at least you still get to go to college. Look on the plus side. Up until a couple of minutes ago, you were getting married to a guy you didn't love, for the sake of your womb. I'd say that's a step up."

"You know what? You're right. I'm so happy still. I don't care. I'll make it work," Charlotte said, looking happier than he'd ever seen her before. "There's more?"

"The wedding is still going on," Diego said, looking at Belle. "The woman has changed."

"What? You're having to marry someone else?" Belle asked.

He went down on one knee, looking at the woman that had completely made him feel whole again, when he didn't think it was possible.

"Yes. I've got to marry a woman. She's so freaking stubborn, and annoying, and if it wasn't for her, I wouldn't be kneeling on this floor right now. The odds have already been stacked against us. Her father hates me. When we get her a dog, he will probably hate me, or she. I don't think I like the idea of another man being in her life."

"Diego, are you doing what I think you're doing?"

"Belle, baby, I'm down on one knee. The Boss said a wedding has to happen, and seeing as you own my heart and soul, what better person to marry than you?"

"You want to marry me?"

"Yes."

"But I might not be pregnant."

"I don't care. When you do, you will already belong to me."

"This is so exciting. She totally loves the chocolate and salted caramel frosting. We've got to get her fitted for a wedding dress. We've got, like, two weeks to get everything organized. Knowing this will be your wedding makes it all so much easier for me." Charlotte got to her feet. "There's so much to do."

"Wait a minute. I want to hear Belle tell me her answer."

"Of course she is going to accept. She has to accept."

"Why do I have to?" Belle asked.

"Because, you two love each other. It's so clear to anyone who sees you. Diego's a mean asshole, but he looks like a big cuddly teddy bear around you. You must say yes."

"Charlotte, get out." He didn't need his ex-fiancée to scare away his current one. He wanted this to work, and right now, Belle looked like she wanted to throw up. It wasn't the idea he was going for.

"But?"

"Nope, get out," he said.

"I could help."

"You can help when I say you can. Get out. I've already gotten you something out of this. Please, leave."

Charlotte didn't put up another argument, turning on her heel and leaving him to talk with Belle.

"You want to get married to me?" Belle asked.

"I do. I want you to have my name. I know I lied when we met. I'm not just a nightclub owner. You don't know how many times I wanted to tell you the truth, but I was afraid."

"You're admitting to me again you're afraid."

"I can't lose you."

"Diego," she said, putting her hang to his cheek. "You will never lose me."

"You're going to marry me?"

"Yes. Of course." Belle laughed. "I told you, I don't share."

He picked her up in his arms, slamming his lips down on hers. "I'm taking you to bed."

"Diego?"

"Nope, I'm not listening to any other complaint right now. I'm taking you to bed, and I'm making love to you, then fucking you."

He held her close as he walked out of the movie room.

Charlotte was waiting, and he shook his head. "Are you going to get her ready to go out? I want to take her shopping for dresses."

"Rain check. I've got my woman for the day."

"Diego, there's not enough time."

"There is always enough time."

Without being stopped, he carried Belle to her rom.

"You know, everyone in the house could hear us."

"Don't care."

"They all know you've brought me up here to have sex."

"Again, don't care." He kicked his door closed, lowered Belle to the bed, and returned to flick the lock into place.

"You can tell me now, Belle. You can either stay with me, and I will make love to you for the rest of the day without any interruptions, or you can go with Charlotte. Spend the day with her, trying on dresses, knowing my dick wants to be inside you."

"Now that is a tough one?"

"Really?"

She lifted the shirt she wore over her head, throwing it to the ground. "Come here."

He removed his clothes as he stepped toward her. They were both naked, and he picked her up, dropping her to the bed. She spread her legs wide, and he moved between them. Claiming her lips, he plunged his tongue into her mouth, relishing her moan. Breaking from her mouth, he trailed his down to her neck, sucking on her pulse.

"You better start playing with that pussy," he said.

He felt her hands move between her body and heard her as she teased through her wet slit. She was already aroused, and he loved the sound. Biting at her nipples, he flicked the buds with his tongue before sucking them into his mouth.

"I'm going to watch you nurse our child. I can't wait to see you full." He placed a hand on her stomach, hearing her gasp as he stroked her.

Staring down at her pussy, he watched her fingers move over her clit, slowly at first before moving down to plunge inside her. In and out she moved. Her arousal glistened on her fingers, and he wanted to taste her before filling her up with his cum.

She drew her fingers up to her clit, and as she pleasured herself, he attacked her clit with his tongue, hearing her gasp.

She was getting in his way, so he caught her wrist in his grip, keeping her in place as he licked and sucked at her pussy.

"Put your hands above your head. Don't move them," he said, spreading the lips of her pussy to get to her clit. She was already soaking wet, and as he licked her nub, the taste of her was incredible.

One touch and he couldn't get enough. He didn't want to stop. Sucking her swollen bud into his mouth, he pressed two fingers inside her, feeling her tighten around his fingers. It was perfect to feel her.

"I'm going to be inside you every single chance I get, baby," he said, muttering the words against her clit.

"Yes, yes, please, Diego, I can't take much more."

He wasn't in the mood to make her wait either. Flicking his tongue back and forth across her clit, he pumped his fingers into her cunt, feeling the first stirrings of her orgasm. He let her come. The sound of her pleasured cries filled the room, driving him wild for more. His cock ached, his balls feeling so full with all the cum he wanted to fill her with. To knock her up.

Pulling his fingers from her pussy, he moved back between her thighs, wrapping his slick digits around his cock. Placing the tip at the entrance of her pussy, he slid up to bump her clit, watching her gasp and wriggle. Each touch to her oversensitive clit had her begging him not to stop.

She was always so responsive. None of her reactions to him were ever fake, and he found it highly addictive. Drawing his cock down to her entrance, he watched her open up, taking him, inch by glorious inch. She was still as tight as she was the first time, but he loved it.

Sliding in deep always reminded him of taking her virginity, of claiming her as his. Knowing no other man would ever get the chance to be inside her. Diego had made her his all those weeks ago, and now, he finally knew she would be his.

His wife.

His woman.

The mother of his children.

She was the one for him.

Diego pulled out of her, seeing her release shining on his dick before he plunged in deep again, fucking her harder.

Belle wrapped her legs around his waist. The heels of her feet dug into his ass, pulling him in close.

"Do you have any idea what you're doing to me?" He put his hands either side of her head, kissing her neck, feeling her wriggle beneath him, thrusting up onto his cock.

"I want you, Diego."

"You have me. All of me. You have me more than any other woman could ever have." She had every single part of him, and he wouldn't hide from her either. He wouldn't tell her lies or cheat.

With Belle, he would be honest, and show her she was worth everything to him. This woman, without even realizing it, had given him a second chance, the best kind he could ever think of.

Pulling all the way out only to slide back inside her, he watched her, took his entire fill of her, and couldn't get enough of all things that were Belle.

She was his life, his very reason for existing, and

as he slammed in deep, he knew he'd made the right decision going to her private booth.

Plunging in deep, he filled her to the top, and as he came, he did so roaring her name. Wrapping his arms around her, he kissed her shoulder, neck, and basked in knowing she would soon be his, all of his.

****

"Isn't taking the test a little pointless now?" Belle asked a week later.

Diego held the pregnancy test, which she refused to take. He'd tried to push it into her hand, but she wasn't having any of it. The last thing she wanted to do was to take that test. It scared her. There would be so many changes.

The first one was her father had told her he was selling his home and moving closer to her. She could understand that. It was the home he'd shared with her mom, and well, being with Diego and finally experiencing love, she wanted the same for him. He'd made a full recovery, much to the surprise of the doctors. Belle didn't doubt it though. Her father was a tough fighter, and he wouldn't let anything keep him down, not even a bullet wound.

"It's not pointless. We're going to be married in a couple of days."

"I know." She still remembered the horrible dress fitting. The woman had picked out what felt like a hundred wedding dresses. Charlotte had loved them all, but Belle had to go on feel.

The moment she had on the right dress, she knew it would be perfect. For two days she had to do that, and she was tired of this wedding already. She'd asked Diego if they could just elope. She'd never been the kind of girl to sit around dreaming about her wedding day.

Diego let out a sigh. It wasn't the first one he'd

given her either. He seemed to be doing it a lot lately, and she wasn't even trying to piss him off or annoy him. It seemed it came naturally to her right now.

"Something is bothering you," he said.

"It's nothing."

"You can't lie to me, baby. I know you. I know when something is bothering you, and it's time you tell me." He wrapped his arms around her, pulling her in close. Every time he did this, she felt safe, complete.

"I'm … what if I *am* pregnant?" she asked.

"Then we'll take care of it."

"Get rid of it?"

"Hell, no. What the fuck? You want to kill our child?"

"No, no, no." She put her hands on his chest, not wanting him to let her go. "What if I'm a bad parent? I can't see." She pressed her lips together, suddenly overwhelmed with emotion. "There's no miracle cure for me, Diego. I'm blind. What if it makes me a bad mother?"

"It's not possible."

"How can you know that?"

"Because I know you, and no matter what, you could never be bad at anything. Our child, our children, will be loved and protected with you around. You're not a bad person."

"You have so much faith in me."

He cupped her face, staring into her eyes. "It's not hard to do. This love I feel for you, it's all for you. Not a moment goes by when I don't think about you. Before I met you, Belle, I was nothing. I was a shell of a man with no direction, no passion, but you've come into my world and completely shattered who I am. You've made me care about you. That kind of love, it doesn't go away easily."

"You always know what to say."

"If you're pregnant, we'll take care of it, meaning we'll plan and we'll prepare. You won't be alone during this. I will be with you every single step of the way. There's no way I'd let you push me aside for this."

She rested her head against his chest. "How did I get so lucky?"

"Luck has nothing to do with this. We've got each other, and that's what has been missing from our lives from the start. I love you, Belle Johnson, and regardless if this test comes out positive or negative, I'm going to always love you. Every single second of every single day of our lives."

She couldn't help but smile. "You're very romantic."

"You bring it out in me." He kissed her lips. "Now, I'd really like to know if I'm going to be a baby daddy or not."

"You could qualify as a sugar daddy. You are old enough."

He grabbed her ass, making her moan.

"You know just what to say to push the right buttons. Come on."

Diego was there as she peed on the stick. She didn't want him to be, but he refused to leave the room. Every step of the way, he promised to be with her. She just didn't realize exactly how close was close.

She washed her hands after placing the stick on some tissue. Diego handed her a towel. "What does it say?"

"Nothing yet. We've got to wait."

"If we were pregnant, would you want a boy?"

"Belle, I'd want a healthy child. That's all I care about."

"I heard Richard talking to you the other day, and

how important male heirs are to you."

"Belle, I don't give a fuck what kind of child we have, just so long as we have one that is perfect."

"What if it has … problems?"

"I don't care.'

"Deafness and blindness?"

He pulled her into his arms. "You are determined to make a big deal out of this when there really doesn't need to be one."

"I'm just thinking ahead to our future and our baby's future."

"Our future is fine, Belle. I just want us to have a family. We'll take care of the rest."

She heard the alarm beep. "That's our time." She squeezed Diego's hands, terrified and thrilled all at the same time. "Tell me. Tell me please."

His lips brushed across her cheek. "We're going to have a baby."

Belle didn't know how she would take the news. She was worried she'd freak out over the smallest detail, but hearing that the pregnancy test had confirmed she was pregnant, she couldn't be sad about that.

"We're going to have a baby?"

"Yes." He lifted her up, spinning her around.

"We need to get married soon. I don't want us to have a huge belly in the pictures or for our child to think the only reason we got married is because of my being pregnant."

"They will never think that."

"We're pregnant, Diego."

"I know, and I've got the perfect way to celebrate." He started to move, and she wrapped her arms around his neck, holding onto him.

"You're so strong."

"I could carry you everywhere."

"I wonder if you'll still feel that way when I'm the size of a tank."

"I may just need a little help, but I'll always find a way to carry you." He lowered her onto the bed, and she gasped as he kissed her neck, moving her back against the bed. He climbed between her thighs. His hands gripped her legs and moved them open, making room for him.

He didn't let her go though. He slid his hands up her legs to cup her pussy. The skirt she wore rode up as he moved aside her panties, and she cried out the instant he touched her.

"Diego?"

"I know, baby, I know. I can feel it too." He plunged two fingers inside her before slowly circling her clit.

She sank her teeth into her lip, not wanting him to stop. "Please."

"Thank you so much for everything you've given me, Belle."

"I've not given you anything," she said, trying to think, but his fingers were making it impossible for her to even make out the words that were coming out of his mouth. Why was he even talking? Nothing made sense, but his touch on her pussy was ... *oh, my.*

"I fell in love with you against all the odds. I love you more than anything in this life, and I know it's because of you. I know it's all down to how you've made me feel, and I fucking love you for it. Not a moment goes by when I'm not thinking about you. When I don't love you. I'm never going to allow you to forget what I feel for you."

"Diego, please. I love you too, so much it scares me at times. Now is not the time to try to analyze our feelings. Please, I need you to keep moving your fingers."

His chuckle was deep, and she gasped as his fingers were suddenly inside her, stroking in and out, fucking her, taking her, and she wanted him, wanting it all, and didn't want him to stop. Not even for a single moment.

He brought her close to the edge, working her body like only he could, drawing out the pleasure. She didn't know how much more she could take before he finally allowed her to hurtle into an orgasm that had her panting and gasping for more. He knew what he was doing, and just what buttons to press to make her scream.

Diego didn't give her the chance to come down from her release as he found his way inside, plunging to the hilt.

"I will never get enough of you. I will never get enough of this. You are fucking incredible, Belle."

He pulled out and slammed back inside, his hands locking with hers as he deepened the kiss. There was no way she could ever doubt his feelings for her. They were everything and absolute, and perfect, just like the two of them. He melted her heart and threw her into a whole new world of pleasure, one she couldn't deny she wanted.

"I love you. I love you so much."

He claimed her lips as he took her. His strokes were deep and hard, but she sensed him holding back.

"You won't hurt me," she said.

"I know. I have no intention of ever hurting you."

He kissed her harder, and his thrusts started to lose control, stroking to the hilt, touching a part of her that had her moaning his name and arching up, not wanting him to stop.

Over and over he stroked that spot, and as she came, Diego followed her, swallowing her cries as he filled her with his cum. Not once did he let her go. He surrounded her, and there was no doubt in her mind, she was safe with him.

Loved and protected.

Exactly what she always wanted.

Chapter Eighteen

"I could hide you," James said.

Belle smiled. "I don't want to run and hide."

It was her wedding day. She was in her room with James and Charlotte. The two people she was close to, not as close as she was with Diego, but he couldn't be here. He couldn't see her.

"You look so beautiful. The most amazing bride in the world," Charlotte said.

"Yes, and she would still look the most beautiful bride if I ran off with her," her father said.

Charlotte chuckled. "It would make you Diego's enemy."

"He's my enemy."

"Dad, you like him. Stop trying to pretend that you don't."

"I need to go and grab a couple of roses from the spares. I'll be back," Charlotte said, kissing her cheek.

The door closed, and she heard her father laughing.

"What?"

"Only you'd be the kind of person to befriend the ex."

"Charlotte wasn't really his ex. They were being forced into this."

"And you're not?"

She and Diego had told her father that she was pregnant. There were a few times leading up to this day that she wasn't entirely sure if he was happy with the news or not.

"No, Dad, I'm not being forced." She placed a hand on her stomach. "I'm marrying Diego Leoni because I love him. You always told me that once I found the one that no matter what, I would know the truth. I would know what true love feels like, and I know it does when I'm with him. It's exactly how you describe your time with Mom. How the two of you met. All of it."

"Belle, you know what he does."

"I know."

"That doesn't bother you?"

"I … no. He does what he has to do, but I know in my heart that he loves me for me. I can't ask for more than that. I fell in love with a man in the mafia." She shrugged. "I'm not going to change him."

"You fell in love with a persona."

"No. Diego wasn't pretending to be someone else, Dad. He simply kept the real life he has from me. He's no different with me. He loves me, and I love him. I hope you can accept that."

"I do accept that. I just always need to know that my baby girl is alert about this. That she knows what is coming, regardless."

"I know that with Diego, it doesn't matter what is coming. I will always have him."

"I'm back," Charlotte said. "Some of your roses have wilted, and we don't want you walking down the aisle with the wrong kind of bouquet."

Her father wrapped his arms around her. "I love you, Belle. Always. It's my job to take care of you."

She rested her head against his shoulder. "I know, and I love you. But you've got to know I'm making the right choice for me. Not for anyone else. I love Diego more than anything. This wedding is because we are in love. He's not being forced into anything. This is what we want."

****

"I could cause a distraction and get you to run away," Richard said. He whispered the words, and Diego frowned toward his not-friend, who had somehow made it as his best man.

"What?"

"You know, I'm giving you an out. I could scream there's a fire."

"There's not a fire."

"Exactly. I cause a distraction and you run like fucking crazy."

"Richard, *you're* fucking crazy. I'm not being held here at gunpoint."

"The Boss wanted a wedding, and you're here. I'd say that's close to being held at gunpoint."

"Okay, if I was with Charlotte, I'd be held at gunpoint because I have no desire to marry her. With Belle, that is entirely different."

"Why is it?"

"I love her where I don't love Charlotte. Today is a win for me."

"It is?"

"Yes, and I will shoot you, and send you off to the emergency room to pick a better man than this. The best man is not supposed to offer me an out on my own wedding."

"Actually, the best man is supposed to do all of this for you. I checked. You wouldn't allow me to hire a stripper for your bachelor party."

"Richard, I'm in love with the best woman there is. I don't want nor do I need to see another woman's tits." He was happy, more than happy with Belle. She was his world.

"Ugh, you make me sick."

"Why? Because I love my wife?"

"No, because you've got that gooey look in your eye. It's so gross."

He was one of the few men who was able to marry for love. The Boss wasn't going to call the wedding off, not after finding out Belle was expecting his child. Diego hoped the first of many.

There were capos who didn't believe he should take a blind bride. They felt he was bringing the wrong impression, making them all look weaker. They could all go fuck themselves.

He wasn't a weak capo, nor would he ever be. His wife was stunning. She was a beauty, and to those that didn't see that, he really didn't care. He hadn't decided to marry her to impress others. He was marrying her because he was fucking in love with her, and not a moment went by where he didn't think about her in some way or another.

"Your moment for leaving is gone," Richard said.

The wedding music started up, and he looked toward the doorway where several bridesmaids appeared. None of them were close to Belle. They had been picked out by The Boss for the day. Belle only wanted Charlotte, but for an elaborate celebration like this, they needed more than one bridesmaid.

Charlotte was the last to arrive, and she sent him a smile as she took her place. She had already enrolled in college, and it was close to home. From what he'd been told Durante sent her to college with a bodyguard who wasn't allowed out of her sight, not even for a moment. He wondered if she would stick it out at college or quit.

His gaze returned to the doorway where his wife, his bride, was walking toward him. This woman. She rocked his world in all the right ways, and now, seeing her walk toward him, her veil down, her father by her side, he knew he was the luckiest motherfucker in this room.

He didn't care what others thought of him or of Belle.

She was everything to him. The love of his life in

all things, and he was never going to let her go. He stepped toward her as James came to a stop. He held her hand, and James touched his arm.

"Seeing that look in your eye, I know now she's doing the right thing. There's no way I could let her walk away after seeing how much you love her." James patted his shoulder.

"I promise I'll love her forever," Diego said.

He helped her up the few steps, taking both of her hands to stand before the priest. Her father had already lifted the veil. Her gaze was on his chest, not that she could see anything.

He didn't mind.

The priest began his sermon, but Diego didn't give a shit about the priest or their guests. He held Belle's hands, stared at her, and simply basked in knowing he was the luckiest man in the world.

They didn't have long, drawn-out vows. They made their promises to each other that would extend to their death. When the time came to slide the ring on her finger, Diego felt at one with her. This was what it meant to finally be with someone. To love them, to honor them, and to always know where they were.

Belle needed a little help sliding the ring on his finger, but when it came to being husband and wife, he needed no further encouragement to take her face in his hands and to slam his lips down on hers.

She finally, after all this time, belonged to him.

There was applause, but he tuned them out.

Belle gripped his arms, and as he pulled back, he stroked her cheek. "You did it," he said.

"What?"

"I thought you'd leave," he said. "I thought you'd find a reason to escape me."

"Diego?"

"I love you more than anything else in this world, Belle. I'm not a good man. I'm a monster. I know I don't deserve you."

She placed her hand over his mouth. "You need to shut up. This is our wedding day. I love you, no matter what. We are different people, but that doesn't stop my feelings for you. Every single day I'm with you, it's the best day of all. There's nowhere else I want to be but with you. I love you, Diego Leoni. I'll never regret this."

Diego glanced over at the crowd. They were all waiting for them to leave, but he returned his attention to his wife.

"I'm going to make sure you don't regret this." All of his life, he'd been sure of many things. He'd always be the best at everything. The strongest, and that he'd always be capo. He'd never allow Angelo to take his place. It was what made him train harder. He was more vicious, more determined, and more prepared than anyone else. He just didn't anticipate Belle. She took him by surprise, but Richard pointing her out that day, he didn't regret it.

Wrapping an arm around her waist, he held her hand and guided her down the aisle. Since their wedding had been announced, he had people ask him if it irritated him the patience he had to show.

There was no patience when it came to Belle. Helping her down streets and in houses she'd never been wasn't a chore to him or an inconvenience, it was a gift. It was his chance to show her that he loved her. That he had no intention of letting her go, nor would he let anyone else take his place.

"Diego, there's no way I'd ever regret this. I love you, and I know you love me. How could that possibly be a bad thing?"

"Come on, lovebirds, let's get this show on the

road."

"Your not-friend made it as your best man."

"I know, we've got to set him up with someone to get him off my back."

Belle giggled. "Maybe we should get him with Charlotte?"

"Now that would be interesting." He took Belle's hand, leading her outside to where a photographer stood waiting patiently. Not that anyone in their right mind would ever complain about waiting around for The Boss.

He didn't let Belle go. Every single picture he stood by her side, holding her, protecting her, loving her, knowing in his heart and mind, he couldn't ever let her go. He loved her. She had given him a second chance, and he wasn't ever going to let that go, not for a second.

Epilogue One

Eight months later

"She's so beautiful," Diego said.

He stared down at his daughter and his wife as she held their child. For the past eight months, he'd been waiting for this moment. She had gone through nearly three hours of labor at this point. Hearing her scream would forever be embedded in his mind. He hated the pain she had gone through as she refused to have any medication of any kind. He'd held her hands through the pain, marveling at her strength. He'd watched her bring their baby girl into the world.

Some men in his world would be disappointed she didn't have a boy, but he didn't care. His daughter was beautiful, just like her mother, and he knew he was the happiest man in the world.

"We did it, Diego. Do you want to hold her?" Belle asked.

"I can hold her?"

She chuckled. "You're her daddy. Of course you can hold her."

He stood by his wife's side, staring down at that tiny bundle, and he didn't think he could hold something so precious. Yet, as he leaned forward to help his wife, he took his little girl and held her.

Placing a hand gently on the blanket she'd been wrapped up in, he felt tears fill his eyes. He'd never been a man to cry.

"Oh, Belle, she is so beautiful."

"Look what we did. You and I." He took her hand, squeezing her, letting her know he felt the exact same way. "So, when do you want to start making another one?"

"Belle, honey, I don't think I'm ever going to

recover. I'm going to always remember you screaming. Let's just keep this one, and not think about another."

She laughed. "I feel fine. It hurt, but I'm fine now. I want us to have another baby."

"Let's enjoy this one." He kissed her knuckles, happier than he'd ever been.

"Is my dad still waiting?" Belle asked.

"James is always there, as is Richard."

"And of course Charlotte," Belle said. "You better go and show her off."

"I don't want to leave you."

"They're going to be worried. When they've seen her and know we're fine, they can relax."

"You care way too much for other people."

"I care just enough, and it's one of the many reasons you love me." She let go of his hand, and with one last, lingering look on his wife, he carried their little girl out to the room where their loved ones were waiting.

Epilogue Two

Ten years later

"I don't want to be another year older," Diego said.

Belle moved to straddle her husband's lap. Their four children were asleep for the night, and they were alone in his study. Diego had built a house just for them out in the country, away from the threat and danger.

She knew deep down they would never be away from the violence, but he'd also employed several men and women to be on guard at all times.

"You're only fifty."

"Yeah, and you're thirty-one years old." He gripped her thighs, moving her into the right position, directly over his swelling cock. "How do you think I feel?"

"I think you feel just as good as you did when we met ten years ago. You know I don't have a problem with your age. You shouldn't either."

"The kids are getting older. Eliza's ten now, and you know she asked me about what boyfriends are good for?"

Their eldest daughter was growing up so fast. Belle would never forget giving birth to her. She hadn't taken any medication for any of her births, and each one had been a trial. By the time she got to hold her bundle of joy, it was worth it. Just like her life with Diego was worth it.

There were always moments that made it at times impossible to enjoy. When he had to leave for long periods of time, or there was danger and he'd have twice as many guards around. She also knew he cleaned off any evidence of what he'd been doing, blood and things like that. Every single night, no matter the cost, he always came home to her. He'd slide into bed, kiss her neck, wrap his arms around her waist, and she just knew, those moments of fear and worry, were all worth it to feel him against her.

"What did you say?"

"Boyfriends only have one purpose."

"Which is?"

"To be kicked in the nuts or hit. I don't mind. Or if she has a gun, to shoot them."

"Diego?"

"I embellished with the gun thing. I'm not a complete psycho. Have some faith."

"I do have faith, but you know what our girl is like." Eliza was strong-willed, like her father, and determined to get what she wanted, again, a trait like her father. She had a good heart though. Family was the most important thing to her, and Belle couldn't fault her for that.

"I do, which is why I kept it to the whole crushing nuts. We're missing the point." He gripped her ass. "It's my birthday."

"I know. The kids are in bed, and I'm right here. So, Diego, love of my life. What do you want to do? Fuck me hard on this sofa, or go to sleep because we know the kids will be up soon?"

He groaned. "You have to go and make those crazy demands, huh?" he asked.

She rubbed against his hardened dick. "What will it be?"

Diego was silent for a long time before finally giving her an answer. "I'm going to fuck you hard and *then* I'll collapse into sleep."

"Happy birthday, Diego," she said.

He pulled her down, kissing her hard, and she knew there was no way life could get any better. He belonged to her just as she belonged to him. They were together, and so long as they were, nothing would ever tear them apart.

The End

SAM CRESCENT

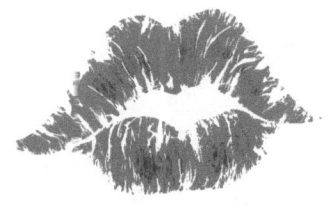

EVERNIGHT PUBLISHING ®

www.evernightpublishing.com

www.ingramcontent.com/pod-product-compliance
Lightning Source LLC
Chambersburg PA
CBHW030117180626
46812CB00002B/458